Book One of the Fallen *series*

FALLEN LOVE

Alex Stargazer

This is a work of fiction: all resemblances to real persons, places, or other entities are either coincidental or used fictitiously.

ISBN-13: 9781707574223

Cover art by Hampton Lamoureux.

For more books, poems, and exclusive content, visit www.alexstargazer.com.

"I love a good book that has magic in it and when you also throw in some angel, demon, and technology in it, that is just three different flavors of ice cream on top. This isn't the first book that I have read by this author and I'm sure it won't be the last. He has a way with world-building that is just incredible." —Ashley, Goodreads.com

"The writing is polished, even compelling in spots. If you're looking for an entertaining read with ambitious world-building and touches of gay romance & erotica, give it a try." —KD Edwards, author of the *Last Sun*.

"To say this novel took me by surprise is a total understatement. This story surprised, astounded, and made me so happy that it is right up there with the top ten books I have read this year out of the hundreds that have come in contact with my eyes and ears." —Sharon on sharonicalogic.home.blog

"Overall, the pacing of the book is realistically paced, the development of characters and plot both mature nicely, the love scenes were well balanced between sensual and sexual, and the supporting characters storylines were developed to a point of wanting to know more about them." —Rion on Facebook

"It was fascinating to experience the changes that occurred in Conall and Mark as their mutual interest blossomed into love—a bond that will be tested when outside forces threaten everything they care about. The paranormal aspects of this book added incredible twists in ways that were completely unexpected. This was an incredible story and I will be waiting for the next book in the series." —Teresa, Goodreads.com

"The plot was both fresh and imaginative, and though I'm not the biggest fan of multiple narrators, in this novel I found I couldn't wait to get back to each character's chapters." —Stephen, Goodreads.com

"Conall and Mark are beautifully written characters with so much depth and not to mention the steamy moments. Just wow. I had read Alex's previous writing and was curious how this book would turn out. Now I cannot wait to see where this story goes next!" —Margaux, Goodreads.com

Part One: Love

To Steven "Tayls" Taylor, who fought many demons but lost. You won't be forgotten.

Chapter One

Conall

They call Dublin the City of Angels. Why, I don't really know; the city is as black as any other in the 26th century European continent. Perhaps it appeals to the Party's vanity: this is, after all, their crown jewel, their seat of power.

There are no angels here, of course—especially not in the Fallen Quarter. Here the light of the setting sun is pale and weak; the darkness moves swiftly, claiming shadows as its own. I am not welcome here. The night belongs to the mutants: to the creatures that roam the moonlit landscape, their venomous jaws salivating at the prospect of prey.

I curse myself for staying up so late—it's past 10pm. Still, I cannot bring myself to regret it: Jason's touch had been so smooth, and his body so seductive against mine. I shiver. Father had warned me that my love of beautiful men would be the death of me—but did I listen? Of course not.

My android guard glides beside me with a disturbing, mechanical gait. It turns its translucent polymer head, the cameras inside its eyes making minute, almost invisible adjustments. Nothing escapes its attention.

Well, almost nothing. I nearly stumble on top of him: he's so still, I assume he's asleep, or maybe drunk—just another Fallen or disaffected Worker. The usual Dublin detritus.

For some reason, I pause. Something doesn't seem right: he doesn't look like any other vagabond. There's a grace to him—almost a hint of something divine. There's blood on his shirt, though he doesn't appear to be seriously injured. Even in the dim half-light, his hair is shockingly blond, and my hand itches to push it out of his eyes.

I know I should leave. He's one of the Fallen, for sure; I shouldn't be helping him. And yet, I can't help myself. Maybe it's because of the way he lies prostrate on the hard asphalt, vulnerable as a newborn. Maybe I'm a fool; an idealist in a world of harsh reality. Or maybe—if I were being honest with myself—it's because he's so impossibly beautiful.

"Hey? Hey, can you hear me?"

He groans again, louder.

"Yeah," he mumbles.

"What the fuck are you doing here? And who are you? No, don't answer that. Here."

I offer him my hand. He grabs it, and I lift him to his feet. The effort is considerable: he's big, I realise, the muscles of his shoulders visible through the thin shirt. I wonder who beat him up. Then again—why should I care?

"I guess I should say thanks. Not that you should have bothered." He laughs bitterly. "I'm dead meat anyway."

"Who did this to you?"

His smile is chilling. "You don't want to know that."

He starts to move away, but I stop him.

"Where are you going?"

"There's nowhere I can go. I can't go back there."

"Go back where?"

"You don't want to know that either."

Again I wonder what I'm doing here. Why am I talking to him—even preventing him from running away—when I shouldn't have looked at him twice?

I don't have time to answer these questions, because just then, the android raises its head, listening. A moment later, we hear it too.

Hsss-click-click. Hsssss.

"Oh shit," he says. "Scarabs."

The android raises its laser, cocks its machine gun, and the green lights in its head instantly turn an ominous red. There's no more time; I have to make my decision. I grab his hand, and we start to run. Behind us, the monsters follow.

★★★

Two dart in front of us, and for a moment, I freeze. They are creatures of nightmare: their legs are spindly, misshapen, and they seem to glide across the road. They hiss again. A split second later, they leap.

The first is incinerated in mid-air by a laser flash, and the android crushes the second. A slick, black-green substance drips from its dead body; the smell almost makes me retch.

I snap back to reality: we need to keep running. The boy is already in front of me.

"How many?" he cries.

"Does it matter? Let the android take care of them." Despite my cavalier words, I'm close to panic. I squint, trying to make out the Upper Quarter. *Not far,* I think. *We can make it.*

The android opens fire, and at a glance I see what the boy meant: there are many, way too many. Several fall in the firestorm, but others clamour to take their place. This isn't a lone attack; this is a swarm. And we're right in the middle of it.

"Run faster!" I scream. "We're almost there!"

But it's too late.

A mutant slams into me with the power of a sledgehammer. I heave against it, fighting with its mandibles: I have to stop those fangs, so gleaming with venom, from sinking in and finishing me off.

And then the weight is off me. Through the corner of my eyes, I see it sail high into the air and into the reach of the android, but my sight never leaves the boy who saved me.

"I had to return the bleedin' favour," he says, hand outstretched. I don't have time to thank him. He lifts me and we're running again. The lights of the Upper Quarter are tantalisingly close. They shimmer behind an immense force-field, designed to keep out mutants and undesirables. Riffraff like the boy I just rescued.

Not that I have time to worry about that right now. "My ID will open the force field!" I cry, and I throw myself forward, fumbling for the ID.

With a flash of the reader, we cross the threshold. We're in.

We breathe deeply, and I collapse against him. The mutants hiss, disappointed, and quickly slink back from the force field. A few are not so lucky, and are noticed by one of the guard towers. Machine gun fire turns the monsters into bloody smears on the ground.

Still, my interest isn't on the monsters—it's on him. It isn't just the muscles, which are hard and powerful against my body. His scent is masculine, and sends a surreptitious thrill through me.

Before, I feared death; but now, I feel very much alive.

"That was fun," I say.

"Fuck you."

***

We walk in silence. He sneaks glances at the clean streets, trying to not look uncomfortable; the Upper Quarter is rather different than the gutter I found him in. But it's only when he sees my mansion that he really starts to understand.

"*That's* where you live?"

"Did you think we in the Upper Quarter lived in hovels?"

"So you're an Upperclassman, eh?"

"Yes."

"And here you are, saving my life like some hero."

"Should I have left you to fight the Scarabs yourself?" He looks away. We both knew what would have happened if the mutants had found him alone.

"But why?" he asks.

I have no idea, but it's not like I'm going to admit it. "Doesn't matter why. Let me find you a room. We should have plenty."

"Won't someone notice me? Don't you have guards?" he asks instead.

"The mansion is large, and father is far away. You can rest easy that neither the staff nor the guards will bother you."

"So do you bring a lot of guys like me to your mansion?" I can't tell if he's being playful or cynical.

I smile, with a trace of irony. "You are a little more unusual. But they shall ask no questions—trust me on that."

Despite my assurances, I sneak him in through a side-entrance. It would not do to tempt Fate, or my father; for both are fickle. I find him a spare bedroom. The room is enormous, and to him, lavish; his gaze is pulled to the thick carpet, the beautifully decorated ceiling, and the bed, which stands imposingly in the centre.

He steps back, shaking his head.

"I'm not born for luxury."

"Well, you better tolerate some."

He looks at me, then. Really looks at me. His eyes are a deep blue, the colour of the raging ocean. There's something in them that I can't read—a guarded emotion, maybe even a repressed desire.

Or maybe I'm just fooling myself.

"Okay."

"Don't you want to know my name?" I ask instead.

He smirks. "Go on."

"I'm Conall."

"Nice to meet you, Conall. Now let me sleep."

"Not going to tell me your name?" I ask, an eyebrow raised in surprise.

"No."

For a moment, I am caught totally off-guard. It makes sense—it's dangerous for a Fallen to know a man like me. Even so, anger builds up inside me, and the feeling is a strange one; it's not in my nature to let someone get the better of me. Especially not the likes of him.

He rips off his bloodied shirt, throwing it unceremoniously onto the carpet. (I make a mental note to come up with an excuse if someone notices the blood.) Then he takes off his jeans. I look away, heading for the door.

"Don't mind the carpet or anything."

"I don't care about your bleedin' carpet, Conall."

I don't intend to let that pass; I swing around and face him. He's naked, of course. The luxury around him pales in comparison; his beauty is of a far greater sort than that. My eyes trace the contours of his muscles, travel up the jawline, and meets his gaze.

Time seems to slow; everything in the universe condenses to that one point. When I look away, it's like a spell has been broken. No: not broken. I would be a fool if I believed that.

The spell is only spinning its web tighter.

Chapter Two

Mark

The morning light shines through the window, bright and blue. The air feels cold on my bare skin, and the bed very warm, and very comfortable. Too comfortable.

"Fuck it," I say, as I remember where I am. I force myself to wake up.

I have to leave; I've already broken enough rules as it is. But where to go? I can't go back to Finn's place. I don't have an ID for a new place, let alone enough quid for a deposit. I try to think of anything beyond the obvious—and forbidden option—and wince.

I move slowly, the bruises still sore. They'd beaten me last night, since I'd pissed off one of the dealers who I shared the place with. I'd never stolen any of his zed (they call it zed because the addicts look like zombies). Hell, I've never done drugs; I'm not stupid enough for that.

But he knew he could lay the blame on me. Finn and I had never been friends: we tol- erated rather than accepted each other, since I couldn't afford to live anywhere else, and neither could he. Yet I never thought that he would betray me like that. Framing me for theft is bad enough, but to make me the resident pervert too? Then again, I should have seen this coming a long time ago.

I want to bash my head against a wall. Instead I close my eyes, breathe deeply, and try to focus. I need to wash my clothes—who knows when I'll have the chance again—but there's no way I can ask Conall about that. So I slip into the corridor, hoping to find the exit, and avoid the servants I was promised "wouldn't bother me."

I don't run into the staff; I'm not that lucky. Instead, the boy from last night finds me in one of the corridors.

"Where *are* you going?" he asks, blocking my exit.

Bleedin' hell, there's no hiding from this guy. "I'm not allowed here. I'm too *inferior*." I lace the word with venom.

"You can at least stay until your bruises heal." He grabs my hand, and drags me off. I don't try to resist, even as his grip strains the bruises; it's a bad idea to fight an Upperclass-man. The law rarely judges in your favour.

He pulls me into a bathroom and rummages in an ornate cabinet for some meds. I wince when he applies the regenerator solution. It's not painful, exactly—it's simply unnerving to feel your flesh knitting itself back together.

"Who did this to you, anyway?" he asks, touching me more gently than he did a moment ago. Maybe he realises that he hurt me—or maybe not. Who am I kidding?

"A dealer and his friends."

"What did you do?"

"Nothing."

"Why'd they beat you up, then? It's not because you stole their booty, right?"

I realise how close he is; his breath tingles the hairs on my neck. He's smiling at me, and I wonder at the subtext of the words.

I give him a crooked grin. "Guys like that never need a reason."

"You lived with them?"

"It's not like I have a choice—I can't afford many places." The odd jobs I do aren't exactly high-flying: nixers, off the record stuff.

"So where were you going when I stopped you?"

"I'm... I'm still thinking about it."

"Why not stay here?" It makes sense; I would be safer than with drug dealers. But it's also dangerous: it's illegal for me to live here, and the Party is much worse than a bunch of small-time dealers. A few punches I can take—but the Party could kill me and no one would ever know

"I can't stay here. I've told you why." In an undertone, I add, "You of all people should know what the Party can do."

He only raises an eyebrow, but doesn't bother asking more questions. He works quietly, applying bandages and pain meds. He looks at me from the corner of his eye; there's something there, I can tell. I try to ignore it.

"Well, stay till you heal."

"Are you alright?" I ask, like I can't help myself.

"The Scarab didn't gets its teeth into me, no; I have you to thank for that."

"You really want to help me, then?" I can't believe I'm asking this question.

He nods, and his expression grows more serious.

"Forget about me—let me go. You can't help me."

"I just did."

His comment surprises me, and I look at him more carefully. I've never been this close to an Upperclassman. His hair is light brown—the colour of hazelnuts. His eyes are green, but intermixed with a dark mahogany; it's like looking into a forest grove, though I've never seen a real forest, only photos on screens.

I head for the door. He stays in my way.

"You know, you could at least bother to ask me where the door is—or do you want to ask my father instead?"

"Okay. You win. Where is it?"

"I'm not telling you until you tell me where you want to go."

"Why do you care, anyway? You're an Upperclassman; I'm a Fallen. It's not the stuff of love stories."

"Love stories?" His expression is strange: he finds it funny, but there's fear there, and the confidence is definitely bluster.

"Yeah. Now are you going to get the fuck out of my way, or is this some sort of inter-rogation?"

He shrugs. I follow him to his bedroom, where he grabs one of his shirts and throws it to me. (I realise my own is still covered in blood.) It's not an exact fit, because I'm bigger than he is, but I don't care; this isn't a fashion runway.

He starts walking. He's wearing dark-grey jeans and a denim shirt. Designer, by the look of it—and expensive as hell. There's a confidence in his stride. I'd seen it before: it's what money does to you.

Finally, he reaches the door. The sun outside is bright; the heat hits us in waves.

"I guess this is goodbye," he says.

"I'm glad you brought me in," I admit, because it's true.

"I wish you'd..."

"Stay? Sorry, I'm not posh like you." He flinches at that.

I start walking, quickly, but not too quickly. I don't need any unwanted attention.

"The gate will open automatically, by the way," he mentions.

I hadn't thought about that, never having been in the place. There aren't any gates in the Fallen quarter, since nobody wants to protect us.

"Thanks for the pointer, Posh Boy." I say it again, trying to annoy him.

"We're not all posh twats, you know," he says as I leave. I don't believe him.

I walk through the gate, out into the streets of Dublin. The city of crime; the city of the night. My city, if I liked it or not.

As I walk, my thoughts are spinning in crazy directions. I know I shouldn't think about him. He's everything I shouldn't like—everything I should *hate*. A rich saviour, comfortable in his mansion while pretending to care. *But he did care*, a part of me thinks. Maybe I'm going soft: a pretty boy says pretty words, and I'm already forgetting how things are really like.

✶✶✶

I move in the shadows, both to avoid the sun—it's quare hot today—and to avoid attention. The Refuse is a den of crime, but it's also patrolled by the Gardá, who will arrest anyone when they feel like it. A bribe would get me out of it. Trouble is, I don't have any "luck money".

I don't know exactly where my uncle lives—we'd avoided each other for more than a year now. Still, I can guess. He wouldn't be in the Refuse; only Fallen live there. But neither would he be far from it.

My uncle is a good man. He works as a doctor; his mission is to save others. He'd helped many others like me whenever he could—by giving them medical assistance, food, or temporary shelter. And he'd raised me.

Of course, Technicals aren't allowed to raise Fallen kids. I still remember when the Gardá raided us at 2am and dragged me out of the house.

The area around me is getting nicer, I notice. There are fewer blocks of flats—built for Fallen, more recently but to shite standards—and more houses, some of them historical. Before the mutants, I know, they didn't have to re-enforce houses with alloys and concrete.

I don't see anyone dealing here, or hawking prostitution; that's another difference between the Middle quarter and the Fallen quarter. (And the Upper quarter too, now that I've seen what it's like.)

I stand behind shadows, occasionally walking so as not to draw suspicion. Uncle usually has his lunch at noon, and old habits die hard.

Eventually, after what is probably an hour, I spot him. His white uniform, greying hair and steel blue eyes are unmistakable. I head towards him discretely; he doesn't show it, but I know he's seen me.

I quietly make my way to his house, and stand in the alley. The new place, I realise, isn't so different from his old one. The walls are hard concrete; the steel roof gleams in the bright sunlight. But that's not what makes it stand out. There's a garden—unheard of in the slums. Bright flowers peak out from behind a little watering pot. Uncle always loved gardening.

He makes a show of closing the door, but when I move closer I see that it's been left slightly ajar. I walk in, locking it behind me.

★★★

"So you're here," he says.

"Yeah," I reply non-committally.

He doesn't bother asking me why. "You can't stay here forever."

He's right, but I still flinch a little.

"I know that, uncle."

Seeing my discomfort, his expression softens. "Come on, boy. Make yourself at home. I'll bring you a cup of tea."

"Thanks, uncle." No one else ever brings me a cup of tea.

I sip the hot liquid, enjoying the rush of caffeine.

"They beat you up, huh?" His eyes follow the marks on my skin, weighing them up with expert knowledge. The regenerator solution might have mostly healed the wounds, but there's no way I can fool a doctor.

"Yeah, but not too badly."

"Someone patched you up?"

I don't bother lying.

"Yeah." Reluctantly, I add: "An Upperclassman."

He raises an eyebrow. "You have interesting friends, boy."

"He noticed I was injured, and brought me back to his mansion. If he hadn't, I might have gotten eaten by Scarabs."

His expression darkens at that.

"There's good in people, if you look for it."

"Even in an Upperclassman?"

"Even in them."

I snort. "I think he just wanted to bang me."

"Well, give him the benefit of the doubt."

I sigh. "Can I stay the night?"

I know the secret police would be onto us sooner or later, but right now, I don't want to risk going back. They've beaten me up once—they'll do it again.

"Sure thing," he agrees.

"Thanks."

He ruffles my hair. Damn, I miss that feeling.

"Don't mention it. While you're looking for a new place, I think you might be able to make some money at the local hospital. We're in need of an assistant with some medical knowledge. They're not allowed to hire Fallen, but they won't look too closely—you'll get the job."

"Not much money around if they're willing to overlook stuff like that."

"Yeah, and none of us are really fans of the Gardá, the secret police, or the Party."

I chuckle at that. "It's nice to see you again, uncle."

"It's nice to see you too, nephew."

Chapter Three

Conall

Diana is always a pleasure to listen to.

Part of it is in the way she speaks—always with a self-deprecating air, always with a rhetorical quip or a clever anecdote. I assume that was the reason father hired her as my tutor, though there seems to be something more to her than simple charm or wit. Call it a mystery.

The topic of discussion today is politics. That's hardly surprising—it's mostly what I study at the Lyceum, a preparatory school for young men of my class and standing. Father claimed good finishing grades would be valuable for my entrance into high politics. I didn't believe him—connections get your far in the Party, not school—but I went along.

"So, back to our previous lesson. What is the essence of politics?"

"Conflict," I reply immediately.

"Indeed, Conall. Now for a harder question: how is conflict resolved?"

"That would depend on the system in question." She smiles again, pleased by my answer. We always did this: the back and forth. She called it the dialectic.

"You can explain the process for the main political systems known to man."

"In our current political system, we pretend that conflict doesn't exist: Unity is Strength. In reality, conflict is always brooding behind back doors and closeted whispers."

She throws back her hair—it's long, and dark brown, though I always imagine it to be electric blue.

"What about democracy?"

"We used to practise that, a long time ago, even if the Party states that history begins with them. In a democracy, conflict was resolved through campaigning and appealing to the demos."

"In theory, Conall. Reality was always a little more subtle than that. Referendums were forgotten or ignored; elected representatives never really represented the populace, being either too reluctant to accept change, or using the populace to pursue their own fanatical ends. Democracy likes to pretend that conflict is resolved—in reality, of course, conflict is never resolved. It's why human politics is so fundamentally unstable."

"Is that why Father is so obsessed with stability?"

"Your father understands politics well. Besides, let's not be so naive as to think there might not be any self-interest at heart." That's Diana: never afraid to tell the truth. It's a wonder she hasn't gotten into trouble. Maybe her standing as a Technical—a class of people responsible for jobs like teaching, engineering, and research—allows her a certain leeway. The Technicals have just enough material wealth to have something to lose; but they are also politically impotent enough to be safely ignored.

We continue discussing the finer points of political science. I'm almost disappointed when we finish.

"It was a good lesson," I say.

"I know."

"Aren't you being a tad presumptuous?"

There's a twinkle in her eye.

"Oh no; the statement was predicated on you, not on me. You clearly found it interesting. You're not always this animated—at times you're close to falling asleep."

"I have a lot of work at the Lyceum as well," I point out in my defence.

"True, but trust a teacher and her instincts."

So we shake hands, and she leaves, blowing me a kiss. I look out the window, follow-ing her progress. The sky is dark and brooding; the clouds are thick and black. I know it's the beginning of a storm. I can feel it: it seems almost alive with malice. Those ominous clouds will smite the city with thunder and assault it with sulphuric acid rain.

Diana seems completely unconcerned. In her bright green coat and vivid red scarf, she stands out conspicuously from the crowd of people racing for cover. I shake my head.

Sighing, I turn my attention back inside. My study is enormous; the ceiling stretches high above, and even the windows tower over me. All of the rooms in the mansion are like this. Still, there are signs of my personality interspersed—a favourite book, an unusual rug Diana gave me, a splash of colour in a curtain or fitting.

I know Father will be meeting me soon. Once he deals with Party business, he returns home, and asks me how my studies are progressing. Usually my answer is straightforward ("excellent, Father," since I very much grasp politics). Sometimes, though, father asks very different questions, and I often hate him for it.

The QCar glides to a halt in front of the mansion, blue light shimmering from its sleek surface. The vehicle is constructed in a tear drop shape: the engineers I've talked to tell me it's to reduce drag during supersonic flight.

I soon hear father climbing the stairs. He knocks—though the motion is perfunctory —before walking in. My father is not a young man: his black hair is marred by grey, and his face is composed of hard, unsmiling lines. But no one would mistake him for a weak man. There's something in his eyes—a power, an intelligence, a menacing ambition. Party members are not to be crossed.

"Hello, Conall."

"Hello, Niall."

"You don't have to call me by my name, you know."

"No, but father gets terribly repetitive after a while."

He smiles just a little. "You should respect those who are in a position of authority, son. That said, a little rebellious streak is not so bad, provided that you keep it carefully controlled."

"I thought you considered rebelliousness a vice?"

"Not in you, son. You need to think for yourself; the propaganda is for those lower down. An Upperclassman needs to be shrewd if he is to survive in politics."

"Is that what you want to talk me about?"

"No." The way he says it leads me to believe he has other things on his mind.

"Then what?"

"You shouldn't stay up so late at that brothel. That android can't protect you from everything, especially in the less guarded parts of the city."

"Thanks for the advice, father, but you've allowed me this freedom and I intend to make the best of it."

"It's a necessary evil," he says.

"Oh yes," I said, sarcasm lacing through my words despite my effort to contain it. "If I fuck guys at the whorehouse, nobody cares. Is that right?"

"It's for your own good, son. You know how they are about that sort of behaviour."

"I don't care what *they* think; what do *you* think?" We've been over this before, but I've never asked him so straightforwardly.

"I don't care who you fancy, boy—there are more important things to be worried about than what goes on in the bedroom."

"Is that how you see me?"

He just sighs. Then, to my surprise, he lays a hand on my shoulder. "I love you son, don't you forget that. Even if it's tough love, it's still love."

With that, he leaves me. I stand looking at the door, feeling angry, confused, and somehow touched. Father can be a bastard. But I shouldn't doubt his motivations.

∗∗∗

The storm hits that night.

It starts with thunder. At first it is staccato; then it increases in frequency until it's a continuous, earth-shattering rumble. The sky flashes green, followed by shades of unearthly blue and violet. Rain can be heard pounding on the windows and roof, though it's acidic thanks to all the sulphur in the atmosphere. My science lessons in lower school had taught me that recent industrial processes, used to make new alloys and ceramics, are responsible for all the pollution.

I sit on my bed and stare at my Com. The tiny device projects a holographic readout; it serves as a portable computer and communications device. There's really nothing for me to do except talk with friends.

You seeing this storm? Stella texts me.

Oh yeah; it looks like a bad one.

Aren't they all?

Yeah, and it sucks being stuck here.

You haven't considered taking the QCar have you? The QCar would survive the storm just fine, but...

Father would kill me.

Yeah, I guess he would. Even being Upperclass doesn't let you do everything. Like most Lyceum students, Stella is Upperclass; you have to be in order to join the Party. Though I suspect that Stella would do her best to avoid the Party—she was there for her parents, not herself. She always told me she fancied being in business or the diplomatic service. Free-

19

dom is the greatest privilige we possess as Upperclassmen.

How are you doing, anyway? I continue.

Oh, you know—assignments. Life. Your tutor is better than mine; I wish I had her.

Yeah, too bad Niall took her off the market. It's common for teachers to act as tutors; the pay is good, and it opens the possibility of family ties. Family ties could mean marriage, one of the few ways of changing Class—though even then marriages have to be approved by the Party. The purpose of the Class system is, after all, to ensure that everyone does the work needed to maintain a strong economy.

Your tutor is weird, though. Like, seriously. Is it true that she walked out just before the storm was about to go off?

Yup.

How? The acid must ruin her hair. I chuckle at that: Stella does have a sense of humour.

Nothing seems to faze her.

Stella sends me an emoticon—a scrunched up face. *Anyway, good night. Tell me if you meet the boy again.*

I'd shared that little secret with her. It's nothing, really, as she already knows about me. I trust Stella—I don't know exactly why, but I do. She's not driven by ambition the same way others are.

That's hardly likely. I say the words casually, though secretly it pains me. Then again, I have to be realistic. He did everything he could to get away from me. And who can blame him? We are worlds apart, and love is forbidden.

Not that I've ever cared about what's forbidden.

Chapter Four

Kaylin

Somehow, I have never loved storms. Yet, in a way, storms are very much like my visions: chaotic, unpredictable, but even so, governed by a complex set of rules we barely understand. I like to delude myself, occasionally, into thinking that storms are more violent and more unpredictable than the future my visions foretell. The delusion lasts only a moment.

"It's a beautiful storm, isn't it?" she asks.

"You would say so, Diana, but you are stranger than me."

She laughs, and her brown eyes flash lightning blue. She tosses her hair back; it moves in the wind like a wave, brown and gold as an autumn leaf. She is dressed in her favourite green coat, and on her shoulder is the red scarf I made for her. The storm howls around us, lashing the buildings with acid rain.

"You think so?" She flexes her hand, almost experimentally. A bolt of lightning shoots from the sky, obliterating a nearby street lamp.

"Histrionics," I say. That's one of the things that separates her power from mine: I rely on absolute control to use my magic, while hers is a magic of wild things, of destruction.

"Oh come on, it's fun."

I shake my head. "Come with me. We have work to do—rebellion is a full time job."

"I'm sure the men will be fine without us, at least for a while. You have faith in them, right?"

"I have faith they will do everything they can, within their abilities; that might not be enough, however. One does not cross the Party lightly. And though they may be professionals, they do not have magic. Rebellions have been tried before, and they have failed—without me, they are doomed to fail again."

"That's a pretty big responsibility you're putting on yourself there, you know?"

"I know."

"Anyway, aren't you curious to know how my mission is going?"

"Ah yes, our potential asset. Does he trust you yet?"

"Piece by piece."

"I don't suppose you could get him to join our cause?"

"Maybe, but it will not be easy. To revile the Party and be sympathetic to its demise is one thing; to put your life on the line, quite another."

Like I don't know as much. "Do your best, Diana."

"Yes, Mistress."

I smile, just slightly. The name started out as a joke, but everyone calls me mistress now.

The storm howls and rages around us, though we walk through it unaffected. We cross empty streets, the denizens of this city staying safely inside—though the occasional vehicle does pass by. I wonder if the driver would consider us strange: two women, walking through a dangerous storm without a care in the world. In my experience, people are good at ignoring what they find hard to believe or impossible to explain. If the world knew about magic, my life would be much more complicated.

We arrive at an unassuming house, and I place my hand on an unassuming door. Runes activate, glowing faint blue; the door vanishes. Inside, the walls are covered with weapons. None would be legal to own: we have laser rifles, pistols, machine guns, grenades and big-bore plasma cannons. Enough to equip a small army, for sure. But to fight the Party head-on? No, that would be suicide. Our approach requires subtlety.

I have work to do. We will speak again later.

Good luck.

I'm pleased to find she's getting better at telepathy. Initially, I couldn't get her to reply, only to listen.

"Grumman, status report," I ask my lieutenant.

"Nothing to see here, Mistress. Business as usual."

"Don't tell me the Party isn't planning to kidnap or kill someone? Are there no more countries left for the European League of Nations to conquer and burn?"

"Oh, I'm sure the Party is plotting to kill someone as we speak. But that's just a normal Party day."

My smile is ironic, and bitter. "Don't I know it."

"Any more visions?" he asks.

"None, but I will try again tonight."

He nods, understanding the dismissal. For a while, I stay, watching my men at work: they analyse maps, compile intelligence reports, and communicate with agents in the field. A few say greetings, to which I reply amicably. Information is valuable currency in our line of work—but even the best spies and hackers cannot know everything. The future, I have come to realise, is dominated by two equally powerful forces: fate, and human intention. We can try to know the latter; the former will always remain beyond us.

But not beyond me. I find a quiet room, sit myself on a comfortable chair, and close my eyes. I relax; the immediate world fades to nothing, and in its place, I see the greater world. A world of infinite possibility—either good, or evil.

Chapter Five

Mark

"Can you grab me some more regen solution, Donaghue?"

I nod at Dr. Liam's orders. I'd been working at the hospital for a few days now; I'd been tasked with a lot of work of this sort since I'd started. Not that I'm complaining, mind you: the work is safe. Pays decently too. I'm glad that uncle had got me the job, even if I have to assume a pseudonym to keep prying eyes at bay.

Oh sure, there are ways to check identities—they wouldn't find anyone with my credentials and assumed name if they looked on the databases. But uncle had been right when he said they didn't look too carefully.

I quickly make my way to the hospital storage, grabbing the regenerator solution and a few other things the Dr. had forgotten to ask for (but which I still paid attention to). Uncle taught me a few things about medicine; if I weren't Fallen, I might even have been allowed to become a doctor.

When I come back, he takes the regenerator off me, and raises an eyebrow at the antibiotics I'd also brought.

"I'd forgotten about the antibiotics, actually. Thank you for noticing on my behalf, Donaghue. You'll make a doctor one day." He smiles. He's younger than most doctors—I'd guess thirty or so—and has a way about him that makes him easy to like.

The patient—a girl who's been attacked by mutant wolves—looks at the wound on her arm. I wince in sympathy. The puncture wounds go down to the bone; her arm looks like it's been passed through a meat-grinder.

Dr Liam applies the antibiotic, and then the regenerator solution. He soon finishes, and works on the next patient. So it goes for a few more hours. Eventually, my shift is over, and I'm free to go. They pay me by the hour, in cash. I'm allowed a bank account, but the Party's agents regularly audit those; it's easier to avoid suspicion this way.

I make my way, out into the sun.

∗∗∗

As I walk past streets that are half empty—I finished later today, and most of the people in this part of town are home by now—I begin thinking.

Although I don't own much, I'd left a few things at the dealers' place that I would have preferred to keep. The most important is my ID: without it, I would be in trouble. But I don't want to risk meeting them again. I wonder if uncle can get me a fake one, but I moot the idea: it would be too dangerous, and I can't risk his life like that.

So, I wait. I know when there will be a moment of opportunity. I walk towards my old neighbourhood, taking side alleys, and taking care to remain hidden from obvious view. I find a place that overlooks my old apartment. I stay there, watching carefully.

It doesn't take long before I see two of them—Brendan and O'Flaherty—making their way out. The other two are away, I know. We follow a rough code: one of us would always be home. We could contact the others if trouble came—either of the legal or not legal kind. My drug dealer roommates aren't stupid; they know how to avoid the dangers of their line of work.

Ironically, nobody would be home now because this used to be my time slot. I'm counting on the fact that they haven't changed the schedule yet.

I make my way to the building. The complex is big; its grey concrete walls, lined with steel, gives it an imposing look. It always reminds me of an institution. The sun is low in the sky now, and its light is blood red.

The steel door opens without a hitch; it's only locked in emergencies, or when night falls. I make my way up the stairs, taking care to avoid making noise. I find our door, and let myself in soundlessly.

The place isn't any more orderly than when I'd left: the remains of food are strewn about, the sofas dirty and the chairs in disarray. Our holographic projector is in the corner —I turn it on, leaving it on a random channel. The noise would mask my movements, and give the illusion that someone is really here.

I head to my old room. It's small, square, and most of it is taken up by the bed. I find my ID hidden carefully inside. I also manage to grab my com phone, a few clothes, and anything else I could carry in the black rucksack I have on me.

Suddenly, he attacks.

∗∗∗

I dodge the knife, knowing he would use it. The kick gets a grunt from me, but he'd failed to hit anything important. I counter-attack: I strike low with my punch, hitting him in the gut. He gasps and backs away.

We stare at each other; him, with the knife; and me, with nothing but my wits and the strength in my shoulders. His eyes are bright green; he has a mop of red hair surrounding a freckled face. Even so, it is the expression that captures my attention. Finn had never liked me; but then, I'd never thought he hated me, either. The look in those eyes makes my stom-ach churn.

"You shouldn't have come back."

"Well sorry lad, but a guy needs his ID. You weren't polite enough to return it when you kicked me out and beat me up." He doesn't look impressed by my sarcasm; instead he spits.

"Stop acting the maggot. I hated the sight of you, and I still do."

"But fuck it, Finn, what have I ever done to you?"

"It's not what you *did*; it's what you *are*."

"And why does that bother you?"

He just snarls and leaps at me. Expecting the attack, I pirouette my body, smashing the contents of my bag into his face. There isn't enough hard metal in there, as otherwise it would have knocked him out. But it did enough to stop his attack. I follow up with a hard strike to his wrist; he drops the knife. What can I say? I know a thing or two about fights.

Enraged, he grapples with me. We fight each other on the floor, but he'd made a dumb move: I'm stronger than him, and he has no idea how to wrestle. Soon I have him in a headlock.

"So what's it gonna be, Finn? I let you go and you promise not to bother me again?"

"I hate you." I want to ask why, but I know there's no point. Everything up to that moment tells me he's beyond rational argument.

"I take that as a no then." I apply more pressure. "Guess I'm just going to have to kill you, eh?"

"You don't have the guts, pussyboy. I bet you're thinking of me right now, aren't you? Wanna stick that hard cock of yours in my arse?" I just blink at his outburst.

He relaxes against me, and starts rubbing against my crotch. My surprise is all he needs. Suddenly, he's out of my grasp, and going for the knife. I don't have time to stop him: I just grab whatever's next to me.

When he attacks again, I swing. I hear a crunching sound; then, deathly silence.

I bring myself to my feet, looking at the damage I'd done. Blood pools on the floor; it's vivid red, and looks so wrong against the grey concrete floor. I lean down, listening for breathing. Nothing. I place two fingers on his throat, only for my fingers to become slick with blood.

I don't really comprehend what I've done. I drop to the floor; tears start falling from my eyes. Sure: he'd tried to kill me. He hated me—for no other reason than because I'm different. I should feel satisfied that he got what he deserved.

But I'm not a cold-blooded murderer. And to see him dead...

I shake my head. I start thinking about the Gardá—would they know it was me? Would they buy it if I told them it was self-defence? *Better leave*, I tell myself. They'll probably just assume it was one of his drug-dealing "friends"—they wouldn't suspect me. None of the others think I have what it takes. *I* never thought I had what it takes.

Until now.

Chapter Six

Conall

The holographic whiteboard is massive, though nobody seems to be paying much attention to it; the teacher, an expert in constitutional law (which is mostly an academic field considering that the Party decides the constitution) is giving a lecture on the details of the European League of Nations, a trans-European inter-governmental entity governed by treaties. It is, I realise, probably the only practical application for the knowledge. The Party may control Ireland, but they are hardly a great power.

Ireland was far too small a state to survive in the military conflicts that had engulfed the world for the past two hundred years or so. Therefore, the Party decided to join the European League of Nations—an arrangement that suits us well. The Party retains control of internal matters: police, taxation powers, and so on. They can leave at any time. In return, they have to contribute to the military budget and provide soldiers.

The ELN has proven to be a successful gambit. It's the joint strongest bloc in the world; its power is rivalled only by that of China. America has collapsed into anarchy, following a series of incompetent presidencies that led them into a great folly: the first, and only, nuclear war. Their democracy proved so disastrous that the ELN abandoned it, in favour of Chinese-style authoritarianism.

"This law is all so tedious," Jake exclaims beside me.

I raise an eyebrow. The boy, who had transferred to the Lyceum after being expelled from a political college in England, has decided to sit next to me this lesson. I can't say I mind, since he's rather attractive. His hair is a perfect, obsidian black; his eyes are dark, mysterious, but also impish with mischief. Arrogance oozes from his pores. I like it.

"I agree, but the Lyceum insists on it. A politician must know the law after all."

He snorts. "The law is decided by politicians, and we don't give a damn what the law-yers think."

I agree, so I ask something else instead. "In that case, why not tell me more about yourself?"

"You've probably heard the rumours already." I have—apparently he had been too badly behaved to tolerate, not doing homework and ignoring punishments.

"Is there any truth to them?"

"Some. But it was I who decided to leave; they didn't expel me. Too much money at stake for that."

"But why come here?"

"They don't seem to care as much here; it makes life easier."

"Fair enough," I say.

"What about you?" he asks. "Any juicy details about your life?"

"Just the standard fare really." I'm not going to reveal my secrets to him just yet.

"Oh really?" His leg brushes mine, and my throat goes a little dry.

"Father is a medium ranking Party member; my mother is a multimillionaire."

"The usual fare indeed," he agrees with a smile. I wonder how much he picks up—I have a feeling I don't want to know.

"So what do you want out of this?" he continues.

"I beg your pardon?"

"Oh come on—what is it? Do you want to advance in the Party hierarchy? Or are you trying to make lucrative connections?"

I flounder for a response; he laughs. "Don't tell me: you're doing this because your dad makes you."

Now I'm annoyed. "What about *you* then? If you're so high and mighty, what's your reason?"

He shrugs. "Money and power. What else?"

I have no answer to that.

The professor eventually finishes his lecture, and we start to leave. He follows me. I try, vainly, to ignore him.

"Are you going to tell me I hurt your feelings?"

"You are a bit of a dickhead."

He only chuckles. "You're right. But maybe you'll like me all the same."

I turn to look at him. Even in the bright sun, he seems surrounded by smooth darkness.

"And why would I do that?"

"I don't know." His hand brushes mine. "Call it a feeling."

I watch his receding form. He walks with an assured confidence—a belief that, no matter what he does, everything would turn out in his favour. And maybe he's right, I realise. My heart is beating double time. I force myself to keep walking.

✦✦✦

I don't pay much attention to the remaining lessons. My mind is a whirlwind: I see Jake's smile, hear his seductive voice, feel the smoothness of his hand against mine. But I also see the boy who saved me; the boy who, rightly, despised me. I wonder when—if ever—I would see him again. My emotions see-saw with the contradictions.

Shaking my head, I try to distract myself by finding Stella.

"How are you?" she asks as we walk out of the Lyceum.

She looks at me with sea-blue eyes; her hair, a bright red, is illuminated by the rays of the sun and occasionally lifted by a stray gust of wind. Around us, other students walk. Behind us, the buildings of the Lyceum stand tall. They are built like their namesake in ancient Greece: white marble, Ionic pillars, resplendent courtyards.

"Fine," I say returning to the present.

"You don't sound fine." I have to give it to her: she knows me well.

"Well..." I walk away from the main throng of students, and start whispering. "It's just that there are two guys I really like."

"Oh? You've already told me about the boy you met in the Fallen Quarter."

"Well, there's Jake."

Her eyebrows shoot up. "*Jake?* The Jake?"

"I didn't know he was called *the* Jake," I protest.

"Are you kidding? Everyone has heard about him. That he got expelled—"

"He told me he chose to leave."

"Whatever. He's still *bad*, Conall."

"What if I like a little bad?"

"Trust me—you don't want *that* kind of bad."

"What do you mean?" I ask, sensing something more to her comments.

"He's a player; he has half the girls in this school under his spell."

"So what?"

She shrugs. "Don't say I didn't warn you."

✦✦✦

At home, I find the mansion empty, save for a few servants. I know father is probably occupied with Party business—he's always secretive about it—so I make myself comfortable. I order the servants to pour me some wine and program the kitchen robot; then I sit down to watch something.

The 3D holographic projector usually manages to keep me interested, especially when it comes to action films (I love explosions). But today I can't even tell if I'm watching an action movie or a rom-com. Figures whizz by my head, but I watch them only with the incurious stare of a zombie.

I try reading instead. The story is a dark tale, of underhand plots and supernatural murders; but somehow, I find myself bored. I skip words, sentences, and eventually whole paragraphs.

I know what I have to do. I berate myself for doing it, even as I withdraw my com phone and call up one of father's contacts. The man doesn't ask why I would be interested in a Fallen boy; he simply listens carefully to my instructions, tells me he'll follow them to the letter, and hangs up.

I lie back on the sofa, wondering what I've gotten myself into. I have a feeling things are going to get interesting.

Chapter Seven

Mark

There's a brooding silence as I tell uncle what happened.

He listens carefully, nodding when I tell him about Finn's hatred. He's not surprised when I tell him what I'd done to defend myself.

"It's not your fault, boy, you know that right?"

I blink, suddenly confused. "Well, yeah, I wasn't the one who attacked him..."

"No: I mean all of it. It's not your fault you had to go back and recover your ID, or your com phone; it's not your fault he had a problem with you; and it sure as hell isn't your fault he's dead. The boy killed himself."

"Thanks, uncle," I say, realising I needed to hear him say that.

"Just giving you sound advice. Don't go back there; you don't want to draw the attention of the Gardá, the other dealers, or the damn Secrets. In fact, lie low—don't let anyone notice you. You're probably right, and they'll just think it was one of his other dealer 'friends.'"

"Maybe they won't even bother to investigate it."

"They have to, although their efforts will probably—hopefully—be *pro forma*." Noticing my confused expression, he adds: "That means they'll make a show of it, boy."

"You know I could never keep up with all your Latin."

"Well, learn it; and learn to speak proper when you need to, too. One day you'll need to pass for something other than a Fallen." Those of us in our Class have a distinct accent—it's hard to describe, beyond slang or saying *dat* instead of *that*. We also have a way with our words that tells everyone where we hail from. It took uncle considerable effort, but I can just about sound like a posh boy if I try.

After that, uncle boils some more tea. I don't think of myself as a tea man (if I need caffeine I would slurp down an energy drink) but I find I myself liking it. I wonder: will I keep drinking it when I leave? The thought brings a cold dread in my stomach.

Outside, darkness has fallen. I say goodnight to my uncle, and try to sleep. Of course, things aren't going to be that easy...

***

There's whispering all around me. There are too many of them—their voices are indistinguishable, but the message is clear.

KILL HIM.

I try and resist. I don't want to kill him; I don't want to become... the thing they whisper about. A monster. Powerful. A being from another world.

I wish he would stop it. He's looking up at me; his eyes are a bright green, and burn with anger. His body lies prostrate below me. I hold a knife to his throat, and though I try as hard as I can, I can't seem to take it away.

Then he smiles.

"Kill me," Finn whispers. "Kill me, pussyboy. Let's see what you're really made of."

"Finn, please," I breathe. "I don't want to do it. I don't want... to become what..."

"Why don't you, Mark? Don't you want power? Aren't you tired of being looked down, spat on, and fucked over?"

And somehow, my hand tightens around his throat. The sharp, brilliant knife cuts a perfect red line through his neck; he collapses, blood gushing everywhere. But even in death, he's smiling.

***

I wake up instantly. The morning sun shines through the window; the room around me is warm, the white sheets glazed by the golden light. I'm safe, I realise. But the cold terror of the nightmare is still there: I see the images whenever I close my eyes. So I force myself to do the morning chores. I throw on a T-shirt, jeans, and trainers. I wolf down some food, quickly brush my teeth, and throw myself out the door.

A sharp pain forces me to stop. I feel around my shoulder blades—but there's nothing. I suppose I shouldn't be surprised: I *did* just get into a fight and kill someone. It's probably just a muscle strain or something. I keep going.

I still have a morning shift at the hospital, so I check in and make myself busy. I am, in a sense, lucky: no one would pay attention to a hospital assistant. I simply bring medicines, help the nurses with the patients, and occasionally call the doctors when I notice something wrong on the monitoring machines.

Time passes quickly—as it does when I'm busy. Soon it's noon, and time for a break. I grab two sandwiches and make my way outside. I sit on a bench, behind the shadow of an oak; I watch the sun make its progress across the sky, trying—and failing—not to think about anything. But the memory, and the dream, are not things I can run away from.

I hear the noises of ambulances, people talking, the rumble of tyres on tarmac, and a Gardá siren. The siren makes the hairs on the back of my neck stand up—but then it recedes into the distance. I breath a sigh of relief. I have more than enough to worry about without the Gardá sniffing me up.

"You look troubled." I almost jump at the sound of Dr. Liam's voice. He simply looks at me, those brown eyes of his narrowed in concern.

"Oh, just tired. I'm not really one for the morning shifts," I lie.

"Is that so? Or is the real reason that you're not allowed to be doing this?"

I close my eyes, feeling cornered. He quickly adds: "I won't tell anyone, Donaghue, if that's your real name."

"How did you figure it out?"

"Nothing in particular. A hint of accent, your body language now, maybe a bit of knowledge that was missing or wouldn't have been taught to you in school. Really, I just pieced it together."

"I... I don't know what to say."

"I understand; you're good at this job, and it's better than the other jobs in your Class. Just be more careful, okay?"

"Yes, Dr Liam."

"You can call me just Liam."

"Okay." I add: "My real name is Mark, by the way."

"Thank you," he says.

He leads me back to the hospital, a gentle smile on his face.

✶

A few hours later, I'm done. Liam waves me goodbye; I wave back. But my mind is on other things.

I make my way to the nearby park. I visit the place often, when I feel overwhelmed at all that life has to throw at me. Others, I know, would end up drinking, doing drugs or gambling—all of which you could easily do in the seedier parts of this city. But not me. Uncle taught me that, no matter how hard life seems to be, I should never do drugs (alcoholic or otherwise). They would only make things worse, in the end. If life as a Fallen is bad, it's not half as bad as what the homeless or the prostitutes are put through.

So I sit on a bench, by a fountain. The damp breeze helps me cool off from the after-noon heat. Few Fallen are here, but that doesn't matter. Parks, along with hospitals, are one of the few public works they let us use. They give us free hospitals because we would spread plagues otherwise; and as for the parks, I guess they didn't feel the need to bother.

I shouldn't be a member of the underclass. Even though most of us are born into it, they called us Fallen. In my case, I *am* fallen: dad had left when my mother died giving birth to me. The children of abandoned spouses are automatically downgraded—the Party say it's to discourage absentee parents and maintain family units. I feel a hint of the old anger, then. Why had my dad left me? If he hadn't, my life would be so much different.

I shake my head. I'd asked myself these questions before; and no answers had fallen from the heavens. I'm on my own, and I better get used to that.

But maybe, something in me says, I don't have to be on my own. That Upperclassman —Conall, because he's not just an Upperclassman—had saved my life. I would have been scarab meat without him. And he wanted me, too: I could tell. I hadn't dared accept that maybe I felt the same about him.

I sigh. No answers are going to fall from the heavens, and God sure as hell isn't going to send me a guardian angel. I have to live the life I've been given.

Chapter Eight

Kaylin

It seems like too nice a day to do what we are about to do. The sun shines brightly, its rays refracted by the puffy clouds that dot the sky. The air is still; the world is quiet.

But then again, there's no time like the present. My men give me regular updates through the com system: they'd been able to spot our target entering his home this evening, and are now observing him carefully. The man is watching TV, they tell me. I almost want to laugh. There he is: a man blessed with a powerful Ability—the ultimate spy—and he's just watching TV. No awareness of who we are. No knowledge of what he really is.

"When do you want to go in?" the lieutenant I'd placed in charge of the operation asks me.

"I would like to observe him carefully—this seems too easy. Surely he would know of his power? And surely he would know that there are those who would do anything to have him?"

"He seems... blissful," the man replies.

"You know what we are like, Eoin."

"Always more than you seem—yeah, I get that." He goes quiet.

I close my eyes, putting myself in that strange, trance-like state that allows the visions to come. But there is nothing: the world around me remains as it is. I open my eyes again, frustrated. It's unusual for my powers to resist my call, and it's especially unusual for them to do so when I need them most.

"Proceed with caution," I order. "I... cannot see anything."

"Really?" Eoin asks.

"Yes. I'm not sure why; it is possible that my fears are correct, and there is indeed more to him."

"Roger that."

There is faint electric sound as they charge their weapons. They're not lethal, of course: they're only tasers, designed for incapacitation. Me and my team move in silently; the TV continues blaring noisily. We knock on the door. (It is always better to start with politeness.) There is no answer.

"What should we do?" the lieutenant asks.

"If we call him out, that may scare him into running. We'll have to go in guns blazing."

Eoin looks at me then. His eyes are a hard blue, barely visible behind his black helmet. A powerful gloved hand reaches out—the signal. Everything explodes into action.

The door falls instantly. My men fan out, weapons at the ready. I hang back, watching. They clear the first room quickly—it's empty. They make their way to the living room door, where we know he should be waiting. A quick hand signal, and we're in.

We are confronted by emptiness.

I stare, certain that he had been here moments ago. Could he have escaped? But we have all the exits covered: it wouldn't be possible for him to evade our notice, unless... Well, it made sense. Things really aren't going to be this easy, then.

"Mistress?" Eoin asks.

"Let me think."

But there's no time to think. Eoin crumples to the floor, his helmet cracked. My men look for the assailant—but no one is there. In the confusion, I see another man fall, and then another. The invisible assailant hadn't run away: he was here, and trying hard to kill us, by the look of it.

"Fire at will!" I order. The tasers would not harm my men.

Blue light flashes everywhere. There is a cacophony of noise; electric zapping, screams, and confused grunts mix into chaos. Through it all, I close my eyes. And this time, I feel him.

I dodge his attack. He tries again, and again I dodge. I am far more powerful than any ordinary clairvoyant. I can sense his intentions—and see before he acts. The third time, I don't dodge: I grab something—his hand—and focus a spell against him. He crumples to the floor, now visible.

The silence that ensues is almost as deafening as the noise. My men aim their weapons at him, though it's entirely unnecessary: he's not going anywhere. My spell ensures that. As my men collect their bearings, I analyse him carefully. He's slight—almost boyish in his stature. Black hair falls over his face, though it doesn't conceal the intense anger radiating from his eyes. His muscles strain futilely against the containment spell.

"Who are you?" he asks.

"I could ask you the same question."

"You're the one who's raided my home and attacked me."

"True. But you might not believe who we are."

"Are you the Secrets? Or some other Party lackeys—someone I've not even heard of?"

"We're not with the Party. In fact, our mission is to topple them."

"Oh really? And why should I believe you?"

I shrug. "I think you will believe me—because I have the answers you've been looking for."

"Answers?"

"Don't pretend: we couldn't hit you because we were *blind*. You have a power."

"How... how do you know?"

"Ask yourself this: how was I able to evade you?"

He pauses, thinking. "You couldn't see me any better than they could."

"Indeed. I could *sense* you; it is one of my many powers."

"So there *are* others like me," he muses.

"Of course."

"And you know all about it?"

"I have them under my thumb."

"So is that what you want, then? Why you came here? To control me for your own ends." It's not really a question, but I answer it anyway.

"Not necessarily; you can say no."

"Really? You'll leave me, just like that?"

"If you say no, we will accept your decision, for no one serves us out of fear or through coercion. But I will ask you to consider this: we are not the only ones who are interested in you. The Party don't know we exist—I've done my best to ensure that. If you don't join us, though, you'll lack the ability to defend yourself, to hide yourself. The Party will discover you eventually."

"Ha! Those bastards will never even see me."

"Perhaps not you. But don't you use the Internet?"

"I... I guess so. You can't live without it."

"The Internet is closely monitored by the Party's algorithms. It's only a matter of time before they get wind of you."

"Fine. I'll run—get out of the country."

"Perhaps you will. But what about your family?"

He looks down, conflicted.

"I know you have a daughter, even though you rarely visit her. And I know you love her—or else you wouldn't force yourself to stay away."

"I don't like this."

I lift the spell. He rises to his feet, shakily.

"None of us do, really. But the Party is a reality: if you want to fight it, join us."

"Can I... think about it?"

"It is your decision."

"Then why did you bring them?" He motions towards my men.

"Let's just say this kind of operation can be dangerous."

He closes his eyes, trying to think everything through.

"We'll be back," I promise him. And so we leave.

✷✷✷

"Damn, that hurt," Eoin complains.

"You're lucky to be alive, you know. That hammer would have killed you without the helmet."

"Yeah." He shakes his head. "That's some power. We could do with a guy like him."

I smile coldly.

"Let's just hope he joins us. Or he's going to find that a hammer won't be much use against a drone."

✷✷✷

The next morning, I attempt to See more. I'm curious as to why I had not foreseen the events of last night. Is he immune, somehow, to my powers? But surely not: I'd been able to sense him, and the spell had no trouble pinning him. No, something else is afoot. I can feel it.

The process of Seeing is not as easy as it looks. To my Familiars, their abilities are as natural as breathing—but Seeing is a different sort of magic, one that requires care and concentration. Worse still is the knowledge it brings: strange, conflicting, and often terrifying.

It's why I prefer to See in a small room, secluded from the rest of the compound. Sunlight pierces a single narrow window; the rest of the room is darker, being populated by thickset mahogany furniture and a carpet of deep red. I find the warm colours relaxing.

I touch a group of bones on the table as I make myself comfortable on the leather armchair. They begin to levitate, and then spin. I close my eyes.

Shadows. Men marching; the rumble of tracks on tarmac. Radio communication, and orders being issued.

An explosion, high in the sky. A mushroom cloud. Destruction.

Seeing is like this—a whole mass of images, of possibilities. Uncontrolled, Seeing presents a useless mass of information. I instead focus, forcing the visions to my intent. But there is nothing. Try as hard as I might, I cannot will the visions to him: something else is there, something that begs for my attention. I can feel it.

So, knowing that Seeing is a process prone to serendipity, I allow the vision to take its own course.

At first it's blurry, and dark. *The looming shadows of a tall building; the dripping of a pipe. A breeze.*

Gradually, details solidify. *A tall, cold, empty space. Two boys. One standing; the other prostrate. Wings. Black, and massive. Power in the air.*

Then the vision explodes into fragments of light.

***

Gasping, I lie on the chair, confused by the vision.

I'm not worrying about the other Familiar now; this vision is something else, something far more important. Its meaning seems tantalisingly within my reach, and yet impenetrable.

"It's tough, eh?" I jump, but it's only Diana.

"Tell me about it. I tried to See whether he would join us, only to be confronted with something else entirely."

"Go on," she continues.

"He had black wings," I say, skipping the details and focusing on what had struck out most.

"Do you think he had some sort of ability, then? Another Familiar?" Her suggestion is a sensible one, but I know it's wrong.

"No—it was something else, of that I am sure. Anyway, you know how my visions are."

"Sure. I assume you want us to focus on the task at hand?"

"You know me well. Let me worry about my visions."

"If you say so, Kaylin, but I don't think you can do this alone. I can tell the Seeing is taking its toll on you. Relax."

I smile ironically. "Since when are you so worried about my welfare, Diana?"

"Since you saved me from the Party, and I joined you in fighting them."

I can't argue with that. I sigh. "What would you have me do?"

She disappears for a moment, and arrives with a bottle of wine. "As I say, relax."

The wine is pleasantly inebriating, but it cannot calm my thoughts. The visions rarely force themselves like that; whatever they wanted to show me today, it had certainly not been accidental. I feel that a force has acted on me today. Something powerful; something grand beyond mortal imagining.

The thought disturbs me even more than the vision itself.

Chapter Nine

Conall

"Sir? I've found the man you asked me to find," my contact informs me through the com phone. I make my way towards my bedroom, hoping to avoid any prying ears.

"Good work, Sean. What's his name?"

"Mark."

A beautiful name, I think, for a beautiful man.

"Where does he live?"

"With his uncle. Illegally, might I add."

I pause, thinking. "In that case, do me a favour will you?"

"Yes?"

"Don't mention this to anyone else. In fact, I would prefer that you hide any trace of his current whereabouts from *those who may be interested*. Do I make myself clear?"

"Sir, this is—"

"Illegal, I know."

A moment's pause. "Very well, Sir—I suppose such a detail could get lost in the paperwork."

"And give me his address, will you?"

"No problem, Sir."

I smile. "Thank you, Sean."

With that, he hangs up, but not before sending me the address via text. Sean is a smart man: he knows not to trifle with those higher up. My father would approve.

Father would not, however, approve of what *I'm* doing. I lie back in my bed, thinking.

My bedroom is my most personal space (even father avoids being in here) and I make the best of it: the decor is all white and cream, a bright, airy change from the overbearing darkness of the mansion.

An Upperclassman meeting a Fallen is rare, but not unheard of. The Fallen are tasked with many things an Upperclassman might need: cleaning, chores, and so on. But the circumstances would raise suspicion; an Upperclassman wouldn't meet a seemingly random Fallen out of the blue. I know I can't just stroll in.

What I really need is cover.

"Stella?" I ask on the com.

"Yes, Conall?"

"I will be sending you a message saying that I'll be there with your friends at that party you're throwing." I've never been particularly good at parties, and Stella's friends were rather obnoxious; they often tried to accost me romantically.

"But you're not really going to be there, are you?" She's smart like that.

"No. Make sure to delete this conversation."

"Okay, gotcha. Have fun with him." With that, the com goes dead.

It's been over a week since I'd last seen him, and a prickle of nervousness cuts through me. Would he hate me? Had I imagined his interest?

I shake my head. For better or worse, I have to try.

The mansion is under constant surveillance, but I have two advantages. First, the cameras are set up to cover the *outside* of the mansion, not the inside. And secondly—I know where they are located. I take a circuitous route, through a side door, and around the garden. After that, freedom.

The afternoon sun shines down on me, bright, hot, but somehow soothing. I move towards the gate, knowing that a motion sensor will detect me; the shimmering force field, barely visible in the daylight, turns off to let me through. I've taken the less used exit—few people are about. I leave the Upper Quarter unnoticed.

∗∗∗

I analyse the house. I'm not surprised he lives in it illegally with his uncle: no Fallen could afford it. The windows are far too large; the garden is too manicured. His uncle, apparently a doctor, is definitely better paid than he is.

I knock on the door, and almost stumble when it's immediately opened. Before I can say anything, he whisks me inside.

"What are you doing here?" he whispers angrily.

"Seeing you. Don't you want that?"

"I do," he admits. My heart speeds up a little. But then he adds: "You shouldn't have come here though. They could have seen you—"

"I took pains to avoid that."

"And if they see me with you, I'll be damned more than I already am."

"Oh? You mean the minor illegality of living with you uncle?" I wave my hand. "I had one of my contacts cover up for you."

He stares at me. "You did that?"

I shrug. "Of course. It's not like *I* give a damn who you live with; in fact I'm glad you're here with your uncle instead of with some *dealers*."

He walks to a sofa, sits down heavily, and sighs.

"You've done a lot for me, Conall. I should thank you."

"You could start by telling me your name."

"You must already know it by now?"

"I still want to hear it from you."

"I'm Mark." He chuckles, and there's a dark undertone to it. "Uncle tells me I'm named after an angel."

I sit down next to him. I've never been shy with a guy before, but somehow, I can barely say the words. "You're very beautiful, Mark."

He looks away then.

"I don't know if I can do this," he says.

"Why? Am I... don't you feel the same way about me?"

He turns to look at me. Those eyes are so perfectly blue—like the glimmer of an expertly cut diamond. My eyes follow the curves of his jaw, noticing the faint stubble there, and the blonde hair that reaches past his forehead. It's like I'm seeing him all over again.

"You should leave. We can't do this; they'll never allow it."

"I don't care what they think," I say. "I only care about you."

"Yeah, well, not all of us are posh boys, Conall. You, they'll turn a blind eye to; me, they'll put in prison and throw away the keys."

He goes for the door. But I'm not having that: I stand in his way.

"What's the point, Mark? What's the point of living if you can't be who you are?"

"I'm not..."

"Don't lie to me." And then, bravely—stupidly—I walk closer to him. I touch his exposed neck, and he shivers. "Are you going to tell me that doesn't feel good? Are you going to tell me you don't want it?"

Before he can react, I push him down, against the sofa. My hips are grinding against his. My hands find their way inside his jeans, to the warm hardness inside...

"Conall," he breathes.

"Yes?"

"Kiss me."

I lean down, at first kissing his jaw, and then his lips. They're warm, and slightly salty, and taste delicious on my own. I make myself comfortable on his legs, while he threads his hands through my hair. I pull back, my breath ragged.

"That felt good," I say.

He smiles; it's an incredible smile. "It did."

Then *he's* kissing me, his tongue hot and powerful in my mouth. It's like being on fire. I feel him hardening against me. I'm hard too, and with a desire I can barely control, I loosen my belt; his own follows a moment later.

He pushes me away.

"No—not yet. Please."

I pull back, frustrated. "Well, I suppose I can't ask too much of you."

"I want you, Conall," he says, "but..."

"I understand." Then I have an idea. "Hey, is there someplace you'd like to go?"

"What do you mean?"

"I *am* an Upperclassman, you know."

He smiles then, just a little. "Somewhere I'm not allowed."

My own smile is wide. "I like your thinking."

$$***$$

I take him to a restaurant. Initially, he'd changed into his best clothes; but I deemed even those too proletarian, so we diverted our route to include a fashion shop. I bought him a smart-casual shirt (he tried to pay himself, but I had none of it) and a new pair of leather sandals—his own sandals went straight to the bin. After I pronounced him present-able, he followed me to the restaurant.

The sun wanes on the horizon; the heat begins to dissipate. Of course the night is dangerous—but not here. *Le Petit Déjeuner,* as it's called, is in the Upper Quarter. A flash of my ID brings us in; the people around us, well dressed as they are, don't take a second look. I thank my sense of fashion.

I've not come dressed particularly elaborately, but then, I'm never really underdressed. My black designer jeans and white designer shirt would never pass off as cheap. Nor would the gold chain on my neck—a family heirloom that father insists I keep safe.

The thought of my father brings a shiver down my neck. What if he finds out? What would he do? Then again, why should I live according to what my father thinks?

We seat ourselves outside, to see the splendour of the Upper Quarter. A waitress comes to take our order.

"What can I do for you, gentlemen?" She smiles at us, her hair raven dark, and her eyes a light blue.

"Some wine for me," I say.

"Any vintage in particular?"

"Whichever is most expensive." She nods, familiar with the vagaries of Upperclassmen.

"And you, sir?" she asks, referring to Mark.

"A cocktail of some sort?"

"Mojito?" she suggests.

"Whatever that is," Mark agrees.

She smiles, takes our order, and comes back with our drinks.

"Enjoy," she says.

Our table is for two, and is therefore more intimate. No one notices as I thread my hand with Mark's underneath.

"So this is what the Upper Quarter is like," he says, looking at the expanse of lights that surround us. The sun is now below the horizon; the sky is a lonesome blue. Night is falling fast, but it only makes the Upper Quarter more beautiful. The buildings here have brilliant glass façades; the shapes in which they are built are geometric. In the very middle, a tower rises into the sky. I knew that's where Big Brother lives—the most powerful man in the Party, and in Ireland.

"It is quite beautiful," I say, "but you get used to it."

"Really? How?"

"Familiarity breeds contempt," I explain.

"Now you sound like my uncle."

"How so?"

"He always has phrases like that—*mens sana in corpore sano* is his favourite, so much that he makes me remember it."

"It is appropriate for a doctor," I point out.

"Yeah, a healthy mind in a healthy body, right?"

"Indeed."

For a while, we stay silent. We watch as the last vestiges of the sun are replaced by the tendrils of night. The wine is good (although I hardly expected anything else). Mark seems to be enjoying his mojito, though I have a feeling he's not used to alcohol.

"So tell me more about yourself," he says quietly.

I sigh. "What is there to say? The mansion you saw originally belonged to my mother, but father received it in the divorce settlement."

"Your mother was rich then?"

"Yes, far more so than father. Though an Owner, I always believed she was more influential than most Upperclass members—they had to obey Party high command, while she could pay for her will to be done."

"What about... your father?"

"He's a party functionary." His eyes narrow at that.

"I don't like politicians."

"I don't blame you," I say, and truthfully. "I've never said this to my father, or anyone else, but—since I've already broken the rules with you—I'll say it now. I don't think the Party is good for this country. I don't think they're as competent as they like to pretend they are; and frankly, the internal schisms, though ostensibly papered over, are serious."

He looks at me, his eyes filled with... something. I'm not sure exactly what. Fear, maybe, and hope. It's a strange combination.

"Are you saying the Party will collapse?"

I shrug. "Collapse is a very big word. Throughout history, parties and nations have endured where contemporaries thought they would implode. But—I won't deny the possibility."

"Could I..." I can see the words are difficult for him, so I say them instead.

"Could you no longer be Fallen? Maybe." I hold his hand tighter in mine.

"But Mark," I say, looking him straight in the eye, "give *me* the chance to make your life a better one."

I pay the bill (it fetched a handsome price) and we leave the restaurant. We quickly make our way out of the Upper Quarter, and to his uncle's home. The door opens quietly.

"Thank you," he says.

Almost shyly, he kisses me. I close my eyes. He's good—better than any of the other guys. None of them ever made me feel this way.

"Thank you," I whisper, "for trusting me." Then I touch my com phone with his.

"You've got my contact details," I say. "We will find each other again."

"We will," he promises.

And with that, I say goodbye. Though there are many kinds of goodbyes, and I know this is one that promises reunion.

Chapter Ten

Mark

I'm crazy. What am I doing with an Upperclassman? He's everything I'm not, and never will be: rich, powerful, and cultured. I should hate his guts. Instead, I kissed him. And I'd wanted more.

I blink in the morning light, then lie back on the bed, sighing. Uncle lets me sleep in an unused bedroom. It's meant for guests, and in uncle's case, that usually means ruffians like me. For that, it's comfortable (more than my room back there, for sure). The bed is solid timber, the carpet is cream, and the walls are covered with paintings of far away places. Mediterranean, judging by the warm colours. A wistful voice in the back of my head wonders if I would ever go there: maybe Conall would take me. We could get married in Spain.

Yeah, and you'll grow wings and fly, I tell myself. Get a grip, Mark.

I dress, wearing my normal clothes (my brand new shirt would remain in the wardrobe). Uncle is waiting for me downstairs; the smell of omelette fills the kitchen. I make myself comfortable on a chair, open a carton of orange juice, and start shovelling mouthfuls.

"You know I warned you about romantic interests."

I look up at him. He looks a me with a mixture of concern, anger, and... something else.

"Yeah, well, I wasn't going to remain celibate."

He changes tack. "Who is he? Judging by the gold chain he was wearing, I take it not someone within your reach."

"You were always observant; I like that," I comment.

"Let me guess: he's the Upperclassman you told me about."

"And a master of deduction, too, I see." I can't help my sarcasm.

He just sighs.

"You know I want the best for you. I know you feel something for him; but I'm telling you it can never work."

I ignore him, downing the rest of the orange juice and helping myself to the omelette.

"You know," he continues at my silence, "you're just like your father. More stubborn than a goat."

I stop. "My dad? He was stubborn?"

His hand moves up to his jaw; he looks away. "I shouldn't have said that."

"As if you could get away with it now."

He smiles a little. "Very well. Yes, your father was stubborn: he was many things, in fact. Complicated. Torn. And he had been walking the dark side so long, we were all amazed he still knew what the light looked like."

"Are you saying my father used to be a criminal?"

"He used to be a lot more than that, although not in the way you're thinking."

My uncle has always been cryptic when it comes to my dad.

"Thanks for telling me," I mumble.

"I didn't have much of a choice, you were right about that. Now, finish your omelette; you've got one more day left of work and then you'll be free for the weekend, to enjoy your boyfriend."

After a few more mouthfuls, I finish the omelette, grab my com phone and prepare to walk out the door.

"And Mark?"

I turn to look at him. His eyes are steel blue in the sun; there's concern there, and love too.

"Please be careful."

I nod, solemnly, before walking out.

✹✹✹

The hospital work is as straightforward as ever. I bring medicines, monitor the machines, and even administer IVs. That's more dangerous: if I do it wrong, an IV would allow an air bubble in the bloodstream, which is potentially fatal. Syringes have to be disinfected in the sterilisation oven, or—if the pathogen is resistant to heat—treated in sodium hydroxide.

I know they're informally giving me the work of a nurse. It doesn't surprise me when, informally, they give me more money as well: six hundred instead of the usual four hundred and fifty.

After more than a week's worth of shifts, I have enough money to buy a nice change of clothing, and maybe even a lower end com phone.

Suddenly, I feel the pain in my shoulders again. I almost collapse; the nurses look at me with worry. After a moment, the pain subsides, and I wave them away. I go and find Dr Liam.

"Liam?"

"Yes, Donaghue?" he replies, using my pseudonym.

"I've been experiencing some nasty pain in my shoulders for a few days now. Could you take a look?" Professional as he is, he immediately finds me an examination room. I take off my shirt; he probes my shoulders. Several forceful touches of his finger don't bring any pain.

"When did they start? Was there something in particular that brought them on?" he asks.

"I got into a fight."

He nods. "That could be a cause, but your symptoms seem rather strange. You say that you only feel it occasionally?"

"Yeah."

"And it's—like needles going through your skin? Not an ache or a tearing sensation?"

"Like needles, yeah."

He shakes his head. "I'll bring the ultrasound here."

The device, I know, is capable of detecting many kinds of injury without the need for an X-ray. He carries it on its wheels. Then he opens a tub of gel, and spreads some on my back and shoulders.

The device beeps, showing a readout of my muscle and skeletal structure. Liam carefully scrutinises it.

"The sonar can't find anything wrong. I should really ask for an X-ray and have the X-rays looked over by a specialist doctor—"

"It's all right, Liam," I say. "I'm sure it'll get better; it's probably nothing."

"If you say so. If anything does change, though, tell me—okay?"

"Sure thing," I reply, before buttoning up my shirt and leaving.

★★★

I prefer to work long hours. It's not because I really enjoy work—this job is the only one I've ever cared about. No: the real reason is escape. Work means doing something. It means getting paid; and since I stay away from drugs, whores, and alcohol, that means saving up money. My bank account has enough for me to live on for a few months. That's more than many Fallen have.

But distraction remains the biggest reason. I have few true friends: too many Fallen are either petty criminals, idiots, or greedy swindlers. Not all of them, though. One I might even consider a friend.

"Hey, Kieran?" I say over my com phone.

"Hey man! Where have y'a been? I couldn't get a hold of ya." Kieran's Fallen accent is especially strong; it always makes me smile.

"I've been in some trouble, but I'm alright now."

"Sure man. Wanna meet up?" Kieran never asks too many questions: something I admire about him.

"Yeah; meet me in the Crescent Park."

"Gotcha." He hangs up.

I sit myself on a bench, and wait. It doesn't take long: soon he's strolling in the sunlight, and waving at me.

I once had a thing for him. His red hair glints in the light; his eyes, I know, are brilliant green, and he has a strong, stocky build. Three years ago, not long after I met him, I tried seeing if he was interested. He wasn't—and I eventually forgot about it.

Still, we remain friends. I shake his hand as he sits next to me.

"So how are things going?" he asks.

"Got myself a new job at the hospital."

"Oh really? They employ us?"

"No, but they don't check too carefully, either."

He whistles. "Smart—and do they pay ya well?"

"The pay's not bad. It's easy work for the money."

"Better than the other Fallen work—am I right?"

"Yeah: better than being a garbage man, for sure."

"So what are you gonna do with the money?"

"Save it, and see if I can buy myself something."

"Not gonna spend it?"

"You know how I am with alcohol."

"Why not—y'a know?"

"Prostitutes? No thanks. Besides," I say, knowing I want to tell him but also knowing that some things should be kept secret, "I have a love interest."

"Oh really?"

"Above my paygrade, if you know what I mean."

He whistles. "How far?"

"Mansion and Party far."

He shakes his head. "You better know what you're doing."

I've been wondering that myself.

"Is the love interest hot?" he continues.

"Yup—soft brown hair, eyes like topaz..." My voice closes off wistfully.

"Well good luck man. You're gonna need it, I tell ya."

I have feeling he's going to be proven right. "Thanks Kieran. You have a love interest of your own?"

"Oh there's a girl, but—nah. Not really."

"Why not?" I ask.

"Well, it depends on what ya call love, innit? Is it just the fucking? Because, yeah; the fucking's good. But if ya mean—oh I don't know. Looking each other in the eyes? Dreaming about marriage? Holidays in far off places?"

"Or knowing you'll do anything for each other, no matter what?"

"Definitely not that." He laughs, and slaps me on the back. "Mark, you sound like one lucky bastard."

"Or an unlucky one," I point out.

"Lucky, I tell ya. Even if you're—" he indicates his intent with a dirty gesture, "love is a rare thing. I hope you don't forget that; we don't all find our soulmates."

"Anyway," I say, looking at the darkening sun, "it was nice talking to you, Kieran. See ya round."

"See ya."

We shake hands again, and he leaves. I look at his receding form. I realised something then: while Kieran might not be the brightest bulb in the street, he could sometimes be very wise.

Chapter Eleven

Kaylin

I stand, a smile on my face, though there is sadness there too.

"So you're ready to join us?"

"I am," he says.

"It is customary, when joining, to choose a pseudonym," I explain. "Our real names can endanger us, if revealed; our taken names, not so much. What will you choose?"

He smiles ironically and without humour. "Would you prefer something ridiculous? Lord Spymaster? Mr Bond?"

My answering smile is amused. "How about... Shadow?"

"I suppose it'll work."

"Good. Men, meet Shadow. Shadow, meet my men."

"Is that what you call them? Just men?"

"We are unnamed, for—"

"Yeah, I get it."

I close my mouth. Around me, my men snicker. They always find it amusing to see me annoyed—they sometimes resent my attitude, especially when my powers allow me anticipate a smart response. I shake my head. We have more important things to worry about.

"Shadow, I am glad you have chosen to join us."

"It's not like I have much of a choice, really."

"Even so, I appreciate it. I have mission for you all: I want us to break into a police station to steal valuable information. After that, I want to destroy it."

Several complaints are shouted out; I weather them calmly.

"I know it will not be easy—the base is well-guarded. But we have a valuable asset on our hands. I intend to make the best of him."

"If you say so, Mistress," they respond.

I smile brightly. They know me well.

✶✶✶

A week later, and following a significant amount of preparation, we find ourselves spearheading the assault.

"Ready, Software Man?" I ask through the intercom.

"Ready, Mistress. I'm patching the live feed on to you now."

A moment later, our hidden cameras turn on to reveal two image sets: the first is the police gate, and the second is our SUV, traversing the local traffic. Within minutes, the two would meet.

"Shadow, are you ready?"

"Yes, Mistress, I am ready when you are," he says.

"Good. We'll give you the signal to enter once the first stage of our plan succeeds."

"Do you think that will be necessary?" he questions. "I think it will be quite obvious once it happens."

I chuckle. "No doubt it will, but wait for our call just in case."

"Mistress, the car is within range," informs Elizabeth, the remote driver.

"Get her going then, Liz."

We watch as the big, black SUV gains speed, overtaking and swerving to avoid the oncoming traffic. She's good: the car is going over a hundred miles an hour.

"The first Q-car will enter the compound in precisely two minutes," another operator tells me. "Then..."

"Then the gate will be open, the force field will be de-activated, and Liz will pilot it straight through."

We watch, raptured by the scene played out on the immense holographic projector. One of their Q-cars enters the compound. A few seconds later, the SUV barrels through. The noise is the most unholy thing I've heard—grinding metal, an ecstasy of tearing and shrieking, followed by a perfect, pin-drop silence.

"Shadow—"

"I'm in."

From now on, it's a waiting game. Shadow can't tell us what he's doing; we can't sneak in cameras or microphones on his person. He threw the microphone away the moment he got in. It would have been too risky otherwise—all electronic transmissions can be detected.

So we wait. I never understood the term "nail-biting," but the nervous, expectant silence seems an apt description for it. The minutes tick by. And then we hear it.

"Mistress, I've picked up Shadow." It's Sean, our escape driver.

"Shadow?"

"Yes Mistress, I got it."

We cheer, and I breathe a sigh of relief. I feel a responsibility to my men, like all commanders do: they are willing to risk their lives for me, and that is never something that can be taken lightly.

⋆⋆⋆

After our mission, I go home. I take the maglev train to Cork; at four hundred miles an hour, the trip takes just thirty minutes. Aside from being faster than a road-based car, I took the train for a different reason: it meant no one would see me leaving and try to follow me. I do not tell my men where I live. Except for Diana, whom I trust absolutely.

Walking from the train station, following a beaten countryside track, I eventually reach a field. A shimmer—almost like a mirage in a desert, but not quite—can be seen in the middle. A flick of my mind rips it away, to reveal a house. (Glamour can be used to hide all sorts of things, but it works more like a broken mirror than an invisibility cloak. It distracts, but true concealment requires greater magic.)

The house seems to belong to another age. It isn't the architecture—a sleek geometric design—that's the reason though. It has cedar cladding, and an elegant tiled roof. They would never survive a mutant attack. But then, they didn't need to.

I open the door; the room that greets me is one of gleaming hardwood flooring, tastefully decorated cream walls, and plush leather chairs. A holographic TV provides entertainment in a corner, though I rarely use it. I make my way to the kitchen, finding myself a bottle of wine kept in the cooler. The last rays of the afternoon sun are falling; the room is lit up in softs golds, the dark accents festooned with halos of light.

I know that things hadn't always been this way. Once, centuries ago, Ireland had been a very different place. It had been rainy and cloudy. It had been free of mutants; the threat of nuclear war had been no more than a hypothetical possibility. And, it had other things: democracy, freedom, and no shadow of the Class-based system the Party had set up over the last hundred years.

They'd told us it was for our own good; that we needed a powerful economy to rival that of China. But really, they did it because it allowed them greater control into our lives, and because certain vested interests had profited from the arrangement.

I feel a pang of hot rage; the same rage that drove me this far, ever since... ever since then.

I've perfected my power over many years. I've read: books about government, about science and technology, and most of all, I read books about history. Forbidden books, not the nonsense that the Party claimed as history. Our organisation is unnamed, but the ideals we subscribe to are born from age-old thinkers, from the successful societies that existed in the 21st century: equal rights and rule of law.

A knock on the door distracts me. I open it, inviting Diana in.

∗∗∗

Diana and I are close. Some even speculate that I am, or was, her lover. They are mis-taken: I'd been with a few men in my life, and I love Diana as a friend—I desire the calm reassurance of *philos* rather than the fire of *eros*.

"What are you doing here, Diana? And at night, too."

"You know mutants don't threaten either one of us, Kaylin." She's right about that. She's simply too powerful to worry about mutants, and I am similarly powerful, though in a different way. Diana could burn them to cinders; I could confuse them with spells.

"It's still dangerous—you're basically a terrorist, after all. If the Party knew about you, they'd be desperate to get rid of you."

She just shrugs. "You'll See it before they act." She's probably right about that, although her confidence in me strikes a nerve.

"Oh, Kaylin. Are you still thinking about him?"

"I almost failed you—"

"But you didn't," she says, her eyes suddenly electric blue. "Even inexperienced as you were—a teenager—you Saw far enough to know what he would try and do. You planted an inside man to rescue me. And the thing with the spell..." She smiles, and sparks fly from her eyes. "That was even more bloodthirsty than what I would have done."

The memory resurfaces...

The Party Commissioner for the Armed Forces, Oscar Wills, always did have an eye for Diana—the fact that Diana never reciprocated his interest was completely irrelevant to him. Secretly, he thought that Diana couldn't really be gay; to him, she was just being coy.

Naturally, Diana treated him with utter contempt. Months passed; he could stand it no more. He would kidnap and rape her if necessary, maybe kill her if she didn't shut up.

I saw this, and planned ahead. It was easy enough to bribe one of his men to free her. As for Oscar, I had something special planned: I asked Diana to cut his nails one day. When the time came, I burned the nails, using them to cast a spell—a primitive spell, for I did not have the Black Book at the time. It accomplished its purpose; Oscar clawed his eyes out, then slit his wrists.

I blink, returning to the present. As a clairvoyant, my memories are more vivid than those of ordinary humans, and it is sometimes difficult to tell past from present—or future.

"Reminiscing?"

"Would you like some wine?" I ask instead.

"Yes, please."

We sit down in front of the mahogany table; the wine is crimson red, its taste pleas-antly inebriating.

"Your plan today was successful," she says. "When are we going to destroy it?"

"Soon."

"How? Are you going to let me have some fun?"

Diana sometimes worried me: she has a penchant for violence. I'm not afraid of viol-ence, but I use it with purpose. Diana just loves destroying things. I guess it's down to her Ability.

"We'll see about the station."

"What about the other Familiars? Shadow can't be the only one."

"I've been able to See all of them up till now"

"Maybe so, but what if the Party does manage to get them first? Or what if you finally meet someone who *doesn't* want to join us?"

"I'm thinking about it."

"Would you kill them if you had to, Kaylin?"

"I..."

"We have to be ready for anything."

I sigh. She's right—sometimes, you have to do bad things. The Party is brutal. And there's rarely room for mercy.

"Let's just hope it doesn't come to that." Deep inside, though, I know I would do it. Whatever power lies in us, it treads a fine line between the dark and the light.

Chapter Twelve

Conall

It's difficult to describe many of the Lyceum students as friends, for friendship is a difficult concept where high politics is involved. But perhaps the two other people I am with come close to that. Stella, as usual, is my confidant; and there is also Aidan O'Connor, a third year boy.

The noon sun shines through a tall window, casting a pleasant illumination through-out the room. Stella's hair shines red, in contrast to Aidan's mop of black hair.

"As I keep telling you, the legitimacy of a government is a nonsense idea. Government *without* the consent of the people is not modern; it was practised for millennia, in the form of kings, popes, barons and bishops. Democracy was a quaint idea that lasted only a few centuries."

Stella disagrees. "But even in those days, the government had to have a form of legit-imacy: the Divine Right of Kings, the word of God, or tradition."

"But these weren't meant to convince the populace that the kings and popes should lord it over them; they were there for the high classes to feel good about themselves. It was power that kept the populace in line. That's the key. Power, through fear of violence or uprising."

"What do you think, Aidan?" Stella asks, frustrated.

"I think both of you have a point," he says diplomatically. Aidan is like that. He is neither confrontational, nor quiet; more skilful diplomat than brash politician, if you will.

"Conall is right when he says that power kept the status quo," he continues. "At the same time, legitimacy remained a pressing issue: that's because power without consent, or at least tacit consent, is inherently unstable. It wasn't just grand ideas about the Divine Right of Kings that made the people consent, Stella; it was, I think, a kind of complacency among the people. So long as things were going alright, the government had *de facto* legitimacy. I think that the concept of *volnost* among Russian peasants fitted in closely with this idea."

Aidan manages to convince both of us with that argument. I continue to admire his skill.

✳✳✳

With the exception of our conversation that day, school bores me. It's been a week since since I kissed Mark, and the memory is like a warm summer on an icy winter's day: pleasant and surreal. I still want him, badly. At nights I dream he's on top of me, his body strong, his voice a dark caress in my mind. Then the morning sun always came, dispelling him, but leaving me with an uneasy yearning through the rest of the day.

Luckily for me, it's Friday. Not long ago, I would have gone to the whorehouse to satiate my desires. With a small smile, I realise Jason would miss me. But I don't feel regret: the feelings that Mark gave rise to were far more potent and complex than simple lust. Sexual desire could be satisfied in a few moments of ecstasy; but love would last a lifetime.

I bring him up on my contacts. He's called, simply, "M". The message I send him is to the point: *I want to see you.*

His response is swift. *Where and when?*

At my house.

Are you sure that's a good idea?

I smile. Father has left on a trip to Germany, to discuss the latest plans for the

European High Military. He's taken most of the guards with him.

Trust me.

Okay, I'll be there soon; can you meet me at the gate?

Sure.

Pleased, I hide the com in my pocket, and make my way home.

✳✳✳

The guard on duty at the mansion is a man I know well, and he's long used to my escapades. He doesn't bat an eyelid when I walk, Mark in hand, through the mansion gate. The sun is still high in the horizon; the light is piercing, the shadows brilliant. Mark looks at the mansion wide-eyed. I smile inwardly.

Once inside, I ask, "Fancy seeing the place?"

"You mean, what—you'll give me a guided tour?"

"Precisely."

He shrugs. "Sure thing, posh boy." The way he says it is unlike the first time, when it had been derogatory and dismissive; it sounds more like a compliment now.

We begin walking.

"This," I say with a flourish, "is the ballroom." He simply stares. The ceiling stretches high above; the designs painted upon it show a gleaming angel, sword alight with fire. Windows stretch to twice the height of a man on the walls. The floor is marble—the colour is a gleaming white, though hued veins are visible, like the veins of some beautiful rock monster.

He whistles. "You dance in this place?"

"Once, about a year ago."

"What for?"

"A special occasion that father organised in order to... make connections."

"Did you dance with a girl?"

"Yes."

"And... how was she?"

"Boring."

I move on, taking him past a labyrinth of corridors. At regular intervals, miniature statues are displayed: of Aristotle, Plato, Oresme, and other famous thinkers. Once in a while, we would come towards a painting, and I would explain that it had been procured under a particular auction for a particular sum. Many were simply replicas, and fetched only a minor price; but others were original works. He looked bemused when I told him one fetched a million.

Eventually, we arrive to the intended destination: my bedroom.

***

I lie back on the bed, surveying him appreciatively. He's come dressed in jeans, as usual, and a nondescript white T-shirt. He isn't clad in designer trousers or expensive leather shoes (like I am) but his beauty doesn't need such embellishments. I could see his muscles rippling under his shirt; his eyes follow me back, the same deep blue as I remember. The rivulets of his long hair shine blond in the light.

"Like the view?" he asks.

"Truly, is it that obvious?"

He only laughs. My heart beats a little faster as he walks towards the bed, setting himself down next to me.

"Very obvious," he elaborates, and then he kisses me.

73

It's only a moment, before he pulls back, but it sets my nerves on fire.

"You better start talking before I rip off your clothes," I say.

Realising I'm serious, he asks, "So just how big of a bigshot is your dad?"

"He's not part of the Inner Circle, if that's what you're asking."

"The Inner Circle? That's like—"

"The highest echelon of the Party. But no; father is only a functionary in the Outer Circle."

"What about your mum? She's the one who owns this place, right?"

"Indeed. My mother is part of the Owner class, and was a very rich woman when she divorced. Still is, in fact."

"But don't you see her?"

I turn away. "I do, sometimes. But... well, it's not that I don't love her. It's that Sianna is very much Sianna."

He raises an eyebrow. "That bad, huh?"

"What about you?" I ask to change the subject.

"I don't have any parents." Realising my mistake, I take his hand in mine. I can feel the warmth running within them.

"I'm sorry."

"Yeah," he says darkly, "I'm sorry too."

"How...?"

"My mother died giving birth to me. As for dad, I have no idea where he is. He left."

"You don't know why?"

He shrugs, though the movement is anything but lighthearted. "Uncle won't really tell me; and I'm not sure I want to know. It couldn't have been for a good reason."

"You don't know that," I point out. "And besides, I think you do very much want to know. I can see it in your eyes."

He looks away. "You're right. But, can we please talk about something else?"

Deciding to use the best icebreaker I have, I call out: "Minnie!"

For a moment, we hear nothing. Then we hear the skidding of feet, the excited bark, the howl of joy; and then, in a single leap, she jumps on the bed.

Mark laughs as she licks him excitedly. That's Minnie—always curious to meet new people. He forces back the overexcited dog, holding her grey fur and looking in her eyes. One is ice blue; the other brown. Heterochromia, I know, is common in huskeys. She sits back, content to receive his attention in other ways.

"I've always wanted a dog," he says.

"I can imagine, though I'll warn you: she's quite a bit of work. Keeps the entire house staff busy walking her—and when they're away, it mostly falls to me to entertain her."

"Where are they, anyway? How come I can just waltz in here with you?"

"Father is away discussing plans for the European High Military, and he's taken most of the staff with him."

"The European High Military? That's no joke, is it?"

"Hardly. He mentioned, for example, that they're thinking of replacing the entire fighter jet fleet with the new model. All two thousand of them."

He whistles. "That many?"

"The Chinese don't even have half. If they weren't so many and so dug in, we could take over their country."

"And would anyone stop you if you tried?"

"The Russians and the Americans have annihilated themselves; the other countries are not strong enough by their own. So no."

He shakes his head. "You scare me, you know. Are you going to be one of them too?"

I realise that had been bugging him ever since he met me. The trouble is, I don't have an answer.

"I... don't know," I say, and not dishonestly. Sure: the plan is there. Father wants me to. I like learning about politics at the Lyceum. But—did I really want to be a shadowy Party figure, engaged in brutal political calculations? Could I face that?

"I don't think you're like them, you know. Call me naïve—but I think you're better than they are."

I shake my head. "Maybe you're right; I don't know. But I do know how I feel about you, Mark."

I kiss him again, closing off any more questions.

✳✳✳

Father would be away for nearly a week, and we make the best of that time. We go to restaurants; he comes to my mansion, and I sneak into his house. We talk about everything: his life, my life, our dreams for the future. I laughed when he told me he wanted to go to Spain, to live an idyllic Mediterranean life.

"You know Spain is run by madmen?" I ask him.

"What, the Communists? I don't care; I like them."

Spain, I know, is the most mistrusted nation in the European League of Nations: the other countries fear their communist party would spread and infect the rest of the contin-ent. But the Spanish government has made no such attempts, preferring to co-operate instead. The Chinese threat is enough to hold Europe together—and I wonder, sometimes, at what would happen if it ever went away.

"I suppose you want to get married there as well?" Spain is considered strange for their acceptance of marriage between spouses of the same sex.

"Why not?"

I laugh at him, though secretly I dream.

Our relationship made great strides in the course of that week. Every day, I would learn something new about him: his taste in food (he detested escargot, when he served them at the restaurant), his dislike of alcohol and contempt for drugs, and even his sex life.

He tells me he's a virgin. We don't talk much about it, but sex is always there in the background. We both want it. But somehow, we don't do it. We both have excuses, when one of us touches the other. We're not ready, and what if we're caught?

Chapter Thirteen

Kaylin

The storm begins as nothing more than a mark on the horizon, as if some divine creator had simply left it there in a fit of carelessness. It moves across the sky with deceptive slowness, engulfing this black city in its embrace. Like a dark hand, it removes the sunlight from the world; the façades of the Upper Quarter are no longer graced by golden light, but by otherworldly hues of violet and green.

Some way in the distance, I can make out Diana. She walks under roofs, pretending to be afraid of the storm. I am staying in a dilapidated concrete tower, which has two advantages—it offers an excellent view of the city, while at the same time concealing me. The wind howls through the empty building, bringing the scent of sulphur and ionised air. I wrap my coat more tightly around my shoulders.

Normally, on a mission like this, I would be in the control room, with the full weight of my organisation behind me. Alas, that would not work this time—the storm interrupted wireless communications. Only cabled communications would work, and my organisation did not have those. Wireless transmissions could be encrypted and broadcast indiscriminately; but a wired connection would have meant a contract with the Internet Company. Those were closely monitored by the Party.

The Bugs are programmed to shut down the force field at 5pm, right? Diana asks. Telepathy has become our only line of communication.

That is correct, Diana. You can test them right now; they should still be on. A bolt of lightning shoots down from the sky, only to fizzle harmlessly against an iridescent blue field.

Now we wait, I telepathise.

For ten minutes, we do just that. It's impossible to see the force field from here: the field is no more than a pale blue sheen, all but invisible under the bright sun or the murky conditions of the storm.

Another lightning bolt shoots down. This time, I see it hit a building—a fire starts burning.

I know Diana will be smiling. And once she starts in earnest, I'm smiling too. Lightning bolt after lightning bolt falls from the sky; the police headquarters are soon ablaze. I watch as men scramble out of the building, frantic. Several more lighting bolts strike, destroying the remaining buildings.

Diana? I say.

Yes, Kaylin?

Those are military police; they enforce the Party's will through violence. They were the ones who tried to kidnap you. Return that favour, will you?

I feel only satisfaction as a score of lightning bolts sweep down and leave them dead. I could be moved to pity dead enemies, or to feel saddened by their necessary deaths. But these men deserved it.

✶✶✶

Alas, my satisfaction is short lived.

Mutant beings—monsters with bone swords. Circling. Salivating. Two boys hide desperately; a street sign.

The vision passes, as swiftly as it came, and cold fear enters my bones. I know I need to keep calm and rational, because panic can mean the difference between life and death.

Diana, I need you now. Meet me in the Middle Quarter, 22 Crescent Street. I run. I trust Diana on two things: firstly, that the she will control the storm so I don't die in a bath of sulphuric acid. And secondly, that she knows how to find me. I'd had all my men memorise the city layout, but pressure can make people freeze.

I don't need to worry. She's right beside me as we run, headlong into the mutants.

Chapter Fourteen

Mark

We lie under a table, me and Conall, watching the monsters with cold dread. Uncle is away on his shift and won't be back until night.

"Should we try calling your uncle?" Conall whispers.

"No way. He might not pick up, the Reapers might hear us, and he can't do anything to help us anyway."

"What about the Exterminators?"

The Exterminators are a government agency tasked with killing rogue mutants, though the job is split with the army and police as well. Everyone in Ireland knows which number to call, but...

"I don't know, Conall. We can only hope they're already coming."

"That's stupid Mark! We *have* to call them."

"If the Reapers hear us..."

"We're doomed anyway."

I sigh with frustration and fear; this is a bad situation. We're trapped in uncle's home, the Reapers crawling outside. Normally, the re-enforcing steel in the house would be enough to keep the mutants out—but then, these aren't ordinary mutants.

The crawl on the ground, moving deceptively slowly. Their limbs are misshapen; they move more like spiders than four-legged animals. Their eyes are bulbous and black. Each is armed with bone blades that can shear through both flesh and metal alike.

The one closest to us is sniffing the ground, probably to pick up our scent trail. It pricks its triangular ears; we stop breathing, though our hearts beat double time.

Everything depends on remaining silent. If it hears us...

The moment passes, and the Reaper turns it attention elsewhere. We breathe a thin sigh of relief.

"Call them," Conall whispers. He hands me the com phone.

I wipe away a bead of sweat from my forehead, and with numb fingers I program it to call the number. I set the volume down as low as I can hear it.

The com phone beeps quietly, the line still.

"Damnit, it's not working. The storm is blocking off the signal."

"Don't you have cable?" Conall asks. "My house has its own connection; it lets me use my com phone even when there's a storm."

"I don't think so... uncle never mentioned it."

"Let me try," Conall says.

But I ignore him. I put my hand on his mouth, quietly forcing him down to the floor. Beyond the window, the entire group of Reapers sits perfectly still, watching us.

Terror grips my chest like a vice. Time seems to slow; life and death hang in the balance. And then, without conscious realisation, I lift myself up and walk out of the house, straight into the arms of the Reapers.

✶✶✶

I don't know what I'm doing. A part of me screams at me to run, though that would be certain death. Another part of me promises that, if I die, at least I might save Conall.

The Reapers move, surrounding me. Up close, they are truly terrifying: their maws are huge, filled with serrated teeth, and dripping a corrosive saliva. They have bright orange fur.

One of the Reapers—the largest—crawls in front of me, stands up, and looks me in the eye. I see the abyss in those dark orbs, but no malice. A strange part of my mind reaches out, and forms a connection with this awful being.

So we stay still, human and monster, predator and prey. Then, without warning, they leave.

★★★

It feels like a long time before I finally go back inside. Conall has his eyes firmly closed; he's paralysed with fear. I gently lift him up, and kiss him. The taste of life is divine.

"Mark? Is that you? Am I dreaming?"

"No, Conall. I'm alive."

"But... how?"

"I don't know."

"Did you convince them to have lunch elsewhere?"

I laugh brokenly. "Something like that."

"I'm just so glad you're here," he says. "I don't know what would have happened if... if I'd lost you."

He holds me tight, and I caress his hair. Nothing else needs to be said.

★★★

Kaylin

"That was close," Diana comments.

"Too close," I agree. "And beyond my power to explain."

"You mean, the Reapers didn't leave because of you?"

"No." I smile thinly. Diana sometimes overestimates me—I can confuse mutant beings like the Reapers with a spell, not with willpower alone.

"Then... how?"

"That is a very good question, and one I would like to know the answer to."

"Okay," Diana begins. "If we want to find out, we should start with who he is. The other guy was Conall."

"The Upperclassman you were teaching?"

"Exactly."

"Did you see how they hugged at the end of it?" I ask.

"Yeah... it looks like Conall has a boyfriend."

"A boyfriend with very unusual powers," I point out.

"Then he's going to need some very unusual company."

"I like your thinking, Diana. You have my permission to discover more about him."

She smiles brightly. Diana always likes spying.

Chapter Fifteen

Conall

No one knows exactly when and how the mutants came into being.

We've lived with the mutant threat for centuries now; they claimed many lives during that time, but the damage they did was ultimately contained and minimised. Our buildings are (for the most part) impervious to their efforts. We have weapons that can easily destroy them, and soldiers who mean business.

Yet me and Mark almost died.

I've become complacent, I realise. And more than that: arrogant. Cocooned, as I am, in the Upper Quarter, I failed to realise the true danger. Not everyone is as fortunate as I am, to have walls and guard towers and 24-hour protection. Mark should have taught me that lesson.

I sigh wearily. I will seek answers to those questions later, when I will meet Mark again. For now, I have my mother to worry about.

✳✳✳

Sianna Danann is many things: businesswoman, financier, and unelected politician are but three of them.

She has chosen to see me in the formal withdrawing room (her favourite in the mansion) and so here I am, like a child expecting a Christmas present. Except, of course, that I'm not a child, and my mother is not a present I would wish to anyone. Her eyes are winter blue; her countenance is cold and graceful. It's in stark contrast to the room around me, which is decorated by panelled dark wood, a carpet of deep red, and depictions of stag hunting on the tall ceiling.

"Hello, darling."

"Hello, mother." I didn't hide the irony from my voice.

"Now, darling, be a bit more enthusiastic. It's not *every* day you get to see me—and, mind you, I fancy you secretly enjoy our meetings, though you are loathe to admit it."

"As you say, mother."

She only laughs. "Yes; ever the rebellious spirit you have. Your father was right about that. But come, tell me more about what you've been up to." She relaxes onto a leather arm-chair.

"I've been studying; I'm on an A for all my classes."

She waves that conversation away. "Your father is all so concerned with your academic performance, but you know what I think of it."

"You'd rather I bribed myself into power than study for it?"

"Oh darling, I wouldn't call it *bribing*. More like making connections. And besides: your father is terribly naive to insist on all this academic nonsense. To achieve power, you don't need good grades at the Lyceum: you need connections, political acumen, and money."

"I suppose a bit of guile and cunning wouldn't hurt either?"

Her smile reveals perfectly white teeth, and a glint in those cold blue eyes of hers that makes me shiver. "Now we think alike, Conall."

"Really mother," I continue, "there is more to life than politics and personal advance-ment."

"Oh? And what would that be, my son? Is there anything else you're not sharing with me?"

I wonder how she does that. My mother seems to possess a sagacity that is almost superhuman; it's like she can look into the deepest recesses of your soul, see what makes you tick, and use it to manipulate you.

"There may be some romantic feelings involved," I say lightly. My mother is a master of this game, but I can play it too.

"Oh? Do tell."

Knowledge is power, so I choose my words carefully.

"There is a *quid pro quo* involved, of course."

"Of course. What would you like me to tell you?"

"Just how many Party figures do you have in your pocket?"

"Enough to carry some influence."

"Good. Because my love interest is a boy."

She raises an eyebrow. "That's hardly surprising, considering what your father has let you get up to."

"There's more. He's a Fallen."

This time she really is surprised. I can tell, though she tries to hide it. "Well, that *is* a pity. Still: I'm sure you could work something out."

"You know I wouldn't tell anyone else about this." That's not entirely true, but then the truth was a flexible concept where my mother goes.

"I know, and you are wise not to."

"Mother... do your best for me, will you? I don't want him to suffer for loving me."

"Of course dear. I will do my best."

Sianna Dannan is a master manipulator, but then, so am I.

★★★

After Sianna leaves, I feel pleased. If anyone is capable of protecting me and Mark, it would be her. Soon, she will have found people to bribe, threaten, extort and cajole. Still, I'm not entirely at ease. The secret police is the reason: they're invisible, deadly, and receive orders only from Big Brother.

They ultimately keep the Party in power. It isn't the army that does it, or the riot police: brute force cannot destroy ideas or uncover plots. The secrets, on the other hand, will seek out dissidents and erase all trace of their existence.

But I'm not giving up. Maybe I'm crazy, for thinking I'm in love. Maybe I'll look back, one day, and laugh at myself. Somehow, though, I don't believe that. Mark had saved my life—twice. And I'd saved his. That had to count for something; that had to be worth more than power.

***

With Sianna in the mansion, the staff are kept busy; it's only too easy for to me to sneak out, make my way past the gate, and find Mark's house.

The sun is bright; the sky is clear and cerulean, the storm clouds of yesterday now long gone. It's warm—but not too warm. A slight breeze is blowing, and it seems to me, in some strange inexplicable way, that the wind whispers to me. If only I could listen a little bit closer...

A door bangs somewhere nearby, and I wake from my reverie. A few more determined steps bring me to Mark's, or rather, his uncle's home. I remark that someone is watering the plants. With a start, I realise it *is* his uncle.

I walk towards him; he continues watering the flowers—roses, I see now, and various other fragrant and brightly coloured specimens—and he acknowledges me only when I begin speaking.

"So you are his uncle."

"That's right, boy."

"You do realise you are addressing an Upperclassman?"

His eyes glint an amused blue. "I'm not scared of you; you're too young, and don't have enough power to be a threat. If I were you, though, I'd be scared of me. Your *liaison* with my nephew has not gone unnoticed."

"And is that a problem?" I say, my voice deathly quiet.

He thought for a moment, then replies, "I'm still thinking about it."

"Well, in that case, you are indeed right. It would be folly to provoke you. So, allow me to introduce myself properly: I'm Conall O'Toole, Upperclassman and Lyceum student."

"And I'm Eoin Kearney, a doctor."

"A Technical?"

"Indeed."

I furrow my eyebrows together. "But Mark is—"

"Fallen, that's right. His father abandoned him not long after he was born."

I open my mouth, but he cuts me off. "And don't even think about asking why. God knows Mark does that enough without you helping him."

I closed my mouth.

"Anyway," he continues, "he doesn't have work on a Saturday. You can find him inside."

"Thank you," I reply, thinking of no response more gracious.

✶✶✶

"I see my uncle gave you the rundown," he comments. He's lounging on a sofa. The room around us is bright; the large windows let in the full efforts of the sun, while the walls are whitewashed and reflect the light.

"I would not want to be on the wrong side of your uncle," I admit.

"Nor would I, if I'm honest. But what did he think of you?"

"I can't quite tell. I suppose I gave him a stereotypical initial impression."

"What—the arrogant Upperclasman?"

"Indeed."

"I hope he saw past that."

"I believe he did, though I'm not sure quite what he made of it."

"How about a different question. What do you think *I* see in you?"

I pause to think. "I think that you used to believe I was a bastard, a spoilt rich brat, and a conniving manipulator."

"You think I thought of you like that?"

"Yes, and to some degree, you would have been right. But I also believe you see more in me: the charm, the wit, the gentle side."

He only snorted. "Are you also going to tell me you write love sonnets?"

"I've written a few poems," I say offhandedly.

"Oh, so you *are* going to tell me you write love sonnets and pontificate on the nature of life while I'm away?"

"They're not love sonnets," I protest, "and I'm not sure you know what pontificate means."

"To think about wistfully?"

"No, it means to express one's opinions dogmatically, especially if one is religious."

He looks suitably chastised by that. "Okay, maybe you are a poet."

I smile. "What about you? Any interesting tidbits about your life?"

"Well, I've been in some strange jobs in my life."

"Go on."

"Like rubbish collector."

I wrinkled my nose.

"Yeah, that's right. But I suppose the most interesting occupation I've had is with medicine."

"That would make sense."

"You bet. I've always dreamed about being a doctor, like my uncle."

"Perhaps you will be, one day."

"Maybe."

I decide to move onto what I'd been thinking about all day.

"Mark... come walk with me. I have some things I want to tell you."

✶✶✶

The afternoon sun shines down on us, while a breeze flits through the trees. A stream gurgles where we walk. The day is hot, though the trees offer plenty of shade; we are comfortable. Mark is wearing white T-shirt and shorts; I've gone with white jeans and a loose-fitting shirt. I realise that our clothes say a lot about who are. Both of us are pragmatic to wear white on a hot day. But, one of us always chooses formal over casual.

"So what is it you want to talk to me about?" he asks.

"You remember, nearly a month ago, when we first met?"

"Yeah. I never said it clearly enough, Conall, but you saved me then. I owe you my life."

"But so do I, Mark. Remember when that scarab was on top of me?"

He stops walking. "I do, now that you mention it."

"Well, it was you who grabbed it and threw it off me."

"It was nothing."

"It was something. And remember when, just yesterday, we were attacked?"

"Of course—like the back of my hand."

"You saved me then too. Mark..." He really looks at me now. "I think I'm in love with you."

His response takes me aback, even if it's what I wanted to hear.

"I think I'm in love with you too."

His kiss is instant, searing hot, and more powerful by how unexpected it is. I thread my hands through his soft blond hair; he holds me tight against his body, his muscles lithe and powerful.

I'd thought I knew what it's like to kiss someone. I've done it more than once, with more than one man. But Mark is nothing like that.

***

Later, we talk.

"So I guess we're officially boyfriend and boyfriend now," he jokes.

"I guess so too."

"So what should we do? Go to the cinema, dine at fine restaurants, read love ballads to each other?"

"There aren't really love ballads; the genre isn't appropriate for it."

He just shakes his head. "Love sonnets then. Whatever."

"I don't know," I say truthfully. "I've never done this before."

"Really? I thought you'd *experimented* with more than a few guys before?"

"Yes, but experimenting is not the same as having a relationship."

"I guess you're right."

"But to answer your question: I think we should enjoy each others' company, in private. My mother will ensure things remain behind closed doors."

"Oh? Your mother knows?"

"She would have found out anyway, and in any case: I've persuaded her to employ her contacts for our benefit."

"You can be cunning. You know that, Conall?"

I smile brilliantly. "Haven't you figured out that by now?"

His lips find mine once more. "Oh, I think you've given me plenty of opportunity."

Chapter Sixteen

Mark

What does it mean to be in love?

It isn't a question I think of often; in fact I've never thought about it at all. I'd been too busy working, staying out of trouble, and surviving—why would I care about love? Love is for poets and rich people. We Fallen care more about Class dowries than fairytales.

Or at least that's what I used to think. Now I'm not so sure.

Uncle quizzed me about my meeting with Conall, and I tell him the truth: we kissed, not for the first time, but for the first occasion when we really felt together. He hadn't said much, except for a grudging admiration of Conall ("that damn boy is smart, I'll give you that") and wishing me luck.

The weekend passes in a blur. I go outside, visit parks, surf the Internet (though I know it's closely monitored by the Party) and even try reading books. I'm not bookish or poetic; the only wit and charm I possess is rubbed off from my uncle. Yet I find myself enjoying some of the books—especially the ones with grit and edginess.

In the end, though, my mind returns to Conall. He consumes my thoughts. I imagine him smiling in the sun; I imagine darker things than that, too. What would it be like, I wonder, to close the lights and feel him in ways I've never felt before?

Sadly for me, Conall is too busy with homework (and being watched by both his parents) to sneak another trip together. My sex fantasies remain fantasies, for now.

But damn, I want them to be more.

★★★

A couple of days later, the pain comes back.

I'm holding a carton of orange juice, when, without warning, the muscles in my upper body clench tightly. I pour orange juice all over my T-shirt, but I can't do anything about it. For seconds—though it feels like hours—I'm paralysed. I feel a weird sensation in my back: it's almost like something is trying to get out of my body.

"Are you okay?" I curse silently. Why does uncle have to notice everything?

"I... I guess I'm fine. Just spilled some orange juice on my T-shirt, that's all."

"You want to tell me that bullshit, boy?" I flinch. Uncle only swears when he's angry.

"Okay. I've been feeling some shoulders pains for a few weeks now."

"And you didn't come tell me?"

"I thought they were nothing."

"You couldn't move your upper body for ten seconds; your muscles looked like they were about to tear themselves apart."

"It wasn't this bad the first time."

He shakes his head, his jaw pulled hard. "Please stay out of trouble."

"I'm trying not to get into any more fights, but it's not like I chose to anyway."

"I know that. I'm just... really worried for you, Mark."

"What? Why? Can't you bring me to the hospital?"

"I can do that. We'll see what we can do."

I have a feeling that he doesn't think it's that simple. Uncle is always impervious to me —I never understood why he doesn't tell me anything about my dad, or what motivates him to act in the way he does.

It's not like me to ponder over mysteries, though. So I carry on—I change my T-shirt, go to work, and forget about it.

***

I have a ten hour shift today; it's long, as most of them are, and I'm distracted all day. I bandage minor injuries, hand out medicines, change IV bags, and help the doctors whenever I can; but I do all of it mechanically, like I'm running on autopilot. It's a wonder no one notices.

At the end of it, I finally got what I want.

"Mark?" he asks over the com phone.

"Hey."

"My mother is finally leaving—thank God—and father is busy with work."

I know what that means. "When and where?"

"Meet me off the Medium Quarter, on Appian Way. Half an hour."

"That's not far. You dressing up fancy?"

He chuckles. "You bet."

I close the com phone. I taste apprehension on my lips, and something else too: desire.

Chapter Seventeen

Kaylin

"Miss Kaylin Connachta?" the man at my door asks.

I don't usually receive unexpected guests. In fact, ever since I've founded the organisation, I've not received any guests at all. The man—a heavy set fellow with thick matted hair, a grizzled beard, and overly large sunglasses—is unfamiliar to me. The other man, who I assume to be his partner, gives me a different impression: of quiet intelligence, eyes sharp blue and probing.

"Yes, that's me. May I ask who are you?" My politeness is only on the outside. Inside, I'm thinking what threat they could pose—and if they are a threat, then how they can be most effectively neutralised. At the moment I'm going for simple murder, but I need to have a better grasp of the situation first.

"I'm Mike and this is Cillian." I have to give it to him: he's good. I would never have detected the lie from the way he spoke or acted. Of course, clairvoyance gives me powers that far surpass those of simple observation.

"Nice to meet you. How may I help?"

"Please, Mrs Connachta, there is no point in pretending. We know who you are."

"Oh do you? In that case, why not come inside, and you can tell me exactly who I am."

That makes them hesitate. Their targets usually show fear, or attempt to escape; this is nothing like what they expected.

"Oh come on? What could I possibly do to you if you came inside?" A lot, but they don't know that.

Reluctantly, they walk in. I notice they're carrying weapons: a pistol, knives, and even a grenade. They could kill me; I'm mortal, not a god. But, I do have the element of surprise.

They sit at the dining table—I even bring them tea.

"So tell me, what have I done?"

"You are suspected of engaging in terrorist activities and committing treason against the Irish state."

"Oh? And how did you come by that conclusion?"

"We've been following you closely, since you tripped our Whispers." I know little about the Whispers, except that it's a system the Party has implemented to look for suspicious activity across electronic devices. I thought I'd covered my tracks—but then, I should never have underestimated their algorithms.

"And?"

"We have observed you disappearing from the grid, then re-appearing. Furthermore, one such disappearance was connected with an incident—I'm sure you've seen it on the news."

"What?"

The burly one—"Mike"—sighs. "Mrs Connachta, we know you sabotaged the force fields of the police building while the storm was raging."

I notice that the quiet one, Cillian, has not said anything. His eyes simply follow me, assessing my behaviour. Neither man has touched their tea; they're not stupid. I know Cillian would be the most dangerous of the two, however.

"If this is so, why bother coming here? Why tell me this? Why not simply take me out?"

"We very much doubt you acted alone, Mrs Connachta."

"Ah, so you intend to have me confess—presumably in exchange for something?"

"We would substantially reduce your sentence. Instead of being executed, you would be made Fallen."

I tread carefully, seeking to obtain as much as information as possible before one of them tries anything stupid.

"So tell me, who do you suspect I am working with?"

"We would hardly tell you if we knew," Cillian replies, the first time he's spoken.

"Who else knows about this? How high does it go?"

"Even if you kill us, our efforts would only intensify," Cillian continues.

"I thought as much."

He's too surprised to react: I press my finger against his neck, and his eyes roll in their sockets before he collapses into unconsciousness.

The other one tries to draw his pistol, but I've already anticipated that move. I concentrate, focusing my power towards a spell. Before his hands reach the holster, they slow, then freeze. His entire body is immobile; he can only look at me, eyes bright with fear. I walk up to him, slowly, maintaining the spell; then I place my thumb against his neck. He too collapses.

I examine their unconscious forms, and sigh. I'm going to need dark magic.

✦✦✦

I bring them to the a basement, a damp, hidden place. Then I seek out the Black Book.

I discovered the Book on one of my worldwide journeys; it originated from India, though I'd found it in the mountains of Tibet. Evading the Chinese authorities had taken some work, but it was well worth it. The book is thousands of years old; the writing is unknown and legible only to me. I know little about its origins, who had created it (no author is mentioned) and how it came to be.

But that doesn't really matter, in the end. What matters is the knowledge it holds.

Cillian wakes up, blinking groggily. I suspect his partner will be out for longer—he has a weaker will.

"Who *are* you?" he chokes.

"That's a good question. I don't see the harm in telling you: I am a clairvoyant and magician. I possess powers beyond the ordinary."

"Yeah, I kinda got the last part."

I smile; he flinches.

"And I suppose you're going to kill me now that you've told me? You can't win, you know; we're onto you."

With a groan, Mike wakes up. He blinks, confused. I suspect his recovery will take a bit longer, so I continue entertaining the discussion.

"I suspect your assessment is accurate, which is why I did not kill you straight away."

"But you could have done, right?"

"Of course."

He curses.

"Yes; you were most helpful in providing the information I needed."

"What the fuck?" Mike exclaims.

"Mind your language, dear." My voice is sweet as sugar, but a deadly strength is concealed underneath.

"I'm not going to mind my language, bitch, until you—" I focus on another spell. His words are cut off with a strangled gasp.

"Silence. You, Cillian, have proven more intelligent, so I will give you the benefit of some explanation."

"You're not really going to torture us, are you?"

"I will if necessary, but I suspect it will not be needed. You see, what I am going to do is rifle through your head and remove all memories of this event. I will then implant a false memory: you came here, you found that your suspicions were misguided, and you need to explain this to your superiors. If you co-operate, things will be much easier for you."

"And if we don't, you'll torture us until you break our will."

"Precisely. You learn quickly."

He seethes with anger, but I know he's weighing up the options—and acting rationally.

"Fine. I submit."

The procedure is relatively straightforward: I take some ink, draw a complex rune on his chest (he stays helpfully still as I remove his shirt), and then take out a knife.

"I thought you said—"

"Don't you worry now, it's just a bit of blood."

He gulps.

"Are you telling me you're afraid of blood? You, a Secret Service agent?"

"We're not actually called the Secret Service, you know. That's just our formal designation." I suspect he's rambling, so I ignore him. I know that he's experiencing something so arcane, something so far beyond what he considers possible, that he's beginning to enter delirium. His partner had already done just that a few minutes earlier.

A drop of blood from him, and another from me, and I'm inside his mind. I search through his thoughts methodically, starting from the ones most present in his consciousness—guilt about his stupidity—and go back to the moment when he opened the door to my home. I neatly excise the memory from his consciousness, taking care to avoid taking any other memories with them. The operation is clean, my spell like a scalpel.

Now for the next part: a false memory. I fabricate a convenient tale, drawing the important details carefully, but leaving the less important ones vague—that's how real memories work.

Once I'm done, I disfigure the rune on his chest. The magic dissolves instantly.

He's sleeping now, the magic having exhausted him. His partner does not protest; the second operation is equally easy. With the job done, I untie them, and call one of my men. They would deposit the two in their car, somewhere in Dublin: the explanation is that after having interrogated me extensively, they had driven back, but fallen asleep from exhaustion.

Some would pale at what I've done. But it's necessary, and I take no pleasure in it. I did not go through more of their memories than necessary. My job requires me to do unsavoury things—but that doesn't mean morality should be abandoned. Without ethics, I realise, I am ultimately no better than they are.

Chapter Eighteen

Conall

I don't take Mark to something as quiet and anodyne as a restaurant. Tonight I have bigger plans: I'm taking him to Club Underground.

The Club's name isn't just for show. For one, it's actually underground—a good four stories beneath the nondescript terrestrial building that houses it. And for two, it's underground in a more metaphorical sense as well: in its depths, the Gardá turned blind eyes. Do some of the things that went on in there above ground, and you would face charges of public indecency and immorality. Do them below ground...

Of course this gives the place an air of danger and secrecy. I've never found any substance behind the morbid rumours; it's all theatre.

Mark and I walk side by side, his presence strong, reassuring, and tempting.

"You sure about this club?"

"Don't worry, I've already been here before. It's not nearly as dangerous as it sounds—it's more about freedom and debauchery than crime noir."

"You know I can barely speak Latin; why are you trying French?"

I smile with amusement. "*Parce que le français est beau.*"

"Not a posh-boy, Conall."

"Because French is a cool language. Anyway, stop complaining—because you're about to see for yourself." We stop in front of a squat concrete building; there are no apparent entryways, and the windows are boarded. But I lead him to an an almost invisible door, where we are confronted by a guard.

Bald, suited, and menacing, Drake did not look like a man you want to cross. He doesn't bother asking for my ID, of course. We get along well.

As we walk down the stairs, a distant booming can be heard. It soon turns into the full throated roar of music. Club Underground meets us with a show: dark blues and neon reds mix to create a kaleidoscope of brilliant light. Parts of the club are lit brightly, and filled with gyrating dancers; other parts remain shrouded in shadow, home to different sorts of activities.

"Dance?" I ask. There's something darkly seductive in my voice, and he replies eagerly.

We move across the dance floor, our bodies entwined in a smooth synergy. Faster we go, overtaking dancers, until the world seems to encompass nothing but us: we are a blur of flashing lights, a symphony of fast rhythms and booming beats, two spectral wraiths in a twilight world between the light and the dark.

Exhausted, but deeply satisfied, we end with the song. We make our way to a bar; there I serve my preferred cocktail (a concoction of Dubonnet, gin, and a lime) while ordering the same for Mark. He tastes it gingerly.

"Your attitude to alcohol always amuses me."

"I think it's a good one—alcohol is dangerous."

"Sure, but it can also be fun."

"I think I've had plenty of fun."

"Oh? Well, for the record, I share your sentiments. You proved a good dancer."

"It's natural."

"Maybe it is. Ever danced techno before?"

"No. But with you—it just made sense."

Another melody comes on. This was one is darker; it begins with no more than a low rumble, and enters a prologue stage of slow beats and discordant strings. Again I offer my hand; again we enter the dance floor. Our movements are slow—languid rather than excited. But soon, the tempo increases, and we begin to move more quickly.

Faster and faster we move. The music reaches a crescendo of booming baritones and shrill synthesiser voices. We become lost in each other: in the thud of our heartbeats, the blood racing through bodies, and the strange connection we feel.

When the song comes to an end, we feel the disappointment that goes with the con-clusion of any good story. We want to keep going: to dance eternally, there in that world of shadows and flashing lights. But all good things must come to an end.

So we make our way to a group of comfortably arranged sofas. The leather under-neath is plush and expensive, for Club Underground caters mainly to guests of a higher sort, despite its position in the Middle Quarter. The alcohol has already fetched a hand-some price.

"I think I could get used to dancing," he comments.

"Ever danced to trance before?"

"That was trance?"

"Yup—progressive trance they call it."

"It was like a whole new world."

"That's what I thought, when I first heard it. You won't find it outside of the under-ground scene, though."

"Why?"

I shrug. "Many think it's too radical; that there's something about it that repels the mainstream consciousness."

"Mainstream consciousness? What's that supposed to mean?"

"I suppose the conforming attitude of the masses."

"The conforming attitude maintained by the Party, you mean?"

"That's heresy, but since this is Club Underground—yes. Trance is, in a way, the anti-Party."

"Some irony that you would enjoy it, then, eh?"

I look straight into his eyes; he looks back at me, desire and defiance mixed in his gaze.

"Let me show you the other levels." I say it with an authority he cannot resist. He follows me, deeper into the lair.

✶✶✶

The upper layer is, in a way, the most respectable part of Club Underground. The levels deeper underground are indeed... darker. The second level is still lit brightly in places, but the dominating mood here is one of shadows: of whispered words, surreptitious touches, sensuous body movements. There are no drugs or prostitutes here, as in the level lower still, and I'm happy with that. Mark has already made his feelings in that respect clear.

"Any more dancing?" he asks eagerly.

"Not yet," I reply, "but don't worry: there will be another song soon enough. Until then, why not try more drinks with me?"

"Are you trying to get me drunk?"

"Not at all. That said," I add with a smile, "getting you drunk would be a pleasant side effect."

He complains half-heartedly, but I soon have him trying a tequila. I myself settle for a glass of wine, finding that my taste for cocktails does not quite outweigh my appreciation of good wine. And it is good wine—I suspect they had some of the better vintages.

"Enjoying the tequila?"

"It's... strong. I suppose I could get used to it."

"I suppose you could get used to a lot of things." My hand finds his in the semi-darkness, and the warmth of his body is one that no amount of alcohol can replicate. From the corner of my eye, I spot Celia giving me a wink. She's an acquaintance of mine in the Club, and is always keen to see me enjoying myself with other men. For once, I'm more than happy to oblige her.

Without warning, I lean into him, and kiss him. At first he freezes, unused to kissing me in public; but when he sees that everything is okay, he kisses me back. His lips are soft and probing: there are questions marks there.

Before I can answer them, another song starts playing. I take his hand for the third dance.

Trance music is about storytelling. And this melody is composed by a master storyteller. It begins with a prologue, a ballad between two strange, electronic pianos; then it draws into a conflict, an interplay of minors and hidden background rhythms. Then the powering crescendo, the apogee of the instruments, draws near.

We seem to glide across the dance floor, like the fallen angels the melody is meant to represent. Our body movements seem mirrored; we are held together by an indelible bond. And when the musical tale finally ends, we stand in each other's arms, breathing hard with exertion—and something else, something more.

Across the shadows I take him, into a private room. I lock the door. Then I start kissing him.

✶✶✶

Before, I kissed him tenderly, with rapprochement and intimacy. But now? I kiss him with desire—dark and burning and overwhelming. I run my hands through his rich blond hair, down to his neck, and through to his abs. I take off his shirt, the buttons quickly succumbing to my expert fingers. I plant kisses over his chest, and lower abdomen, until...

He moans as I take him in, his hands resting on my shoulders. At first I only tease him—a gentle touch of my lips, a suggestion. Then I pleasure him more eagerly, my lips forming powerful circles. He's rock hard now.

"Oh fuck it, this is just as good as I thought it'd be."

I chuckle darkly. "Glad I'm not disappointing you."

"Conall—you could never have disappointed me."

Needing no further encouragement, I continue stroking him. His fingers wrap around my hair; he pushes me in more deeply, his body hungrily meeting mine.

Then I stop. At his expression, I rise up, kissing him again. A little known fact: a kiss after a blowjob tastes divine.

"Is that it?" he asks.

"Hardly." I take off my own shirt; he needs no further encouragement. He kisses me on the jaw, then all over my upper body.

"On the bed," I growl.

He complies easily, holding my ass between his hands as he lifts me. Then my jeans fly off, and it's my turn to moan in ecstasy. He's inexperienced, but makes up for it with enthusiasm.

"You know I want more," I breathe darkly.

"I..."

Sensing his fear, I smile.

"Then let me."

His body is large, and muscular, and much stronger than mine; but in my arms he's as compliant as chocolate caramel. I turn him on his back, kissing him on the nape of his neck, until my lips go lower.

At first he resists my efforts, being tense, the sensation unfamiliar. But soon I begin to convince him: he relaxes, and then shudders as I go deeper. He lets out a soft gasp as my tongue forms circles around the hardness within; he moans loudly when I repeat the action more aggressively. I give him everything I have. His body tells me he wants it, and more.

"Conall..."

"Turn around and look me in the eye." He does as I tell him. His expression is lost.

"Wrap your legs around me—hold me tight while I stand." He complies instantly.

My cock is pulsing with anticipation. At first I only touch him, grinding against his body with my erection; then I go in.

His eyes widen. I lean down, kissing him. His body tightens against mine; I kiss him tenderly.

"Relax, but hold me firm," I whisper.

"Yes sir!"

I smile with amusement. Then I'm inside him again, his body warm and soft next to my tumescence. My movements are lithe, powerful; his are strong, guiding. He gasps as I find him deeper, and closes his eyes. I growl, low in my throat, and speed up my action.

"Mark, open your eyes," I whisper.

They are brilliant blue against his face—he's like an angel, I realise. My own little piece of heaven.

Harder we go, until we can't go any longer. I explode with pleasure. He arches his back, his legs wrapped around my body, until he, too, joins me in ecstasy.

★★★

"Hot damn," he says.

"An admirable sentiment," I agree.

"I always wondered what it would be like to get it, you know."

I smile teasingly as I kiss him, having collapsed on top of him once we were done.

"And I take it felt just as good as you thought."

"Just as good as I *dreamed*."

"We should get back, you know," I point out.

"Oh? Where to?"

"My bedroom."

"I like the sound of that."

I chuckle with amusement. "I'm sure you do—though we've put the cart before the horse, so to speak."

"True. And we should... clean up."

"I have an en-suite shower."

He shakes his head, still amazed by my wealth, likely. "To your bedroom, then."

The journey back is like a dream; the night is dark, but the lights burn brightly, and his strong arm stays wrapped around my shoulders. What could I say? My own little piece of heaven.

Chapter Nineteen

Kaylin

"So the Secrets finally picked up on us, eh?" Grumman asks.

I've just explained how I was attacked by the Secrets, the extent of their knowledge and their motivation. My men watch me quietly; there's admiration in their expressions, and fear too. I haven't described the precise details of the ritual, but I told them what it did.

"That is correct, Grumman. We were compromised."

"So what are we going to do now?" one of them asks.

"Well firstly, we need to review our IT systems—particularly those that use the Internet. Software Man, I'm disappointed: you told me you'd cleaned up all traces of my presence on the Internet."

"Mistress, I—"

"Don't bother with excuses. Just get on the job."

"As for the rest of you," I continue, "we need to carefully reconsider our tactics. If one of us is approached by the Party's agents, or is captured, or killed—what do we do?"

"I thought we already established that," Diana comments.

"Our original policy was to play the fool, and wait for rescue. Otherwise—if and only if the attack is meant to be lethal—we use force. But I believe we need a third response: information gathering. Simply killing the agents was within my power, but it was the wrong response to the situation."

"But how do we gather that information? We don't all have your abilities, Mistress." Trust Diana to point out the flaws in my plans.

"No, but you're all smart enough to figure out how to do it. Chances are, they're not going to know everything—they'll want to interrogate you, or convince you to be a double agent. Go along with it; take it as an opportunity."

"I like your thinking," Grumman comments.

"Onto other matters. Diana, how is X doing?" We've taken to calling Conall X, in order to protect his identity as best we can.

"X is distracted with Y."

I raise an eyebrow. "Distracted?"

"As in XY, yes."

That comes as no surprise, really.

"Come with me," I order.

We make our way to a quiet room; I make myself comfortable while Diana recounts her findings.

"Have you discovered more about Y?"

"Yes: his name is Mark, and he is a Fallen."

"A Fallen—really? With an Upperclassman?"

"You bet. I don't know what they're thinking."

"They're in love; we were once in love too, you know."

"True," she admits.

"But you are correct: this could prove a dangerous situation. Is there anything else you know about Mark?"

"Not that much, really. I know that he lives with his uncle, who's a Technical—"

"Oh?"

"And that's because Mark's dad abandoned him. He's living with his uncle right now, in fact—illegally, might I add."

"Interesting. As yet, though, I still do not know exactly why they are important."

"You haven't had any more visions?"

"No. I shall attempt to glean more tonight, though my efforts have proven in vain so far; it seems that the visions will come only when they think the time is right."

"Damn visions."

"Welcome to the club, Diana."

"Anything else you want me to do in the meantime?" she asks, changing subject.

"I will need you for other tasks: let them be for now. If they've escaped the notice of the Secrets so far, then clearly they're wise enough to avoid detection. Drawing ourselves in too closely may put them at risk."

"As you say, Mistress, though I am mighty curious to know what's up with those two."

"Some am I, Diana. So am I."

★★★

The night is dark; the sky, a perfect velvet black. Stars shine in its depths, multitudinous and bright: entire worlds could be there, far away, alien. Maybe they are happier than we are on Earth. The freedom! To not have to worry about the Party, or the mutants, or the crushing responsibility of command.

I sigh.

"You always did enjoy watching the stars, didn't you?"

It's Doireann who speaks. Friend, and sometimes lover, Doireann (whom I usually called Dorian for familiarity's sake) is a man I care for—enough to keep my full powers secret from him, in any case. He only thinks I'm a bit special; he didn't realise I'm the leader of a paramilitary terrorist organisation, or that I can kill a man with a single muttered spell.

Sometimes, I wanted to tell him, but I never did. No one should have to endure what I do.

"You know me well." I return to the conversation.

"So why did you bring me here, Kaylin?"

I shrug, though from the way his eyes narrow, I'm not fooling him.

"Life is tough. I thought: why not bring a little more lightness to it?"

"So that's it, eh?" He smiles.

Though Dorian was no longer the man I met (and fell for) ten years ago, he is still handsome. His eyes are iridescent blue in the starlight; his posture is tall, and strong, and just a little bit arrogant. His dark hair is framed by equally dark stubble.

"You could say so. Come; there's wine in the cooler. Bring some here and make yourself comfortable."

He obliges. I suddenly realise that I had gotten used to ordering men in my life. I don't quite know what to make of that; there is surely some philosophical significance, though it escapes me.

"How's work coming along?" I ask.

"Being a banker is not really an easy job, you know. But I still prefer it to the alternatives." He could say that again.

"I've been promoted," he continues.

"Oh? Congratulations."

"Thank you. What about you though?"

"You know I'm not allowed to tell you."

"Ah, the secrecy part. Very well—we all do what we must. How about life in general?"

"Life is life. Sometimes it's dangerous; at other times exciting. Occasionally it's even a little boring."

"I never took you for being a philosopher, as well as a spy."

"I keep telling you I'm not a spy."

"But what else could you be—with the secrecy and that special ability of yours? Besides, it's not like you would tell me if you were."

I laugh. The man's curiosity is part of why I like him: he would have been boring otherwise, and there is nothing I dislike more than boring.

"What do you think about the wine, anyway?" I ask.

"It's excellent, even by my tastes. The Irish weather is very febrile for the crop."

"Not that many years ago, no one would have conceived of growing grapes in Ireland."

"No?"

"The warm weather we've experienced seems to have been here forever, but that's only because we have short memories. Barely a few centuries ago, this island was rainswept and cold."

"You would know better than I, Kaylin, although I do wonder where you get all this information from. I've never heard of half the things you say."

"The Party does its best to keep the information under wraps."

"Oh? Aren't you supposed to be on their side?"

I laugh, though a little bitterly. Banishing thoughts of the Party from my mind, I turn the conversation to more light hearted matters: the years we spent together, as friends and sometimes as lovers; the hardships and surprises; the days when everything seemed so much simpler. The night air is cool against our skin; the stars glitter brilliantly.

I cherish that moment, knowing darkness is never far away.

Chapter Twenty

Mark

I wake with his body pressed against me. His skin is smooth, soft, and warm. I'd thought that the best bit would be what I could see: his brown hair, the sunlight that picks out stray strands, like gold. God, he's hot.

And yet, it's the other senses I notice more. He has a nice smell—something light, but with a more masculine undertone. I can hear his heart beating, regular and reassuring.

"So this is what's like," I whisper.

He smiles just slightly. "Oh yes."

"Were you awake the whole time?"

"Oh yes."

I laugh. "I can't help it; I'm new to this love business."

"Well, don't worry—you're doing great."

"So you enjoyed last night?"

"Hell yeah. Although, getting back home did prove a little difficult."

"Really didn't feel like putting your clothes back on, eh?"

"Nor finding our way home."

"Won't anyone notice me in your bed?" I ask, suddenly conscious of the possibility.

"Probably not. The mansion is large, as you can see, and—" He doesn't say any more. We both hear it: footsteps, walking up the stairs, getting closer...

"Quick: hide in my wardrobe."

"Your wardrobe? Won't it—" But he pushes me in, silencing any questions. A few moments later, someone walks in.

"Good morning, Conall."

"Good morning, father."

"Had fun last night?"

"The Club is as good always."

"Though you didn't stay up nearly as late, I noticed."

Despite the fact that I can't see him, I know Conall would be giving him his nonchalant shrug. I stand still, and quiet, in the darkness of the walk-in wardrobe. It isn't cramped; in fact it's so large, it's almost a room in its own right.

"I'm just here to tell you I'll be away for a while," his dad continues.

"Oh? Party business?"

"It's related to that, yes. I'll be part of a delegation to China."

"Oh really? I thought diplomatic relations were, eh, frosty."

"They are, but some things need to be discussed—that's the way it is."

"How long will you be away?"

"About a week, depending on how the talks go."

"Have fun."

"Yes, son, I'll have fun." Even I could hear the sarcasm in his voice.

"I can only wish you the best, father."

"Indeed you can," his father comments. Then, as he begins to leave, he adds one final comment. "And you, I am sure, will have plenty of fun."

I imagine Conall would be giving him the wide-eyed innocent smile.

After some minutes, Conall comes and opens the door for me.

"That was close," I point out.

"Indeed. Lucky for the wardrobe."

"How many clothes do you have, anyway? Does it need to be so big?"

"It's mostly full, actually."

"Speaking of clothes, you aren't wearing any." He looks down, as if suddenly aware of that fact.

"Well, yes."

"How come your father didn't think that weird?"

Conall shrugs. "It's not as if he doesn't know about my sexual escapades."

I don't know what to make of that, so I took a different tack. "Well, put some on. We have a week to ourselves, right?"

"We do, with father away."

"And I can cut down on my shifts."

"Then it's perfect."

I like the sound of that word.

"Are you sure you want me to put my clothes on, though? We can't leave until father is gone. And the bed is empty."

There was a hint of smile in those eyes; I couldn't resist it. My lips found his, and our bodies entwined on the sheets.

✳✳✳

Sometime later, we get up, dress, and make our way outside. The Saturday morning is busy: there are people of all sorts—Fallen, Workers, Technicals—doing various sorts of things. They seem happy. I realise that I have never considered myself happy before; the world before me had seemed alien. And in a way, it still is, except now I have my own happiness.

I hold Conall with one arm over his shoulder. People might have thought we were friends, but they would have been wrong. The day is hot—like summer is—but not nearly as hot as in the last month. Eventually, summer would give way to autumn, when leaves would fall and the nights would lengthen. After that, a short, but cold, winter.

"So what are we going to do with our newfound freedom?" he asks.

"I don't really know. But no more clubs or parties, please."

He pouted. "Why not?"

"Too much debauchery."

"Oh! I'm surprised you know the word, to be honest."

"I've picked up a few things," I explain by way of answer.

"Okay, how about flying?"

"Flying?"

"It'll be fun! I even have a pilot's licence."

"And what are you licensed to pilot?"

"Well... it's called an ornithopter."

"A what?"

"You'll understand when you see it."

"Okay, whatever. I swear you'll be the death of me, Conall."

With a smile, he orders a taxi, and drives us to the airfield.

✶✶✶

I expect a massive concrete monolith, stretching everywhere as far as the eye could see. That's how I knew airports, anyway. But this is nothing like that: it's compact, the main building covered in glass. The taxi leaves us. Conall doesn't need to pay; the fare is already covered by his membership card. We walk to the gate. Conall flashes his ID, and we were

119

in.

"How come you know how to fly, anyway?"

"Call it a past time. Father encouraged it, since he thought it would instil discipline, responsibility, and spatial awareness."

"And keep you out of trouble?"

He chuckles. "That as well."

"Your dad is weird, anyway. Why do you call him father?"

"Our relationship is... complex."

"That's one way of putting it."

"There's our ornithopter," he says, pointing at... well, the ornithopter.

It's hard to describe, because I can't believe something like it could exist. It's like a giant dragonfly: it has transparent wings, attached to a cabin. Spindly-looking legs keep it steady on the ground.

"There's no way that thing can fly," I point out.

"Oh, but it does. Come on."

"I am *not* going in that thing—it looks like it's about to take someone's head off."

He just rolls his eyes. "Trust me, Mark."

Reluctantly, I follow him. Inside, the ornithopter resembles a plane—it has instruments like one, at least, although the strange-looking joystick doesn't seem as normal. Conall puts on a headphone set, and begins talking with air traffic control.

"Delta 341 here."

"Roger that. You are cleared for take-off."

I continue looking around, but the cabin is pretty bare: there's just me, him, and the cabin walls, which are mostly made from some sort of transparent plastic.

"So how does it take off?" I ask.

"It has two joysticks"—he shows me a smaller one, in his left hand, next to the larger one on his right—"which I can manipulate to give 3D instructions. The bigger one controls forward, backwards, left and right movements; the other one controls altitude."

"So to take off, you just lift the smaller one?"

"Correct."

"Let me see you do it."

He presses a small red switch—I guess it's the on-off—and lifts the joystick. I watch, open-mouthed, as the wings begin flapping. Not spinning; flapping. There is no sound, except for the rush of wind. We're in the air, maybe a couple of metres above the landing pad.

"Wow."

"It has that effect."

"Can you start flying forward? How fast does it go, anyway?"

"It flies at about seventy miles an hour, give or take."

"That isn't that fast, right?"

"Not really, no—even trains reach higher speeds than this. Jets are a totally different beast."

"Is that why you wanted to fly a Q-car?"

"Yup. And it can go straight up."

"Like 90 degrees?"

He nods.

"Glad I didn't let you kill me."

He just laughs. Then, suddenly, he shifts the joysticks, and we're shooting into the air. The world below us turns into a patchwork of light green, dark green, and yellow. An expanse of blue I realise is the ocean.

"How come it's so silent?" I ask, feeling eerily out of place in this world of sun and sky.

"The wings are driven by electric motors."

"And can you do acrobatics in this thing?"

"Some, but I'm not going to try."

"Why not?"

"Because, as you say, I don't want to kill you."

He gives me a playful punch. But then my shoulder goes numb. I stand unmoving in my seat, paralysed. At first he doesn't realise what's wrong; but then his eyes widen in con-cern.

"Mark? Is something wrong?"

"I'm fine," I reply. It isn't technically a lie, because the paralysis had faded off. But for a few seconds, I had been scared.

Chapter Twenty One

Conall

There's a lot to a relationship, I realise. I used to think it's all about sex. And indeed: I'd loved the sex. But what I had called relationships are nothing in comparison to what I have with Mark. It isn't about infatuation; it isn't about being daring and breaking the rules (although being with him did give me that kind of high). In the end, it's about feelings—affection, humour, personality. I love his sarcastic quips and no-nonsense attitude to life. I loved the fact that he always speaks plainly, without bullshit.

In fewer words, I am in love with him. I don't like that word—love. I used to think it's exaggerated, even fabricated; that Romeo and Juliet were just stupid kids playing a political game they didn't understand. But now? Now I suppose that love is the ultimate politics.

After the plane ride—in which I gave him a tour of the ocean, much to his amazement—we part ways. We want to be together forever, but I still have homework and he still has responsibilities. We would meet again on Monday, and have the week to ourselves.

Still, I'm not completely free of romantic interests that day...

***

"Hello Conall." His voice is dark, and makes me shiver.

"Jake? What are you doing in my house?"

"Well, I haven't seen you in a while, and decided to stop by. Finding your address wasn't terribly difficult."

"And how did you get in?"

"Your guard was quite happy to permit me entrance once I informed him that I was here to see you."

I could understand what the guard had thought of that.

"And now you're here in my library, where I am supposed to be studying the works of Hobbes."

He waves his hand. "Hobbes was just a conservative who misunderstood social structure and the so-called 'state of nature'. Really, he's terribly dull."

"Oh? So you *are* familiar with him? I thought you didn't bother with the reading material."

"For the most part I do not, but occasionally I partake." Something in his wording makes me squint my eyes at him. He looks back, a sardonic smile plastered on his face. He seems completely at ease in the library—he even caresses the books, examining the titles.

"Is there a hidden context in those words, Jake?"

He just smirks. I notice that he wears black jeans and a black T-shirt; he seems strangely in tune with the dark browns and polished woods of the library.

"The context is yours to interpret. Anyway, I suspect you have other interests."

"Oh? And what would you know?"

"I spotted you with him—the blond pretty boy."

Now I am surprised. "He's not a *pretty boy*—he's strong enough, and hard enough, to turn you into mush." My words are said defensively, I realise.

"He does have some impressive muscles, you are right. But no more about him. How are things with you?"

"I thought, since you've clearly been spying on me, that you would already know."

My words have no effect on him. "Hardly."

124

"Well, I've been busy. The Lyceum; my flying—"

"You fly?"

"Light aircraft, yes."

"Interesting. Go on."

"And of course there was the Club—"

"No? I didn't peg you for the type."

"Well, I'm not nearly as spoilt or as naive as you seem to think."

"And I take it you were there to partake in the more daring activities?"

"Oh yeah."

"Well, well. It seems I have underestimated you."

I don't know what to make of our bizarre exchange. I suppose I should see it from his perspective: here is an attractive man, clearly a potential partner...

"Why are you really here, Jake?"

"To see your wonderful library."

"Don't try sarcasm with me."

"Oh, well, if you *must* be a spoilsport. I'm here because I find you fascinating, Conall. You interest me; you dare me to discover more, with your confrontational attitude and the reluctance with which you reveal secrets."

"So—I'm a game?"

"I wouldn't call it a *game*. More like an interest."

"If you want me to tell you more, at least tell me more about yourself."

"You are already aware that I am English?"

"Of course."

"And that I am, as one might say, poorly behaved."

I smile. "You've made that clear. Why not tell me about your hobbies, your family, that sort of thing."

"My parents are obsessed with power." Mine are the same, so I can't comment.

"And as for my hobbies," he continues, "aside from drinking, gambling, and other such questionable activities, I have an interest in cars."

"Not Q-cars?"

"No; they are soulless machines. I prefer real cars, with tires and loud engines."

"I suppose you have a collection?"

"I do—I have a Ferrari, an Aston Martin, and my personal favourite."

"I'm guessing that's a Rolls Royce."

"Correct. It seems you know a thing or two as well."

"Machines have always interested me, though planes attract me most."

"Do you want to fly something faster one day? A jet?"

"Absolutely. But first I have to avoid killing myself on a slow flyer." That draws a laugh from both of us.

"Anyway," I continue, "I really do need to finish my reading. Next time, try the door-bell, will you?"

"Next time." He's smiling as he leaves. I have a strange feeling that I would come to regret that moment one day, although I don't feel guilty about it. I am in love with Mark. Jake—intriguing and pretty as he is—will never match up.

Chapter Twenty Two

Kaylin

They say that in a dream, you cannot truly feel fear. After all: the dream is a place of imagined horrors, a world devoid of the pleasant logic of waking reality.

But they are wrong; the fear is all too real. Because the world I am seeing is not some fantasy concocted by my imagination; it is as real as the grass beneath my feet, or the air in my lungs. And my mind could never dream the horrors that she inflicts.

I know her name, as surely as I know her thoughts, or the dark marrow of her being. She is Sheilia.

A smile, and a hint of her many powers, gets her past the guards and into the reception area. She waits patiently. (She has lived for thousands of years; patience is easy for her.) The purpose of her visit is clouded by numerous other concerns, but I get the gist of it: meeting a Party member. A high-ranking one, not any lowly functionary.

Through telepathy—mine or hers—I overhear the thoughts of the people nearby. Several men observe her surreptitiously, captivated by her beauty. A few women gaze jealously. The receptionist, a young woman, wonders if Sheilia is open to sex. She smiles at that, and makes her way to the desk.

"Hello, how... how may I help you?" the receptionist asks, flustered.

"Call me Sheilia." Though the name is not requested, this immediately puts the other woman at ease.

"What can I do for you, Sheilia?"

"Are you Enda's private secretary?" she asks, referring to the Party member.

"Well, *technically*, I'm not."

Sheilia raises an eyebrow. "But in practice..."

"In practice, he likes it if I take care of his business."

The Dark One smiles; the receptionist blushes, almost swooning. I have no interest in other women, but it is easy to understand what she sees: the graceful figure, curvaceous, and beautiful as any claim to Aphrodite. And I understand the things she does not see, too. The power—almost like a thrum, invisible but intoxicating.

"So tell me your name," Sheilia continues.

"Annabelle," she blurts.

"Well, Annabelle, I would greatly appreciate it if you could put me in touch with En—" The dream world flickers, a kaleidoscope of colours dancing across my vision. Dreams are notoriously unreliable like this: it's like watching an old analogue TV with bad signal.

"Quickly, you understand. I am a busy woman, and, well—this is terribly important, you see."

"Yes, but Enda is a busy man too. I don't know—"

"Oh, I'm sure you can do something to convince him. His other business is not as important, I can assure you." With a twinkle in her eye, she adds: "I know you've already convinced him before. And I would be happy to repay you for the favour."

The meaning behind her words is left unsaid, but is all too clear. The poor woman blushes, her heart rate doubling.

"When you put it like that..."

A few moments on the com phone, and she announces: "He's ready to take you in, now."

"Thank you, Annabelle. I will not forget this."

With a smile, her stride cool and assured, she takes the lift. She opens a grand mahogany door, finding herself face to face with Enda Burton, Party Commissioner for Law and Justice.

＊＊＊

The office is full of splendid elegance and assured grandeur. The table is huge, execut-ive style, and made of hardwood. A skylight lets in rays of brilliant sunshine. The man at the table is less impressive—he is too short, his eyes too small, and his hair too close to being bald—but he nonetheless exudes power. Not power of her order, but a power non-etheless. And one that is useful in attaining her ends.

"Good afternoon, Commissioner Enda."

"Hello to you too, though I don't know why on Earth Annabelle insisted on you being here. You were scheduled for later. Crazy woman."

Sheilia only smiles. She makes no comment on the man's hypocrisy. Instead, she makes herself comfortable on a leather-backed armchair, and waits.

"Okay. What do you want?"

"Well, truth be told, *Enda*"—she says his name with a salacious tone, and something in him takes notice—"I want a favour."

"Oh?" he asks, more alert now. "What kind of favour would that be?"

"It will seem rather strange, and you may wonder why I am even asking it."

"Nonetheless, I want to hear it; you make me curious. I haven't even asked for your name yet."

"Sheilia," she adds warmly.

"A pleasure to meet you." I don't understand how the man's hostility has molten so completely. She must be a master manipulator.

"But yes. My favour. You see, there is a man—well, I call him a man, but he's more of a

129

boy really—who I suspect has committed murder."

"And you're coming to *me*? Why haven't you reported him yet?"

"Well, that's the thing. I *suspect* he has committed murder, but I cannot prove it definitively." Her words are a lie, but he believes them utterly. "I want you to arrest him; this will allow me the opportunity to obtain suitable evidence."

"Are you sure you need him arrested? Can you not seek the evidence and then make a case? Not that I doubt you, you understand."

I realise why she picked him, beyond his position. The man is a fool.

"Well, I quite agree, but you see, I can only collect the evidence if he's in prison."

"You think he has contacts in the prison system we can track?"

Her expression is amused. "Something like that."

"What's his name?"

Again the dream world flickers, going vague around the edges; a noise like static cuts through my ears. I curse inwardly. Names are powerful things, and dreams cannot always reveal them.

"Then I shall consider your offer, most gracious and beautiful Sheilia."

She rises, but I sense she is not finished. Of course not: the man has only said he will *consider* her offer. A little more is needed.

The man stills as she leans closer. A menacing power suffuses the room—invisible and yet so terrible. Her kiss is merely a brush of the lips, but I see the darkness that suppurates from her mouth and invades his body.

"Consider it carefully, my dear Enda." With that, she leaves, her hips swaying arrogantly. The man licks his lips, eyes burning with lust, confusion, and the red gleam of possession.

★★★

Alas, she is not done yet.

A smile, a few whispered words, and a hint of her power convinces Annabelle to leave early—with her. They walk to Annabelle's car, and make themselves comfortable on the drive home.

"So how was it?" Annabelle asks.

"I convinced him to aid me in my business, though is he a poor specimen of a man. I pity you."

The other woman winces. "Yeah, dat's how things are here." Away from her job, her Fallen accent is more noticeable.

"And I think you deserve better," Sheilia continues.

The car stops. They get out. The door opens; they kiss. Annabelle closes her eyes in ecstasy, but the Dark One's thoughts are on a very different plane. The sex is brief, but passionate, Annabelle driven by all-consuming attraction; and Sheilia too, though her sexual desires are intermixed with less natural things.

I want to close my eyes. I want to stop dreaming. But I cannot: I am a prisoner, trapped here, forced to confront this evil.

Annabelle's screams are as much surprise as pain. Soon they turn to gurgles of agony, and then fall silent. Death is a sweet release.

Sheilia casually walks away, her wings utterly black, her form utterly inhuman. Annabelle's eyes lie open, her neck twisted at an impossible angle. There is pain, there, but something else too: betrayal. She thought Sheilia cared for her. And why not? How could a being so beautiful, so charming, hide such festering evil, such black passion?

Blissfully, the dream ends.

Chapter Twenty Three

Mark

The day is perfect. It's hot, yeah, but the breeze is cool; it's sunny, too, and dry. Conall giggles as I spray him with water from the park fountain. Children laugh around us. Conall's eyes are a perfect chestnut brown in the sunlight; stray strands of his hair flicker with the wind.

Everything is perfect. Until they came.

We don't notice the Q-cars—at least not at first. We don't notice the navy blue uniform of the Gardá, until they're close enough to tell why they're called the Shades. And when they speak my name and tell me I'm under arrest, I want to fight. But we both know it's too late.

"What are the charges?" Conall asks, his voice cold with fury.

"Murder," the captain replies.

"What?"

Conall's voice is shocked. I'm left numb. It would have been better if they'd tried to pin me for moral corruption, or for living illegally with my uncle, or for any of the other stupid Party laws. At least then I could have comforted Conall—told him everything would be fine, a good lawyer would get me out. But even though I want to reach out, to tell him it's a lie, I can't; I did murder Finn. It had been self-defence, sure. But would they believe me? Would Conall?

The policeman handcuffs me. I want to resist, to bash his head against the concrete; a voice deep inside even promises me I'll enjoy it. But I don't.

"Follow me," the Gardá orders.

"I'm an Upperclassman, I'll have you know." Conall is still trying to overrule them with his authority, though I want to tell him not to try.

"We know."

"I demand you let him go; you have no evidence."

"You're right. But we don't need evidence to arrest him; only suspicion. You know the law."

"On whose suspicion is this based on?" Conall asks skeptically.

"We've been ordered by Commissioner Enda. Here—I have the official Order." The Gardá unfurls a stamped piece of paper; Conall takes it, looks over it, and then gives it back. He's visibly shaken.

The policeman moves me forcefully towards the Q-cars. Conall follows, though he's not under arrest.

"I want to go with him," he demands.

The Gardá shrugs. "It's none of my concern."

Conall sits next to me in the back of the Gardá's Q-car.

"Tell me everything," he orders.

✳✳✳

I begin slowly, my voice low, my throat cracking. I start with the day when it all began: the moment when Finn told my ex-roommates I'd stolen their drugs. It had been a lie, sure. But that didn't matter; it's easy to doubt someone who's different from you. And I had been a damn idiot, too.

Oh, I tried to keep it secret; I tried to pretend. I'd never had anyone until Conall. Before that, I'd watched porn, but always when they were away. Finn had suspected. He'd

133

shown them the porn—told them I was a pervert as well as a thief and a liar.

"And that's how I found you."

"Yeah."

"I understand why you didn't want to talk to me about it. But I'm glad you have—even now."

"Thanks," I say quietly.

"But what happened after? Why do they think you murdered Finn?"

I swallow. "I didn't have my ID, so I went to get it. I tried finding a window of opportunity—I didn't want a confrontation. But Finn found me. He attacked me with a knife."

"So it was self-defence?"

"Damn right it was."

"How did you kill him?"

"I bashed his head with a lamp."

He closes his eyes, thinking. "And the knife? Would it have had fingerprints? Blood?"

"He never got me, and it would have my fingerprints as well as his; I disarmed him."

"That's not good."

"I *know* that, Conall."

He sighs. "You should have told me—before."

"Yeah?" I ask bitterly. "And what would you have thought, Conall? A Fallen guy you just met, confessing to have killed someone?"

"It was self-defence; you said so."

"You wouldn't have believed me. No one ever does."

"I..." He wants to say it, but we both the know the truth: he would've at least suspected. Maybe he wouldn't have offered to keep me in his home.

Maybe he wouldn't have fallen in love with me.

★★★

The Q-car stops, and we exit. I walk, heart heavy, to my cell. The Gardá they'd sent to accompany me is stone-faced; Conall, beside him, mulls over my words in silence.

"You could try and escape," he whispers.

"There's no point, and you know that as well as I do, Conall."

The Gardá opens the door to my cell. I turn around, and Conall locks eyes with me. I can't tell exactly what's going on in his head—there's anger in those brown eyes of his, but also worry, and something that I want to believe looks like love.

"I'll come back for you, Mark."

"I..."

"Don't fear, and don't despair. It *was* self-defence." And then he kisses me. It's gentle—just a touch of the lips. The Gardá looks away, pretending he hasn't seen the exchange.

The cell closes with an air of finality; Conall walks away.

★★★

They serve me food twice: the first not long after I arrive here, and the second in the evening. The cell is bare; there's nothing to distract me, not from boredom—and not from my thoughts.

I want to bash my head against the wall. I wish it had all been different; that I had never had to kill Finn, that my father had not abandoned me... that nothing would stand between me and Conall.

That life would be perfect.

Yeah, and angels will sing you hymns. Get a grip, boy. Realising there's nothing else I can do, I put my head against the threadbare pillow, try and make myself comfortable on the lumpy mattress, and go to sleep.

⋆⋆⋆

I wake up, bleary-eyed. Shadows of half-remembered nightmares lurk in the corners, though I ignore them, focusing instead on the electronic beeping. A prison warden is at the gate.

"Where are you taking me?"

"This is just a holding cell; the main prison is further down."

"Prison? I haven't been put on trial."

"Sorry, but I'm not the one issuing the orders."

"Then who the fuck is?"

The guard looks away. "Someone high up."

"What—the Commissioner? The guy who ordered me arrested?"

"Yes."

I blink, trying to think past my confusion. Yesterday had been... chaos. In between the conversation with Conall, the arrest, and thinking about how I killed Finn, I'd forgotten *who* had put me here. It doesn't make any sense: why would the bloody *Commissioner* care about me? How could it possibly interest him?

"But... why?"

The man shrugs, though he looks at me with pity. "I don't know, mate."

I swallow my anger, and follow the man out. The corridors are grey concrete. There are no windows; the only light came from fluorescent tubes above. I spot security cameras, and I know there are other security measures in place—ones that I *can't* see.

We walk for what feels like an age, though it couldn't have been more than a couple of minutes. There's nothing to indicate a break from the monotony—at least visually. But two other things alert me to the change. First, the noise: I could hear conversations, shouts, even taunts. And something else—something that pricks at a sixth sense. I can only describe it as the atmosphere of violence.

He opens the door, leading us into a hall. Inmates with orange jumpsuits look at us, their eyes sliding over him, but settling on me. Something inside me raises its haunches: I meet their stares, knowing my eyes are hard as stone. They look away.

We arrive at another cell, which the guard opens. I don't ask any more questions; I walk in, and sit down. He locks it.

"Hey, you my new cellmate?"

I turn to see another man, or maybe boy is a better word. He smirks at me, eyes blue and hair blond.

I ignore him.

Chapter Twenty Four

Conall

I am furious.

They have no right, I tell myself. *He did nothing wrong; he shouldn't be in prison.* I know these things are true, but I also know that in the real world, things don't work like that. It doesn't matter if imprisoning Mark is unjust: if the Party wants him in jail, then he would be in jail.

Somehow, I have to get him out. My hands tighten with rage.

"Darling, calm down," Sianna says from the front of the Q-car. She'd picked me up once I'd left the prison and called her. Frankly, I'm surprised; I didn't expect she would care.

"I don't want to fucking calm down."

"And mind your language."

"Since when do you care?"

"I only care because I can see how distressed you are, and despite whatever you may think of me—I do care about you, Conall."

I have no reply to that.

Soon, the Q-car slows down. I look outside, seeing the mansion towering high above. It looks like a prison—just one that's more luxurious than Mark's.

I let myself out without a word, stalking angrily towards the front door. Father is wait-ing for me.

"Son—"

"If you don't have anything positive to say, don't fucking say it."

For a moment, he simply closes his mouth. It's like watching a fish trying to breathe air.

"Conall, please let me say what I want to say."

He never uses the word "please". I stop, turn around, and look at him more carefully. His eyes are blazing, just as I know my own are.

"You never told me about him."

"You wouldn't have approved."

"Maybe not, but you should have told me. If you had..."

"What?"

"Maybe this wouldn't have happened."

"If you're so damn powerful, *father*, why don't you just order him to be freed?"

"You and I both know I can't do that."

"Then shut up." I storm past him, up the stairs, and into my bedroom. He doesn't follow; he's smart enough not to do that.

Once I close the door, I let it all out. My tears are hot and salty on my face. I would have made some sort of poetic reference—"sweet, bitter tears; a love forsworn and cruelly torn asunder". But even poetry couldn't reach me now. I feel only grief, sharp and inescapable.

✷✷✷

I sleep poorly that night, my dreams dark and disturbing. I dream that he's suffering in prison; I see leering faces, and scrunched up fists, and bruises on Mark's boyish face. Morning chases away the dreams, though not the pain.

At the Lyceum, I remain sullen, and pay no attention to the teachers. Friends and colleagues try to cheer me up, but I am inconsolable. Only Stella understands.

"What happened, Conall?"

"They... they arrested him."

"What? Why?"

"They think he committed murder."

She puts the question as gently as she can. "And did he?"

"It was self-defence. God, I wish I could have stopped them. I wish... dammit Stella, I wish he'd told me. I wish the world would be a different place. I wish—"

"Conall, you have to calm down and think straight." I try to still my ragged breaths, realising that she's right. Wishing wouldn't do me any good; but maybe there's something else that might help me.

"What are you going to do now?" she continues. We're outside the Lyceum, in a nearby field that's usually used for playing football. There's no game today, so the place is empty—just as we need it.

"I don't know"

The breeze picks up, and her hair becomes a wave. The sun shines down, though it's low in the sky, this being late afternoon.

"You need to keep eating, you know."

"And drinking," I offered.

"And sleeping."

I smile just a little.

"I don't know if there any easy solutions; I'm not a lawyer. But I know that you need to try."

"What if there's nothing I can do?"

"There has to be. The way you talk about him, Conall... it's obvious how much he means to you. I wish I'd met him. Makes me wonder what kind of man he is, to make you really care."

"Are you saying I didn't care about anyone before him?"

"Be honest, Conall. Until him, you only thought about sex and having a good time; your love interests were just playthings."

I know she's right, though it's hard to admit.

"What if he'll be there forever?"

"He won't be."

"How will we survive? As a couple, I mean?"

"You have to try," is all she can say.

∗∗∗

I try to follow her advice, though the dreams keep on coming—dark and vivid and menacing. I see fights, improvised knives, and blood.

I don't go to the Lyceum on Friday. I'm too exhausted from the lack of sleep, and besides: I can afford to miss a few lessons. Instead I prowl the mansion, like a caged animal. Father doesn't try to talk to me.

I want to say that I used the time to come up with some sort of brilliant plan, but in truth I did nothing like that. Mark has been taken away from me. I want to shout, to scream, to blame the universe for everything. And you know what? The universe doesn't care.

Chapter Twenty Five

Mark

In a way, life in prison isn't as bad as I thought it would be.

Maybe it's because of Declan, my cellmate. (I tried calling him roommate, but he told me this isn't a "fucking hotel".) He's taught me the ropes: who to avoid, who might be your friend, and who was plotting against you. I'm not sure exactly why he's doing it—I haven't exactly been nice to him—but soon I'm glad. The prison is... an interesting place.

There are three men I have to watch carefully. Sam "the Crusher" is the guy everyone in the prison tries to keep on their good side. He's big, mean, nasty—and not as stupid as he looks. Caleb "The Gorilla" is a black man, tall, heavyset, and not very bright; he is manipulated frequently. Finally, there's Cutthroat Sean—everyone stays away from *him*.

Our routine is pretty simple. At night, we're locked up in our cells. As morning comes, they let us outside so we can exercise. I make the best of that; I need to be strong in this place. In the afternoon, we would be back inside, and we're allowed to play cards, watch TV, or read a book. In the evening, things depend on the guards' mood: if we're nice, they would let us stay up late. If we aren't (or if they're just in a bad mood) they would lock us up in the cells.

This afternoon, me, Declan, and a few other guys are sitting at the table, eating lunch. The food is nothing to write home about: a kind of porridge, only it's made from meat, and doesn't taste too bad if you don't look too carefully.

"So, Mark, what'dya here for?" It's Brandon who asks, a Fallen and a car thief before he came here. He looks me at me up and down, eyes black and probing.

I know it's a dangerous question. I have no idea what they think of murderers—I've heard stories from Declan.

"I helped my friend smuggle stuff in lorries." I throw in a bit of truth, since I had once helped smuggle some things in a lorry.

"What'dya smuggle?"

"All sorts of stuff—drugs, mostly."

"Cool," he says, before going back to his food. Inwardly, I breathe a sigh of relief.

"So how are you fitting in?" It's Declan who speaks this time.

"I guess things could be worse."

"No shit."

"What's that supposed to mean?"

"I mean, you haven't been beaten up or threatened yet. That's good going."

I only shrug, as if I can't bring myself to care. So they go back to their lunch, ignoring me.

I try not to think; I try not to remember anything. But I can't. I hear uncle's words again—*they'll make a show of it, boy*—and try not to notice the irony. And of course, I think of Conall. Is he hurting right now? Is he disappointed in me? Does he still even care?

I finish my food. I play cards with the inmates, winning a few games and losing others. From the outside, it looks like nothing is wrong with me: I'm composed, I laugh at jokes, I even smile a little. But inside, it's torment.

★★★

As night comes, the guards bundle us into our cells. I ask for a book—some pulp mystery—and try to follow the plot, though my heart isn't in it. Opposite me, Declan has closed his eyes.

For a moment I think he's sleeping, but then he asked me a question. "Mark, why did'ya lie?"

My eyes shoot up. "What are you talking about?"

"In the canteen, when they asked what you did to come here."

"What makes you think I was lying?"

He shrugs. "I might be wrong; ya might not be lyin'. But I've been here a few years, and I notice things, ya know? It looked like you were lyin'."

"Well, even if I was, I wouldn't tell you."

"That's okay. I get it. You don't trust me: if I were you, I might not trust me either. But let me tell ya somethin' kid."

"Oh yeah," he continues at my expression, "I can tell you're a kid. How old are you?"

"Nineteen," I say.

"Well, I'm only 25. I wasn't much older than ya when *I* came here. At first it was tough. It's why I taught you the ropes—'cos I didn't want you to go through what I did. So: I don't know if you trust me any more now that I've told ya, but I promise you, boy, I can keep a secret. And I think that if ya tell me the truth, well, it might be easier for ya."

So I tell him. He listens carefully; I realise that while he looks like a teenager, and sometimes acts like one, he's really a man, and decently smart.

"That sucks, kid. All in self-defence? You were right not to say anything—there are some bad types here who would give ya crap, 'specially if they have a friend of a friend who knows one of your dealers."

"Well, I'm just glad you understand."

"I do, Mark, I do. I really don't think you should be here, but ah, you know what they're like."

"What about you, Declan? Why are you here?"

"Stupid stuff really. I was a bad kid; I made a lot of mistakes. One got me in prison."

"That sucks." I wonder how my life would have turned out if uncle hadn't been there. But then, I realise with a bitter irony, my life *has* turned out exactly like that: he and I are in the same place.

"Brothers?" I ask.

"Brothers," he agrees.

★★★

Morning comes again. We eat breakfast; we go outside. Declan doesn't talk to me, or even stay next to me, but I know he's keeping watch. I'm not sure why he's hiding our association—but it must be for good reason.

Then I begin to guess. Two guys and their friends approach me. I recognise the leaders: the Crusher and the Gorilla. I try to gauge their facial expressions—but they're unreadable. I count six guys in total, way too many to fight, if it came to that.

"You the new kid?" the Crusher asks.

"Sure am."

"What's'ya name?"

"Mark."

"Nice name."

"Thanks."

"What you here for?"

"Smugglin'." I inject a bit of the Fallen accent uncle had tried to keep out of me. It isn't good for them to think I'm academic.

"So tell me, kid, and tell me the truth when I ask ya: who are ya gonna join?"

"What?"

The Gorilla laughs. "He doesn't know! He doesn't know!"

"Shut up," the Crusher orders. "Of course he doesn't know—he's new. Here's the deal, kid. There are two sides in this prison: mine and the Cutthroats'. You are either with us or against us."

"Is there any way I could be neutral?"

"You could, but I wouldn't be recommendin' it. You'd end up like the Invisibles."

"The Invisibles?"

"There are a few of them: James, Declan, O'Grady. You probably seen 'em around. They're invisible; ignored and without friends. Nobody will be there to defend ya—or take revenge—if one of us wants to fight ya. So: which is it?"

I know the situation is dangerous, and that I have no idea what the Cutthroats' team looks like, but I don't think I have much of a choice. The guys in front of me look mean enough.

"I'm with you."

"Glad to hear it, boy. One of my guys will smuggle ya a note in the middle o' the night. You'll be part of the club soon."

"I'm sure it'll be great." He doesn't detect the trace of sarcasm. I watch as they walk away: six men, convicts, and who knows what kind of criminals. I know I would have to watch my back from now on—the Cutthroat would be onto me, even if I protest my innocence.

"You sure that was smart?" Declan asks me once we're back in the canteen.

"Not much I could do about it."

"You'll be part of a side, expected to fight, to associate with them, and to take hits for the team. You ready for that?"

"I can always leave."

He laughs bitterly. "They'll never let you leave."

I don't argue, knowing he might be right. I change subject.

"How long do you think they'll keep me here?"

"What—you don't know your sentence?"

"They haven't convicted me yet."

"That's crazy man." He's genuinely surprised. "They have to give you a trial... eventually. Who's keeping you here?"

"The Commissioner."

"The *what?*" He brings his voice down to a whisper. "The Party Commissioner for Justice, you mean?"

"That's the one."

"Why the bleedin' hell would he be interested in you?"

"I wish I could know."

He shakes his head in bewilderment. "I hope you'll be alright, man."

None of it sounds good. So I eat my food, mechanically, and try not to think about anything. Not the Commissioner, not the Cutthroat, and not Conall. Definitely not Conall.

∗∗∗

It starts not long after we've eaten lunch. The change is subtle: there is nothing obvious to show for it, no ostentatious displays of aggression. But I can feel it, like ice on the back of my neck. Violence.

I feel a powerful conviction, all of a sudden; I don't know what it is, don't even realise that I'm acting on it. I find myself walking towards Declan, grabbing him, and throwing him with me to the floor.

It's a good thing, too. A split second later, something flies above our heads—a bottle,

147

by the look of it. There is an audible crash, as it collides with... none other than the Crusher.

"WHO THREW THAT?"

There's no response, but we can all see who did. It's a guy with dark hair, blue eyes, and a grizzled, almost misshapen face. He looks mean, but not so mean as to hide his fear.

The silence is perfect; you can hear a pin drop. And then, instantly, everything erupts into chaos.

Everything that had been on the tables is now in the air—knives, forks, plates, and bottles. The noise is indescribable. Everywhere I look, I can see bodies moving: in attack, in defence, but no one except us is outside of it. Punches are thrown, and blood starts to flow.

"Are they crazy?" I shout over the din.

"It looks like the guy who threw the bottle at me was one of the Cutthroats' men. They've taken it as a provocation, and now they're settlin' their differences."

"Let's get out of here." He wordlessly agrees.

But where to go? We can't go outside, because the exit is thronged with battling con-victs.

"The cells man, the cells," he says.

So we make our way along the walls, trying hard not to be noticed. They don't pay attention—they're too busy fighting, throwing punches and upending tables. Slowly we move, until we reach the corridor that will lead us to the cells.

But it's blocked. His smile shows crooked teeth (and some that are missing entirely).

"Not much of a fighter are you?" the Gorilla asks.

"I'm not stupid," I point out.

"You're stupid 'cos you're a traitor, and you know what we do to traitors."

I try to argue my out of it, but I can see there's no point. The Gorilla is out for blood.

Declan has hid behind me, the poor bastard. The fight rages behind us.

I should be afraid. But something has awoken inside me: a darkness, a burning malice. It sends electric tingles through my shoulders and arms. My body feels immensely powerful; I can conquer the world.

He springs at me, and I meet him head on.

Chapter Twenty Six

Conall

Everything seems grim. The sky is low, the clouds are grey, and the wind howls against the building. A greyness permeates the world; it is as if Ireland had been replaced with the netherworld, a Limbo where the denizens are tortured in agonising melancholy. Inside, I am as bleak as the world outside: the despondency is crushing.

I've never been lonely before—not really. Even in the vast mansion, there are always people. I have friends I can call on. And usually, I enjoy my own company.

But not now. There is nothing anyone can do about it; the guards try to cheer my up, father tries to talk to me, but I am inconsolable. Even Stella, talking to me on the com, can get little more than curt answers and non-committal grunts.

I wrap myself in a raincoat, heedless of what damage the rain and the wind might do to my designer trousers. No one tries to stop me as I leave. I walk, and I walk; the rain pours down, and the wind rages; but still, I feel nothing. The grief had been sharp, at first. Now it's just a howling emptiness in my heart.

I don't know what I'm going to do. Mark isn't in prison because of some trivial crime, or the ire of one Garda; he's being held under the Commissioner's orders. Even mother and father can't possibly overrule the Commissioner himself.

Since I have no idea what I'm going to do, I try to not think about it. I put one foot in front of the other; I am soon soaked, and cold, but still I walk. Time passes, though I take no notice. I must have walked a good couple of miles until I stop.

I realise that what I'm trying to do is pointless. I can't forget about him, no matter how much I walk—and no matter how much I suffer. So I do the only thing I can think of.

I'm going to see him in prison. I don't know if they'll let me; but that's immaterial. I have to see him again. I would sooner brave Hell itself, than be stuck in this Limbo state.

Chapter Twenty Seven

Kaylin

The morning finally awakens me from the dream. I drag myself out of bed, exhausted; the mirror shows shadow under my eyes, though they are not so much of sleeplessness as they are of foreboding fear. I still see her in the back of my mind: the horribly wrong angle of her neck, her blank eyes, the cold, uncaring pose of her murderer. I wash my face, throw on some clothes, and attempt to eat something. The daily ritual usually calms me—but not now. Too much is at stake.

I need to discover who and what she is; I need to know *why* I saw her. My visions, I had learned, were not without purpose. Learning to understand them often proved to be the difference between life and death.

Diana? I need you.

Kaylin? Even through the telepathic bond, I can hear her exhaustion.

Yes, sorry to wake you. It's important.

Okay. Where... where can I find you?

I'll be at the command post. Make sure you're there.

I focus my power away from the telepathy (using it does not come without a cost) and prepare myself. Before I know it, I'm out of the house.

✶✶✶

They mutter among themselves, their voices a mixture of irritation and worry. I have gathered all of my men in the central auditorium, here in our Dublin base. The place is not nearly as large as the name suggests—the base needs to be small enough to conceal in a crowded city—and so they line the walls, some sitting on repurposed chairs or on the floor. Diana is at my side, a frown on her face.

"Good morning." The tenor of my voice is unusually formal. A heavy silence falls, laden with expectation.

"I have had a vision, and not an ordinary one. I have dreamed."

Diana looks confused, knowing that my visions come in a trance-like conscious state. She doesn't know about the sleeping visions—the rarest. And the most terrible.

"I saw a being with black wings; I followed her, watched as she persuaded a senior Party official to do her bidding. Watched as she murdered someone."

The silence is broken by confused whispers.

"What are you talking about?" Shadow asks. For once, I don't know if I should admire his blunt demeanour.

"I don't know what she is, before you ask. But I had a sense of her. She is powerful—perhaps more powerful than any of us."

"Is she a Familiar?" one of them asks.

"I... I do not believe so. There is something else about her, something alike to us, yes, but also different in a way I can't put my finger on."

"What do you want us to do, Kaylin?" Diana whispers.

"We need information. We need to know who she is, what she is, why she acted."

"What about our other operations?" asks Grumman, my operations manager and senior lieutenant.

"Yeah. I thought the bastards in the Party were our enemy?" Shadow continues.

"Our operations can be resumed at a later date; this is more important."

"What makes you so sure?" It is Diana who asks. She doesn't sound skeptical—only interested in my response.

"You haven't seen what I've seen." Complaints follow from more of my men. I close my eyes, sighing in frustration. Diana lays a hand on my shoulder.

"Kaylin, look: I know it's hard for you, but it's hard for us, too. We've been working on this for a long time. We need to understand why this is so important that we have to focus the bulk of our resources on it."

I realise that only one thing can quell their doubts: they have to see what I saw.

"Silence." The voices die off. They may not accept my leadership without questions, but they recognise authority when it's used.

"There is something I can do that will convince you. I need you all to place your hands on the table, palm out; you have to form a circle." They follow my orders. They know about what kinds of Abilities I possess, but that doesn't mean I haven't kept a few secrets.

"Clear your mind. Try not to think about anything." This would be easier with proper spell-craft, but lacking that, a circle is the best option. I focus my power, drawing the vision back from my subconscious. Then I *push*—I force it out of me, and into their minds.

They gasp in shock, Diana closest to me. Then they fall back, dreaming my vision. I sigh, take a chair, and wait. This is going to be tough.

✶✶✶

Moments later—though it feels as if aeons have passed—they begin opening their eyes, dragging themselves out of chairs.

"I need a feckin' drink," Shadow exclaims. Murmurs of agreement rise out, and it's not long before everyone has a beer in their hand. Or, in quite a few cases, whiskey. I notice a new respect in their eyes. They thought everything was easy for me; that I saw the future while they floundered about in ignorance. Little did they know that the visions have a price. All magic does.

"So," Diana continues, her voice remarkably steady, "you want us to do some sleuthing."

"That's one way of putting it."

"And—if it comes to it—some fighting."

I hesitate. "We need to learn more before we even consider that option. As I say—as you saw—she is powerful."

"More powerful than a team of us?"

"Maybe so."

"This sucks, Kaylin."

I laugh, though bitterly. "It does. And we need to prepare ourselves for the worst."

"The worst being?" Diana prods.

"That she is not a one-off. That she is part of something bigger—something far worse than the Party."

They mull my words in silence. Then Diana poses another question: "Who is this person she's going after? Why is he important? What's his name?"

"I also want to know," Grumman adds.

"I don't know. Dream visions are unreliable like this; they are not powerful enough to reveal names."

"We got Sheilia and Annabelle's names though? And Enda's?" Diana asks.

I wave my hand in contempt. "Sheilia is not her real name, and Annabelle is dead. As for Enda, he is weak; a tool, not an actor."

I rise, wearied, and begin issuing orders. I'm not going to let fear paralyse us: knowledge is power, and knowledge will help us defeat her.

Chapter Twenty Eight

Mark

He's a strong motherfucker.

I dodge his first punch, but his second catches me on the shoulder; I stumble back. He presses his attack, but despite his strength, he's a bad fighter: he overreaches, letting me get a punch on his stomach, and then another straight against his jaw. He backs away, his eyes black with rage.

"You'll pay for that, you little pussyboy."

"Bring it on, you stupid ape." If he's going to be an asshole, so am I.

He bellows, springing at me. I dodge and block most of his attacks—but not all of them. One hits me in the chest, and in my weakness, he hits me in the face. The pain is deafening; it's like I'm seeing stars. But I keep going. He's strong, but I can beat him.

I half-pretend I'm still winded; he comes in triumphantly for another attack. But it's a ruse. Without warning, I kick him in the knee—hard. He goes down. Before he can get up, I aim a kick at his face. He would have done the same if it had been me.

"Fucking cunt," he spits.

"You attacked me."

There's no point in arguing, though, because he grabs my ankle and twists. I fall, but manage to get my other leg to hit his wrist. He lets go.

We both drag ourselves back up. I heave lungfuls of air; I feel blood pumping through my body, my heart beating double time. He doesn't look any better: he's bleeding from one of my punches, and one of his eyes are getting swollen.

"Not such a big guy after all, eh?" I mock him.

I intend to provoke him into another stupid charge, but he does something else—something much worse. He attacks, I dodge, but something else hits me. I feel a sharp pain; I back away, finding my hands slick with blood. He holds a shard of glass in one arm.

"Nobody fights fair in prison, pussyboy." My head is swimming—I must be losing blood, I realise—and I almost can't get away when he attacks again.

"I'm going to kill you and that little bitch boy of yours."

The pain stops, then. The dizziness is replaced with a bright clarity; all of my senses seem sharp beyond anything I've ever experienced. I see my blood on the bottle shard, bright red and gleaming. I see the pores on his skin, the madness in his eyes, the harsh artificial lights and the gleaming concrete floor. I feel a black rage; a powerful darkness grows inside me, obliterating any pity.

When he comes for me, I simply take hold of his hand. His eyes widen as he tries to pull away, but I hold him like a vice. He screams in pain when I twist his wrist, breaking several bones, and then crush what remains.

He screams and he screams, but the anger I feel is relentless. My other hand reaches for his throat; then I lift him, and slam him into the wall. He crumples in a heap.

★★★

The fight ends not long after that. Gas seeps in through ducts; the inmates fall gasping on the floor, stunned by the neuro-agent. Several androids and guards handcuff them and drag them into their cells. Tables are returned to their rightful place, or else the pieces are collected and replaced with new tables. Within minutes, it's as if nothing had ever happened.

In the cell, Declan initially doesn't say anything. He just looks at me. I don't respond; I just lie on the bed, close my eyes, and pretend it's all right. But my mind is on fire. I have so many questions—why had he attacked? What is it about me, or Declan, that evokes such hate? And how had I done... what I did.

Finally, after several minutes, I say, "Quit that."

"What?"

"The whole looking-at-me-like-I'm-crazy thing."

"Well, aren't you? Did you see what you did to his wrist?"

"Did you see what *he* did to *me?*" My anger flares. He shrinks back.

After a few moments, I say more quietly: "Declan, what's wrong? Why are you really acting like this? I'm sure you've seen this before. And heck—I'm sure you agree with me. So what's up?"

"I'm afraid of ya, Mark."

"Why?"

"Because what you did wasn't natural."

"What do you mean it wasn't natural?"

"I *saw* it, man. He'd cut your throat. And... and then the blood disappeared. It was like fucking magic."

"Maybe the cut wasn't as deep as you thought, and—"

"Don't lie to me, and sure has hell don't patronise me. I know what I saw; I've been here long enough to tell when a wound is nasty. And how do you explain what you did after he cut you? You just grabbed him like a rag doll and threw him against a wall like he weighed fuckin' nothin.'"

I don't have any answers. I've been trying to figure it out myself. Surreptitiously, I place my hand around the place where I had been cut. My fingers come back clean.

✶✶✶

I would talk more, and think the events through more carefully—only a guard comes in and interrupts us.

"Which one of you is Mark?" he asks.

"I am. What do you want with me?"

"There's someone here to see you."

My heart leaps. I can't help it; the fight, the guards, the whole grueling place had made me miss him. It's all I can do not to run out of that cell. Instead, I follow him obediently. A few of the inmates gave me hard stares, but I ignore them. I could deal with them later. I hope.

We walk for a few minutes, until until we reach a set of force fields. The guard placed his finger on a scanner; the force field flashes off. I walk inside. I hear a faint electric hiss as the force field is turned off in front of me.

He looks... well, he doesn't look good. There are bags under his eyes; I wince in sympathy. Some of the buttons on his shirt aren't tied properly. And the expression he wears is harsh; there's a pain there, the kind that makes me think he's going to punch someone at any moment.

Still, his eyes soften when he sees me. He doesn't kiss me—there are cameras—but he still takes my hand in his. His skin is warm and soft.

"How have you been doing?" he asks softly.

"Could be better. I was attacked by an inmate."

"What? Why?"

I shrug. "I don't really know. But he got what he deserved, don't worry."

"How is this place?"

"It could be worse I guess. They let us out in the day; they don't keep us isolated or locked up. The food is edible, and we get holographic TV."

"You still shouldn't be here."

"They can hear us, you know."

"I don't care—and besides, they know full well I'm right. They haven't put you on trial; they have no evidence."

"They do what the Commissioner says," I state, knowing it's true.

"Maybe I can bring you a lawyer—"

"This isn't something a lawyer can get me out off."

"Well, what else do you want me to do?" The frustration in his voice is clear.

"Oh I don't know—use some of that Upperclass mojo of yours, sprinkle some fairy dust, and make everything happily ever after again." The bitterness in my voice is poison.

"Mark, this is your best shot!"

"But what's the fucking point? I don't want to think..."

"To think what?"

"That we're just setting ourselves up for disappointment."

"Well, fuck you Mark. I didn't come here for you to tell me you're just giving up."

"Conall, please—"

"Don't bother, Mark." He gets up from the chair. "Coming here was a mistake."

"Well, I guess you might as well forget about me. It'll make things easier for you. You can be what you were again—a spoilt little posh boy who likes to debauch himself with drinking and whores."

"Who told you about that?"

"I could guess; it was obvious enough. And," I continue, knowing I shouldn't but angry enough to plough on regardless, "I'm sure you'll have a good time when you're older, too. A nice job in the Party, plenty of money, and maybe even some power too."

"Power is nothing if it can't save you, Mark."

I laugh bitterly. "Then rise through the ranks! Make yourself Big Brother, for fuck's sake."

He only shakes his head, and leaves me. When the guard comes back, I'm tempted to say nothing; but Conall is not the only person I wanted to see. I convince the guard to let me use one of their cable phones.

∗∗∗

He picks up the phone as soon as I ring it.

"Uncle?" I ask hopefully.

"Mark! I got the news from the Garda—I didn't believe it at first, but…"

"I'm in prison, yeah."

"This sucks, kid. Are you alright? Are you hurt?"

I've always told uncle the truth—but do I even know the truth anymore?

"I don't know. I'm not physically hurt, but—something inside me—it doesn't feel right. I had to hurt someone, or they would have hurt me."

"That's prison." His voice is gentle, but matter of fact.

"And Conall… we just had a fight."

"I expected that."

"You did?"

"You're both going through a tough time."

"Well, he wants to hire a lawyer for me. I don't know if it's worth the bother."

"Is it true the Commissioner himself is holding you?"

"Yeah."

He curses under his breath. "And for murder? How? And why the Commissioner himself, of all people?"

"I don't know."

"We need more information. I'll try and see what I can do, Mark—you hang tight in there. Don't let anyone mess with ya."

"Thanks, uncle."

"And good luck."

I only hope I'm not going to need it.

★★★

Declan is smart enough not to ask questions, which I appreciate. I'm in a despondent state for the days after my conversation with Conall. I barely eat; the food tastes like cardboard. I don't talk to anyone, and the other inmates give me a wide birth. I don't ask what happened to the Gorilla, though I'm pretty sure he won't hurt anyone again. I don't see him around, though several of his buddies—the Crusher's men, I realise—give me nasty looks.

Then I begin making calculations. Trying to join the Crusher had been a mistake; the Gorilla hadn't liked me and would have found a way to hurt me. In a way, it's good that I fought off him off. Firstly, I learned who the enemy is, which prevents me from being betrayed; and secondly, it makes them just a little bit scared.

Even so, I know I can't count on it. Individually, one of them wouldn't dare attack me. But what if they gang up on me? I need allies. Conall, I realise with a stab of pain, isn't going to be able to get me out—if he even still wants to.

And so I look for the Cutthroat.

"You the Cutthroat?" I ask. I guess there's no need to be indirect with him.

"That's me." He doesn't look scary from the obvious perspective: his build is closer to slight than muscular. Still, I can tell he's dangerous. Part of it is the way he holds himself— he's like a predator ready to spring. Part of it is the eyes; they're like flint, hard and merciless. And part of it is that sixth sense of mine that told me when the fight would start, before.

Yeah, I still don't know what the hell that is.

"So what do you want with me?" he continues.

"Your protection."

He looks me up and down. "From what I hear, you don't need protection."

"Against one guy? Sure. But the Crusher isn't alone."

"You're right—you think smart. Of course, my protection doesn't come without a price."

"I understand."

"So you swear to protect me, your fellow men, and be loyal to us?"

"Yes."

"One more thing: why did the Gorilla try and fight you?"

"I don't know."

His eyes narrow. "You're not lying, but I don't think you're telling me everything, either."

"You don't want me to tell you everything."

"It's okay—I think I already know."

"Oh?"

"There's word round the street that a certain Upperclassman visited you today. I put two and two together. Anyway, don't worry about that; I'm not the kind of guy who cares. I just want to make sure you're loyal. And I think you definitely are—because the Crusher's guys hate you know, especially with that hanging over your head."

"Okay." I guess an Upperclass friend would make them hate me.

"Glad to see you in the team," he finishes.

Soon, I find myself in his circle. I thought his men would be suspicious of me, but no: they congratulate me on beating the Gorilla. I smile and laugh, but it's full of unease; I don't know what they might want from me. And nor do I want to find out.

Chapter Twenty Nine

Conall

I hate what I said.

But I had been angry, and distraught, and he'd told me what I didn't want to hear. And in the end, I have to admit he's right: there is nothing I can do. I should forget about him; he and I aren't meant to be. Doing so would be kinder for the both of us.

So I leave the prison that day. I don't stay much at home—too many questions are still being asked—but go, instead, to the park. It's been three days since that conversation, and while I still sleep badly (and still miss him deeply) I think that perhaps, just maybe, I'm getting over him. I walk the gravel paths, enjoying the bright sunshine. Summer is drawing to a close; then autumn will arrive, and the trees will begin to shed their leaves, and the ground will become a rich smorgasbord of browns and greens.

The air is warm and sweet, while the breeze blows just slightly. It's a perfect day to be free. I would have enjoyed it even more if Mark had been free with me; the thought makes the pain resurge.

But then I see someone that makes me pause: it's Jake, lounging on one of the benches. He's some way off from me, but even in the distance, his expression fascinates me. It's contemplative—almost numinous. Then he turns, sees me, and waves. I walk up to him.

"Fancy seeing you here," I say.

"As I say, there's more to me than debauchery. How are you?"

"As good as can be in the circumstances, I guess."

"Oh? What circumstances would those be?"

"They... they got Mark."

"What? As in prison?"

"Yeah."

"Convicted and everything?"

"No, but... it's under the Commissioner's orders. My parents, even with their influence, can't get him out."

"That must suck."

"Yeah, it does."

For a few moments, there is silence, broken only by the cry of a bird.

"Hey, I know this might come across the wrong way... but I want to be here for you, Conall. I can see you're in a tough spot, and I know—*know*—your parents don't understand what you're going through."

"Thanks, Jake. I never expected that from you."

He smiles; the expression turns his features into perfection. Those dark eyes of his seem full of an infinite compassion.

"It's the least I could do."

✶✶✶

I see Jake a lot in the days that follow. He listens when I speak, in pain-filled sobs, about Mark; he helps me rejoin life, through humour, sarcasm, and some eloquent persuasion. I start speaking to my parents, to Stella, and then to the Lyceum students at large.

But still, I talk most of all with him. Constitutional law never seemed so interesting until now, but we talk whenever we can: in the cafeteria, through the breaks, and in surreptitious places outside of the Lyceum. Eventually, I let him into the mansion, and there we talk at length about, well, everything. We debate politics—he is well versed in Irish politics as well as that of England—and history (which is really just past politics) and other, smaller things like pineapple on pizza. (He detests it, calling it "an abominable invention".)

I know something has happened when he asks me to visit his mansion.

It comes out of the blue. We're walking together in one of the parks (Dublin has a few); the sky is bright and clear, the water of the river is as cerulean as the sky above, and the world seems held in some state of gorgeous suspended animation.

"Would you like to see my home, Conall?"

"I... I would like to, yes. When can I come?"

"Right now would be fine. My parents visit me every odd week or so, but otherwise I have the place to myself."

So he bundles me into his car (a purring Rolls-Royce) and drives me there. The architecture is distinctly Gothic: the lines are angular, the windows tall and flat, and there are even some gargoyles in sight. It's quiet; the area is a little outside Dublin, and more secluded than my own mansion. He talks with a guard on the intercom, who de-activates the force field for us.

"Don't you get mutants round here?" I ask.

"Of course we do. But the automated cannon and lasers do a fine job getting rid of them."

We walk to the door; it is opened by a butler. Jake thanks her (female butlers have become fashionable lately) and leads me upstairs. I hold the rail, enjoying the perfect smoothness of the wood. A vast expanse of space stretches around us; the house is like something from a fairytale. My own mansion, though grand, seems a little unimaginative in comparison.

"This place is..."

"Eccentric?" he suggests.

"Cool, more like. You have quite the imagination—I take it was built under your direction?"

"Indeed. My parents' estate in England is rather more conservative; I thought this a refreshing change."

"It must be tough living away from them."

"Actually, no. I wanted to come here; it let me escape from their attention."

"Were they too overbearing?"

"Yes... you could say that." I wonder whether my own parents would fit the description.

Jake opens a door, to reveal... a banqueting hall. Only I struggle to comprehend it, even used to opulence as I am. The ceiling is curved and stretches well above our heads; the floor is made of flagstones, and decorated with saint-like figures. A table lies in the middle: it's long, and built of solid mahogany. It looks—not quite medieval—but not far off either. A fairytale conception of medieval, maybe.

"Wow," I say.

"Yes, I am quite proud of it."

"But what do you need it for?"

"Ordinarily I eat in the kitchen, but sometimes I bring guests. We enjoy the formality of eating here."

"Before debauching yourselves?"

He smiles just a little. "Yes."

He seats me next to him, and then rings a bell. (It really is that old fashioned.) The butler comes in; he orders some drinks, and a dinner of venison and hazelnuts. The wine arrives almost immediately: it's a deep burgundy red. Not long after that, pleasant smells emanate from somewhere nearby, until dinner arrives in a plateau.

"How is the food?" he enquires.

"Excellent—the venison is soft and the hazelnuts are just a little bit crunchy."

"The wine?"

"The same."

"Then I will let you finish dinner first."

I eat ravenously—I'm hungrier than I realise—while he eats demurely, delicately cutting the venison and gently biting the hazelnuts. Soon, I am done, and he lies back to examine me.

"Can I be honest with you?" he asks.

I hesitate. "You've done a lot for me. I guess you deserve the right to be frank with me."

"I want to be here for you, Conall, but I'd be lying if I said there wasn't more to it than that."

"What are you trying to tell me, Jake?"

He leans closer. His fingers touch my leg, lightly, and then he traces a pattern on my jaw.

"I want you, Conall."

And even though I know it isn't right—even though his memory still burns bright—I accept Jake's kiss. His lips are warm, and delicate; they are like the petals of a rose, velvet red, and rich with promise. Soon the rest of his body is entwined with mine: his hands caress my hair, and the nape of my neck, and his legs hold me tight as he straddles me.

"Master?" We both jump. But it's only the butler, who appears perfectly unfazed by our intimacy.

"Oh Laura, you sure do have timing."

I think I see a hint of a smile on her face. "I'm sorry, master, but I thought you might want to know it is getting late, that's all."

He waves her comment away. "Thank you for the solicitousness, but I am perfectly aware. You are excused."

She performs a formal bow.

"Wow," I say, once she'd left.

"Yes, I do take this business seriously, as you can see. But where were we?"

"Jake... I enjoyed the kiss." That is true, and there is no point lying about it. "But I'm not ready to go any further. I'll see you later, okay?"

"Very well, I can wait. I hope you enjoyed tonight; I didn't want to make you uncom-fortable, what with..."

"No, no, you were right to act on it. It's just, well—it's hard for me."

He nods in sympathy. "No pressure."

So we shake hands, kiss briefly, and I steal off into the night. My head is a whirlwind of emotions: guilt, yes, but also desire, and the hope that this thing with Jake could turn out to be something more.

But then, would I have to give up on Mark? It is a question I do not want answered.

✶✶✶

Kaylin

"Kaylin?"

"Yes, Diana?"

We are in the Dublin base; I am busy poring through the Black Book, reading page after page of apparently inane stories. I have ordered my men to look for any trace of

Sheilia—in records, online, in camera footage, or even a vague anecdote in a newspaper. So far, nothing.

"Mark has been imprisoned by the Party."

I pause, looking up at her. "When was this?"

"A few days ago. I got word from one of our men stationed at the prison; he just told me that Mark got into a fight with another inmate, and the other guy is..."

"Dead?"

"Mauled is the word he used."

"This isn't good. Who is responsible?"

"The Commissioner for Justice."

I shake my head. "And the charges?"

"You know what they're like—a litany of dressed up complaints. But the main thing is murder: some drug dealer he shared a room with, apparently."

"We have to get him out of there."

"Sure, but how? An armed jailbreak? That's risky—even for us."

"What about his boyfriend, Conall? He must be in a tough place right now."

"He's refused to turn up for his tutoring sessions, and I hear from his father that he's been skipping school as well."

"Has he hired a lawyer yet?"

"I don't think so—"

"You don't think so?"

"I'll look into it."

I grab my com phone, calling Grumman. He answers on the first ring.

"Yes?"

"Grumman, bring me Shadow, and post some men to watch Conall. I need full information on the situation with Mark ASAP."

"Sure, on it. You think this might have something to do with your dream?"

I pause, exchanging a look with Diana. "I'm not sure yet."

"We don't know who she wanted imprisoned, true, but it seems like too much of a coincidence. Especially given how interested you are in Mark as well."

This is why I love Grumman: he knows what the Hell he's doing, and he neves misses an important detail.

"You're right."

"And I bet you're planning a jailbreak, too?"

"Diana thinks—"

"It's a bad idea, I know. But I'll look into the prison anyway—just to see what we're up against."

"Thanks, Grumman."

Diana is smiling; I know that smile all too well.

"Can I burn it all to the ground?"

"I can't guarantee anything."

Even so, I can't help but smile. Even in the worst moments, her destructive humour lightens my mood.

Chapter Thirty

Mark

"They're putting you on trial. In three days," the guard tells me, his voice rough.

"A trial? Finally! What are the charges again?"

"Murder, as you know."

"Have they found any evidence against me?"

"That's not my place to say... but I've heard they're planning to use that little incident with the Gorilla against you."

"Fuck him, he attacked me. It was self-defence."

"That's what you keep saying." He shrugs. "If I were ya, kid, I would plead guilty and serve my time."

"Fuck you."

"Well, it was just my advice, that's all." He doesn't seem to care about my outburst—and I guess he wouldn't, since he's probably seen it all before.

The guard leaves, and I sigh with frustration. On the one hand, it should be good news: a trial means that maybe I could get make a case, and be free. But on the other hand, it reminds me that this place—the place I've unwillingly come to call home—is not where I belong, and that I have no idea why the Commissioner really wants me here. He wouldn't care about some murdered Fallen to personally issue an arrest warrant. No: something else is going on. I just don't understand what.

But I don't have time to think, because just then, the pain hits me.

It's in my shoulders—obviously—though it feels like it's now progressed to the rest of my back. I don't have any words for it; I just endure it, racks of mindless pain, spasms of silent agony. I don't even ask where it came from, or why. There is no why. There is only pain.

After what feels like hours—or maybe aeons—it stops. Opening my eyes, I find Declan above me, his expression worried.

"Mark? What's wrong?"

"I... I don't know."

"Does it hurt?"

"Yeah. It hurts."

"Where?"

"My back and shoulders."

"Has it hurt before?"

"Yes—I felt it before I came here. It was sporadic, though, and never as bad as this."

"Take off your shirt; let me see."

I do as he tells me.

He looks at my back, and his expression seems to fall apart.

"When did you get the tattoo?"

"What tattoo?"

"The bleedin' big tattoo that's on your back, that's what. You telling me you don't remember?"

"I don't *have* tattoos, Declan. Let... let me see." He takes me to where a small plastic mirror hangs off a wall. He then takes one of the plates they bring food in—it's made from a reflective plastic—and raises it so that it's at an angle to both me and the mirror.

And then I see... It's blurry, and it doesn't make any sense, but I can't deny what's in front of my eyes. Wings. I have a tattoo of two wings on my back.

***

Declan had gone very quiet after he saw the tattoo, and I didn't blame him. I have no idea what it is, or how I got it. I can think of lots of rational explanations—maybe someone drugged me and did the tattoo—and none make any sense.

But right now, I have more important things to worry about.

I had to beg the guard, and he'd only agreed reluctantly, but now I have access to a phone. I call uncle.

"Mark? Is everything okay?"

"They're putting me on trial for murder."

"Do they have evidence?"

"Not about their original case, no."

"But...?" he asks, sensing there's more.

"I had to defend myself, uncle. One of the inmates attacked me—I told you about him before—and, well, I messed him up bad."

"Typical of them to use that against you. But at least you're getting a trial; that means you should get a lawyer."

"I thought about that."

"Have you considered calling Conall again? He'll get you the best lawyer money can buy."

"I..."

"And he's an Upperclassman. He stands a better chance of saving you—please understand that. I've tried my best, but I'm only a doctor. This is beyond my power."

I sigh with frustration. "Okay, uncle. I'll think about it. Have you managed to find any more information about why they're holding me?"

"Sadly not. We'll have to wait for the trial. Good luck, boy."

"Thanks."

I shut off the phone, and close my eyes. It's not going to be easy: to talk to him, to hear his voice, to know that I am at his mercy.

***

"Conall." I keep my words to the minimum, and to the point.

"Mark! Is it really you?"

"Yeah, it's me. I'm calling from prison."

"Are you okay?"

"I'm alive and I'm not hurt. Listen... I need your help. They're putting me on trial—for murder. I need a lawyer, a good one too."

"When is the trial?" he asks.

"In three days."

"And you want me to help you?" The way he says it—almost offhandedly, his tone curt —makes me cringe.

"Yes, Conall. I'm asking for your help. Please don't be an arse."

"I'll think about it."

"You'll think about it?"

"Okay, damnit, I'll get you a lawyer. I just don't want..."

"What?"

"I don't want you to think that everything will go back to the way it was—to us."

"I never asked for your love, Conall."

"I know that. And I'm sorry, for what it's worth."

"Save me your pity. Tell your lawyer to show up."

I close the phone, not giving him time to reply. The guard comes in and walks me back to my cell; I'm almost glad to go back. I can survive the inmates and the guards. What I can't survive is knowing that Conall might not care about me anymore; that, for him, it was all a bit of fun, and not worth any hard times.

I don't cry that night—I've not cried in a very long time. Instead, I hear voices. They whisper to me, in my dreams—they tell me how powerful I can be, if only I let go of Con-all.

I lash out at their invisible promises; the tattoo on my back seems to burn like fire.

Chapter Thirty One

Conall

The conversation with Mark left me feeling cold, and bitter; yet I have no wish to admit I'm wrong, or to entertain the thought that I can't give up. I'm a fool—an idealist. It shouldn't surprise me that all my dreams with him would turn to dust: that the Party would imprison him, a Fallen.

I start to walk. I leave the house—no one tries to stop me. I realise this is my coping mechanism: whenever things go wrong, I walk. I see Dublin almost in its entirety. The sky-scrapers and cubes of the Upper Quarter are lit in myriad reflections by the bright sun above; the daintily manicured Middle Quarter seems strangely peaceful, even when I stop at his old home. His uncle isn't there, but the nostalgia seems desperately real.

Then I walk away, to the Lower Quarter, and then the Refuse. No one tries to accost an Upperclassman in the middle of the day, although a few shifty characters do give me looks. I ignore them—I have bigger things to worry about.

I find myself ordering a taxi, and typing Jake's address on the destination screen. It's Friday afternoon: I left the Lyceum quickly, and sat silently at home. I didn't want any con-versation. But now I realise conversation is exactly what I need—just with the right man.

He responds on the intercom. "Yes?"

"It's me."

"Come in, Conall!" The force field flashes off, and the metal gate opens without a sound. I walk through.

He opens the door before I get there.

"I didn't see you today," he says. "What happened?"

"I... I wasn't feeling well. They're putting him on trial."

"What? Now?"

"Later."

"Well, not much you can do. Come in."

I come in. The mansion is as much the fairytale castle as ever—I even spot an oil colour of a vampire on one of the walls—but I lack the enthusiasm to appreciate it. It is only when we stop in a small withdrawing room, and when he touches my hand, that I feel... something.

"If it helps, I'm sorry."

"Yeah, but you're right. Nothing you or I can do. Why not tell me about something else instead? How was England?"

"Different in many ways politically, but still similar in others. We have the same weather. The same rolling hills and green fields..."

"Now you're getting cliché."

He smiles. "Just a little. My parents are Peers in the House of Lords—

"You still kept the name, didn't you?"

"We English do love our tradition, yes. We even kept the Commons, though of course, it's powers are far reduced; it's seen as more of an anachronism really. But then..."

"You also love your anachronisms. How's the King doing?"

"Quite nicely."

"And... did you have friends there? Do you visit often?"

"I visit, yes. And I did have friends—but not close friends. Do you know what I mean?"

"I do."

"And while I had plenty of fun, I've found that in time, the fun isn't so fun anymore. Not without friends."

"But you still have fun, right?"

"Of course. Why do you ask?"

"Well, I could do with some right now."

He chuckles. "Would your idea of it include a strong drink?"

"Yes indeed."

He disappears for a second, and comes back with a bottle of whiskey. "Aged," he adds, "and Scottish—you would approve."

He withdraws two glasses (crystal, of course), pours the whiskey, and raises a toast.

"To the future," he says.

"To the future," I agree.

I down the whiskey; it's smooth and strong. I relish the feelings it brings—the freedom from my thoughts, the necessary abandon. Jake doesn't argue when I ask him to pour a second glass ("it's very good whiskey") and only suggests the wine when I ask for a third.

"I should have you realised you were a drunkard," he comments.

"It's nothing I can't handle."

And it looks it isn't anything *he* can't handle, either. His body is languid and relaxed; his expression interested and amused.

The wine is a Merlot—a very fine example of an otherwise quotidian choice. The two of us make short work of the bottle. Feeling pleasantly inebriated, we try playing cards. He beats me, but we still have a good time.

As the sun draws lower across the sky, I think of leaving.

"Jake... I had a great time."

"I'm glad."

"I should probably leave."

"Will you go to his trial? Get a lawyer?"

"I... I don't know."

"Then why leave? What can that accomplish?"

I realise he's right.

He touches my hand, tentatively. "Why not stay?"

His eyes are dark, and seductive. His fingers are soft against my own. I stay.

✶✶✶

Everything seems so wrong, and yet so right. He kisses me breathless; he rips off my clothes, and I undress him just as enthusiastically. His body is smooth, and supple—I draw him close, savouring the feel of his muscles, the masculine scent of his sweat. The world around me seems to spin, the alcohol burning the fears away. I let it all go.

"Let me see you on that bed," I breathe.

He complies with a knowing smirk. And what a sight he is: lithe muscle, and dark, fathomless eyes. I straddle him, kissing him deeply, and he threads his hands through my hair.

"Do you want to be on top? Or should I?" he asks. The question sends a thrill through me.

"Go on."

He flips me over with ease. He kisses my back, his strong arms massaging my shoulders. Then he kisses my neck, his stubble grazing my skin.

It's only when he goes lower, his lips caressing the top of my ass, that the doubts settle. Even in my drunken stupor, my body refuses it. It's all so very wrong. I've been with many, many guys—big and strong, agile and flexible, dominant and submissive. I've fucked and been fucked; I've let my body have its fill.

But it's not those memories that come. Instead, it's Mark: his blue, angelic eyes; his vulnerable body, the night I found him; his will to fight for life, no matter how hard or unfair.

"Conall? Is something wrong?"

I sigh. "I'm sorry."

"Conall—"

"I should want you with all of my heart, all of my body—because you deserve it. But I... just can't."

"You would prefer a convicted murderer?"

"I still love him, no matter what."

"Well then you're a fool, Conall!" He lifts himself off me; the sudden cold hurts. "Leave."

"Is that all you can say to me, Jake?"

"You want me to be clearer than that? Okay: fuck off."

I sigh, and put my clothes back on—I can feel the after-effects of the drink wearing off, and with it, the feelings return. I'm a fool; Jake is a player. I should have expected this, even if it seems bitter.

Worst is the knowledge that the real love of my life is wasting away in prison. He deserves better; he needs me to be strong, because there are some demons which cannot be fought alone.

Chapter Thirty Two

Conall

"Mark?" I ask on the phone. Some contacts from my mother had allowed me to get him another phone session.

"Yeah?" He sounds dejected, almost like... he's given up. It chills me to think that.

"Listen... I was wrong. Damn it, I was a fool. You're innocent of murder; you only defended yourself. I was a fool to be so hard you—you're the one in prison, not me. And I'm sorry. I still love you, and if—"

"I still love you, Conall."

It amazes me: the way he knows what I'm thinking, and the way he knows what I'm going to say.

"Thank you." I take a deep breath. "Your trial is tomorrow; I've just hired a lawyer to look through your case. She's charging me a fortune, don't worry."

"Glad to hear it." There's a hint of irony in his voice.

"Stay strong, okay? I'll see you tomorrow morning."

"I will. And Conall?"

"Yeah?"

"I can't thank you enough. These last weeks... they've been hell. I needed someone to be there for me—I needed *you*."

"But I wasn't there."

"Now you are; that matters. See you tomorrow." He closes the phone.

I breathe deeply, feeling apprehension, but also a sense of... gratitude. It's like a huge, invisible weight has been lifted from my shoulders—I realise that, all this time, what I needed was love. And hope.

∗∗∗

The day is bright; the air is hot. Summer may be waning, but its grip has not abated yet. My mother's car feels uncomfortable despite the climate control. Her chauffeur is driving it—the lawyer is next to me in the backseat.

She doesn't look impressive or intimidating: an older woman with grey hair, and a stiff black business suit. Yet mother assures me that she is fearsomely intelligent—and very good at tearing down prosecution cases. Mother herself had perused her services when she was accused of fraud; the case had been dropped, despite mother's considerable enrichment.

"Does he have a chance?" I ask her quietly.

"Of course." She speaks quietly, in an unhurried pace. "I would consider it an affront to my legal career if I lost this case; the prosecution's arguments are ludicrously weak."

"But it's the Commissioner's order!"

"Even he can't do just whatever he wants; there is rule of law in this country."

"For Fallen?"

"Even for Fallen. They go to jail only because they lack proper legal defence."

I mull her words in silence, quietly hoping. Outside, the streets of Dublin gradually give way to the court building: a squat, gated, and fortress-like thing. No one has ever been stupid enough to attack public buildings—but it pays to be secure.

The chauffeur speaks to a man on the intercom, telling him our case number. The car glides in to a main area; we leave quickly. Inside, the building is no more welcoming than it is outside. There is concrete everywhere, lit by bleak white lights.

I follow the lawyer to a plenary chamber, where I come face to face with Mark.

∗∗∗

My reaction is instinctive and overpowering. I stride forward, embracing him, his hair soft against my hands. Almost shyly, I kiss him on the neck.

"Miss me?" he asks, in that low, amused voice of his.

"Yes."

It's almost too much to bear: the feel of his smooth skin, the bulging muscles of his arms, the perfect blue of his eyes. A detached part of me notices the signs of his imprisonment—he has a stubble, which is pleasantly scratchy against my jaw. (Another, more primitive part of me makes sure to remember to ask him to keep it; the sex will be fantastic.) He smells slightly more strongly, too.

"Are you okay?" I ask him.

"I'm physically unharmed," he adds, shrugging. "The inmate I fought didn't stand a chance."

"What about..."

"Mentally? I feel better with you around—let's just say that."

"Good day," the lawyer says quietly, nodding to him.

"Is she my lawyer?" Mark asks bluntly.

"Yes, she is. I would praise her illustrious qualities... but I think that would be unnecessary."

The stern woman almost smiles at my compliment. But she soon turns to business.

"Mark, listen carefully; I'm going to outline the details of your defence. You must stay quiet: speak only when prompted, and say only what I tell you to. It's not what you may be used to as a Fallen, but it's how the law works. Understand?"

Mark nods seriously. It is time for his trial.

***

Some say nervousness is like a weight on your shoulders; others compare it to a queasiness in the stomach, or a sort of twitchy jitteriness. For me, though, the feeling is more akin to a pressure around me. It's as if the whole room is ready to explode.

The judge is in front of us—we sit on the right side of the court room, and the prosecution sits on the left side. There are no jury members; the Party doesn't believe in them. The session is recorded and filmed.

I notice that there are three prosecutors—none of them are the Commissioner, which shouldn't surprise me. All of them wear suits; one is bald, one is old, and one has a smile I don't trust.

"Why three?" I whisper to the lawyer, as one of the court staff reads out the case.

"It seems they're determined."

She does not sound at all perturbed; I realise her confidence really is absolute. I don't know if that's a good thing.

The first prosecutor rises, and begins presenting evidence. I turn to Mark; I try to project strength, confidence, compassion. I hold his hand tightly.

***

Mark

I should be nervous. Conall is—I can tell. Yet I feel... something else. It's a bit like certainty, mixed in with a bizarre sense of elation; it's not a normal emotion, at least not like any I've experienced.

My back seems to itch, and while I hold Conall with one hand, my other hand grips the table. I see hairline cracks forming on the wood. In fact, everything seems to be in perfect clarity: I see the bored expression of the judge, hear the snarky tone of the prosecutor, and feel the calculating intelligence of Conall's lawyer.

I feel something else, too—almost at the edge of my consciousness. I can only describe it as a force of evil, moving fast towards us. I close my eyes. The sensation only intensifies, and now the itch travels from my back until it seethes under my skin, like a vicious dog on a leash.

"The defendant was arrested on the basis of our informant, who told us that he had various criminal contacts in the prison system."

I want to laugh.

"We considered it prudent to arrest him, both under the Public Protection Act, and on the Criminal Surveillance Act."

So he kept talking, until it was our turn.

"My client cannot be arrested under the Public Protection Act, since article two, paragraph three of the Act explicitly states that the Act cannot apply based on suspicion of an intended crime. The Act can only be invoked if there is clear evidence that my client intends to commit a crime. The prosecution has presented no such evidence."

"Oh, but we have!" another prosecutor begins. "You see, we believe the defendant killed one Declan O'Sullivan. We found the defendant's DNA on the murder weapon."

My lawyer is unimpressed.

"Without even considering a case of murder, your Honour," she says, referring to the judge, "the prosecution's case cannot rest on the Public Protection Act. The next paragraph in article two of the Act states that it cannot be invoked as part of a separate offence—it only applies in cases where the defendant has a history of crime, or there is some other exceptional element. An anonymous informant is not exceptional."

The prosecution pipes up again, but the judge cuts them off.

"I dismiss the charge placed under the Public Protection Act. The State's case is not a proper legal use of the instrument. The court is dismissed; we will reconvene after the break."

The judge leaves, and Conall breathes a sigh of relief. The lawyer smiles, just faintly, pleased with her victory. The itch continues under my skin.

✱✱✱

Kaylin

My team have been working furiously to trace Sheilia's whereabouts; I've been devoting my time to the Black Book, trying to discover its secrets. Neither endeavour has been success-ful: my team has come up empty, and the Book seems reluctant to reveal much..

I expected as much from the Book; it is fickle, and I sometimes wonder if it has a mind of its own. But I never expected my team of experts—programmers, spies, well-planted bureaucrats—to be so empty-handed. It's as if the being we are seeking does not exist in this world, except perhaps occasionally.

"We should stop with this nonsense and return to our normal business—if you don't me saying, Mistress."

"I trust you to speak your mind, Grumman."

"So?"

"We will continue with our present efforts; the matter at hand is too important."

"If you say so, Mistress."

Before I can snap out an irritated retort, Diana strides in.

"Mark has just been put on trial."

I divert my attention away from Grumman and the book, suddenly tense. "Right now?"

"Yes. Conall is with him, and he's hired a lawyer. I understand the case is going well."

"But the dream—" I don't get to say anything more. A vision hits me: I see Mark, standing tall, beautiful but inhuman. A woman whispers in his ear—Sheilia. Mark is smiling; it is an ugly and frightening smile. Then, the vision changes. I see destruction, and black wings across a burning sky.

"Kaylin?"

I snap back to the present. "We need to get to Mark, now. He is in danger. Grumman —organise the team. Diana, you're coming with me."

"What do you plan on doing? Breaking in to the courthouse and kidnapping them?"

I stop. "Something like that."

"We need to plan, Kaylin. We can't just barge in. Besides—it's unlikely Mark will come to harm while he is on trial."

I shake my head. "There is more to this than the Party, and there is more at stake than Mark's physical safety. Now move! Quickly, before it's too late!"

✳✳✳

Mark

"How is the case going?" I ask the lawyer.

"It is too early to tell."

"But it's good that they dropped the charge?"

"The charge was one of many... but yes. I'm confident the rest will follow."

Conall is frowning; he doesn't believe her. I'm not really interested in her response, either. I'm just trying to distract myself from whatever is going on inside me. Everything seems too loud—I can hear voices from across the building. Everything seems too bright, even the dimly lit plenary room.

Then I hear it.

"What was that?" I ask.

"What do you mean? I didn't hear anything," Conall says.

"It sounded like an explosion."

Moments later, the lights go out. The room has no windows; the darkness is complete, and there is total confusion. I hear a whistling sound—a split second later, a thump. Something tells me our lawyer is down.

Another whistling noise passes by, and I try to grab whatever it is. A rush of air tells me I just missed. Conall grunts, then falls to the floor. A third whistling; something hits me in the neck. It feels like a dart.

For a moment, I feel a weak, sagging drowsiness. I force myself awake; the feeling vanishes. But then something—someone—tackles me, hard. I push him off, trying to stay on my feet.

Another whistling, but I dodge—I feel the dart missing me. I realise three things, in this moment: one, we're under attack. Two, they want us alive. And three, if Conall and the lawyer have fallen unconscious, I should pretend the same.

So I drop. Soon after, someone places a cloth over my head.

"Is he asleep?"

"Seems like it, captain."

"Good. We need to get out of the court—if the 'power cut' is too long, people will start to get suspicious. Move."

Robotic arms grab me, and lift me. An android, I realise. We're not being kidnapped by just anyone—these are Party agents, for sure. I don't know what they want with me, but something tells me it's not good.

"What about the lawyer woman?" the man asks.

"Leave her."

I feel the hot sun on my face, and then I'm forced into the interior of a car. I wonder how they managed to get us out so quickly, but I know I have more important things to worry about. Like: where are they taking us? Would anyone realise we've been kidnapped, and by who?

I strain my ears. A mechanical walking sound tells me the android is moving away—probably to the inside of a Gardá car. We're probably in an ordinary, unmarked car. An electric whine, and the rumble of tires, tells me we're on the move.

I wonder where Conall is. Could he be in the car with me? If I move, they might realise I'm not really unconscious. So, instead, I do something else—I reach out. I feel him next to me, not physically, but like a mental presence.

The car ride is short. We stop, the door opens, and they bundle us out.

"The Commissioner will want them awake," the man says.

"Then give them the antidote."

They inject me with something, and remove the cowl.

"How long will it take?" he asks.

"I don't know—a few minutes at most. The Commissioner will be here soon."

Their footsteps tell me they've walked away. I open my eyes.

***

We're in a large, though dimly lit room. There floor is a concrete slab, and a table is arranged in front of us; the only source of illumination is an LED shining above the table. I see two soldiers next to it, and I can tell there are two more soldiers behind us.

Conall wakes up with a groan—I put an arm around him, helping him up.

"Where are we?" he asks groggily.

"Speak quietly," I say. "We've been kidnapped by the Party's agents; they're bringing us to see the Commissioner."

"They have no right—"

"Shut up. They have the right of might, and I need you stay calm and pay attention—it might be our only way out."

"The right of might! I rather like that. I'm sure Big Brother would approve of it also—it fits well with the Party mantra."

The man giggles at his own joke. I take him in: he's bald, a little short, a little fat, and wears an expensive suit. He's just walked in from the door in the corner; it's probably the only way into the room.

"The Commissioner for Justice, Enda Kenny, right?" I ask.

"You know me! This really should not come as a surprise, I suppose. I seem to be very well known."

"What do you want?"

"That's no way to talk to your superior!"

"Forgive me if I don't really give a shit about your Class."

There's a crackling sound as something hits me—something electric.

"I punish disobedience most severely, you understand, especially from someone in your position. A Fallen, a criminal, and a big mouth!

"But to answer your question... Well, perhaps I ought to backtrack a little."

I close my eyes. The taser didn't hurt as much as I thought it would—didn't hurt at all actually. But it's better to make him think I'm weak.

"You see," he continues, "I have an acquaintance—a very interesting woman, who has promised me great things. She requires your continued presence in prison; the little incident with the Gorilla was not sufficient, apparently."

"You still believe I have criminal contacts?"

"Well, she explained to me that it's a little more complicated than that. Nevertheless, it is none of my concern: my end of the bargain stipulates that I keep you in prison."

"Why bother with a trial?"

"I thought the trial would go smoothly—I didn't realise you had an Upperclassman friend. Imagine that! The plan was for you to be sentenced appropriately; and besides, I would have had to give you a trial eventually. The Law is strict, and it's a terrible pain to wipe the records. You've been quite inconvenient."

"So what do you want? I give myself in, plead guilty, and you let me go?"

"Almost, but not quite. You'll have to fire that pestering lawyer of yours—and you cannot simply walk free. We will say that you tried to escape in the power cut, and my agents caught you in the service of justice."

"How convenient."

"Now you understand! I didn't realise a Fallen could be so bright—it almost makes me wonder why she is so interested in you."

He smiles, and then I feel it—see it, even. A fire burning behind his eyes. Something is inside him, something dark.

I spit. "Fuck you."

His face falls, almost comically. "Well, that is terribly impolite. It seems I need to do some convincing."

A soldier walks up to me, and hits me with the butt of his rifle. No pain; I ignore it.

"You're going to have to do some more convincing."

"She did say you were to remain alive... but perhaps your friend could take your place instead."

My blood goes cold.

"Stop," I say.

"So you acquiesce to my plan, after all?"

"I do."

I'll figure something out—I need to find out who this woman is, and then, maybe...

"It is not so simple, alas. Your promise is weak; I need some more commitment."

I watch, horror-stricken, as two soldiers grab Conall, and another punches him in the kidney. He gasps, then vomits.

"Are you going to torture him?"

"A little. As I say, commitment."

Another punch—to the jaw this time. Conall's eyes spin. I want to close my eyes; he shouldn't have to suffer like this, especially not for me. All of this is my fault, in the end. But I can't close my eyes: I need to see him, to suffer with him, to... protect him.

It's impossible, my mind tells me, but something inside me responds: *No.* I hear voices —whispering around me, thick and fast. I wonder if I'm going insane.

Power surges through me: strangely smooth, fluid, and intoxicating. If this is madness, it feels good. At the same time, my back burns in pain, though the pain seems insignificant now.

I move with blinding speed, grabbing the first soldier and throwing him at the wall.

Before the other two can respond, I smash their heads together; they crumple to the floor, lifeless.

"Oh... interesting." The Commissioner seems too stupid to feel fear.

I hear a mechanical *click*—the fourth soldier, behind me, has just cocked his rifle.

"Impressive, but terribly pointless. Alas, you brought this down on yourself. My loyal man over there has his sights on your friend; it would be unfortunate if something were to happen to him."

I hear the man's breathing, feel him tightening the trigger...

I move without thinking. In a flash, I'm in front of him. I grab the man by the throat, and squeeze; he goes red and then white.

"Let us go, or I will kill him," I say.

"Go ahead; he will have died doing his duty."

I don't know what to do; I've run out of options. So I squeeze, and the man dies.

Such an easy thing—death. Life is so fragile, so easily taken away. And the power inside me wants more. It grows and grows, breathtaking in its sheer, unbridled force. It's like a little bit of God, though a terrible, destructive God.

My wings tear through my back; I feel alive. I turn my eyes back towards Conall, and the Commissioner. Conall is down on the floor, only half-conscious, I can feel. The Commissioner looks at me open-mouthed.

"You...? You're like them?"

I walk calmly towards him. "Like who? Tell me."

"No... it wasn't meant to be like this. She promised me it would happen *after*!"

I recognise the flicker of power within him now—it is something like my own, but much weaker, and its does not belong to him. It's a parasite of sorts, a detached, omniscient part of me observes: it manipulates him, feeds on his desires.

My fist explodes through his skull. His corpse falls to the ground, brain and blood spattered everywhere.

"Mark? What's going on?" Conall, groggy and confused.

I hold Conall in my arms, stroking his hair. He whimpers.

"It's all right now," I say. "He's dead."

Slowly, Conall turns to see the Commissioner, his blood pooling from his head onto the floor. Then Conall turns towards me—and sees my wings.

"Mark? Am I hallucinating? Are you an angel?"

I guess I'm an angel, though the concept seems alien to me.

"You're not hallucinating, Conall. It's real. I love you."

"Can you fly?"

I don't know, but I'm going to try. I look around—the door is where I remember it, but it's too risky to go through it. I look up.

"I'll have to go through the roof."

I summon the power within me; it responds eagerly. I focus it to my hand: a blue ball of fire ignites. Fascinated, I send it upwards. It blows a hole clean through the concrete.

I feel the cool breeze brush my wings, and see the sky—so blue and vast—tinged with the low afternoon sun. We can't fly through there, to be seen by anyone... or can we?

Instinctively, I grab the shadows in the corners of the room. They unfurl around us, shrouding us with their comforting darkness. Now, I imagine myself flying; I feel the air, so alive, and compel it to obey my will.

The initial gust lifts us both into the air, but I hold it back, and allow us to drift back down. Controlling it is an art—and getting it wrong could kill Conall. So I focus carefully, imagining us to be light as feather, and agile as a bird.

The slightest whisper of the air lifts us from the ground. I gradually increase the power, until we're outside—out into the sky. Faster and higher I fly. A sense of euphoria overtakes me, and I laugh; it's as if I don't have a care in the world.

Held tightly against my arms, Conall whispers, "Mark, if this is a dream, then I want to keep dreaming."

I only smile, and he falls asleep blissfully. I continue flying, darting past buildings, cars, and people, unseen as the night.

Conall thinks I'm an angel. Flying, like this, I can believe it.

Part Two: Wings

Chapter One

Conall

Slowly, I wake up. The sky is lit in pale blue hues by the emerging dawn; the grass around us is misty with dew. The air is cool, though not cold. For a brief, blissful moment, everything seems perfect.

It takes a few more moments until reality catches up, and my mind begins to ask questions. Am I hurt? How did Mark get us out of there? Where is "here"? An answer is immediately presented when I realise that the cushioning warmth around me isn't just Mark's body—there's a velvety softness to it, far different to the hard lines of his muscles.

With a start, I realise I'm enveloped in his *wings*. I gaze at them, open-mouthed. They're long, graceful, and perfectly black. I touch a feather gently: it's soft, but at the same time, incredibly strong.

"Hey," he says.

I turn to meet his eyes. They are the same perfect blue, his hair the same golden blond. He's still my Mark. The boy I loved; the boy I moved Heaven and Earth to get. Or, well, he seems to have done most of the moving.

"Hey," I reply.

"How... how are you?" he continues.

I smile sardonically. "We weren't like this even when we first met, Mark. Are you going to tell me you've become a softy?"

He chuckles darkly, the deep tenor of his voice vibrating against my body. "I'm no softie, Conall. Never have been—and sure as Hell never will be."

"You do seem to have gained a few extras, though."

He flexes his wings, ever so slightly. "These, you mean?"

"I didn't remember you having them before. I know I said you were my angel and all, but—come on."

This time, he laughs. "Yeah, well, I didn't know either." The humour falls from his face. "Do... do you remember what happened?"

"No, but I guess you killed him. And he deserved it, trust me."

"Thanks, Conall. I needed to hear you say that."

"Why? He put you in prison, after all."

"Because I *enjoyed* killing him, Conall. I've enjoyed doing a lot of things like that, lately."

I gulp. "Lately? As in, it's related to—"

"To me being *this*."

"What are you, Mark?" I breathe. "You can't... it can't be possible."

"I'm not an angel, Conall." He laughs. "I'm much worse than that."

"You're... a demon?" The word sound bizarre—like something out of a horror film.

"Something like that, yeah."

"How do you know?"

"I told you: I *want* violence. It's like a siren call."

"I didn't realise you read mythology," I joke.

"Well, it looks like I am a myth."

"You're still my Mark. I'm serious," I add, when I see his expression. "I still love you. I know... that we went through a tough time when you were in prison. That we—I—said some things I shouldn't have. But I do love you. I love you even if you're a demon."

"Even if I'm a monster?"

"I refuse to believe you're a monster—I *know* you're not."

He mulls over my words, his eyes half-lidded. I raise myself on my elbows, draw in close, and kiss him. His lips part smoothly. His tongue tastes of musk and tobacco; his strong arms wrap around me, deepening the kiss. After a long moment, I break off.

"Did you discover a newfound love of smoking while you were away?" I ask sarcastically.

Again that deep chuckle. "No, actually, though I don't think cigarettes will kill me."

"Oh."

He smiles at my bemused answer. "You know, I was thinking you'd give more than a kiss. I haven't been with you in weeks."

"Did you masturbate in prison?"

"Yeah. Had to be careful about it, too—it's not exactly full of privacy there."

I laugh out loud. Then I launch myself on him.

"Let me make it up to you."

✦✦✦

The first time had not been perfect. I had been unfamiliar with his body, and he had been a virgin. The sex had felt good—but otherwise it had been short.

His lips are sweet and seductive against my own; his jaw is perfectly square, and rough with stubble. (I love that stubble.) I cradle it in my hand, looking him in the eye.

"Am I doing good?" he asks.

"You are."

"Could you... could you touch my wings?"

"Oh?" I draw my hand over his right wing; he shivers with pleasure. I touch his other wing, and then both wings at the same time. He shudders.

"I'm going to have so much fun with you," I promise, savouring the possibilities.

"I bet you will."

"Turn around and lie on your back," I order.

I examine him, amazed. His wings meet his body at the top of his spine, next to his shoulders. But they haven't torn through the fabric of the shirt—instead, I see that they are ink black, like shadows. I feel a weird tingling as my hand passes through.

"You are amazing," I exclaim.

"Thanks," he remarks.

I take off his shirt—it's that horrible orange jumpsuit. His back, aside from the wings, is the same as I remember: taut, muscular, like a Classical statue. I rub his neck and shoulders; then I go lower, bypassing his wings, until I hit the top of his trousers. I remove them. He's bare underneath, skin perfectly formed, ass tight and well-defined. I kiss him there, and he moans.

"My wings, Conall," he cries out.

Smiling, my hands reach out to touch them. I keep kissing him there, but thread my hands through his wings. Instantly, he softens. I kiss him more deeply; he moans more loudly this time. My hands explore further, touching his wings at the edges, curling over individual feathers, and gripping them tightly.

"Hold them *harder*," he begs.

But I tease him, touching his wings gently. My lips form strong circles inside him; I feel him shiver uncontrollably. I kiss him with everything I have, and then—slowly—the tension building, he cries out.

"Looks like you still like it up the ass, Mark."

"You're amazing, Conall."

"But you're right: I'm curious to see where this will lead."

I grip his wings, hard, and kiss him again. He cries out.

"*Harder.*"

I tighten my hands, using all my strength. Secretly, I'm afraid I'll hurt him—but he only growls with pleasure. Hands and lips in tandem, I work, until he climaxes again. His body convulses with ecstasy.

He turns around. Those eyes of his are like blue orbs, illuminated by some strange, otherworldly fire.

"Fuck," is all he can say.

"I gathered as much," I point out sardonically.

"Damn, Conall, but I've never felt anything like that."

"It's novel for me, too, you know."

"I bet." He leans in, and kisses me. His arms lock around me; he pulls me down, trapping me with his legs.

"Do you like this?" he asks.

"I believe I was the one on top."

"Yeah, but I thought you could do with a change of scenery."

I laugh. "Well, then, I *do* like this. Show me what you can do."

He takes off my shirt. His body coils around mine; our chests are touching, but that's not nearly enough, and he twists until our upper bodies are locked together. He radiates heat. His skin is smooth, his muscles hard. His wings also wrap around me, embracing me with their velvet touch.

"I guess this is the man-to-man position?" I quip.

"You could call it that," he says, nonplussed. Then he takes off my jeans, rips off my boxers, and places my raging hard cock against his. I close my eyes, lying my head on his shoulders. I groan as my dick grinds against his.

"So, are you liking the man-to-man?" he asks, an amused undertone in his voice.

"Unconventional, but intimate."

"How about something more conventional, then?" Before I can ask, he wrestles me to the ground. His cock throbs against me.

"Hah, you can't do it that easily," I point out.

"Oh?"

"You'll need to do some convincing."

He shrugs. Then his lips are inside me, and I can only close my eyes, captured in bliss.

"Could you reciprocate?" he asks. Realising his intent, I open my mouth, taking him in.

He overwhelms my senses. He is everywhere, tugging my body in opposite directions —the sweet ecstasy of his lips, the hungry lust of his cock.

I'm surprised when he breaks it off, pins me to the ground, and fucks me.

"This what you wanted?" I ask.

He kisses me, by way of answer. His hands take my hair, his fingers playing with the individual strands. I gasp when he goes in more deeply, shudder as he keeps going, and melt into the kiss. He accelerates, until I burst in an explosion of pleasure.

I feel his withdrawal like a stab of ice, but then he's grinding against my dick.

"Are you trying to—"

"Make us both come?" And his hands wrap around us, and we really do come together.

★★★

The sun rises, bringing warmth with it. The heat isn't as bad as it was, summer now drawing to a close. I lie on top of Mark, stroking his hair. His eyes are closed against the sunlight; his face seems angelic, the skin filigreed by gold. I wonder how he could ever be... evil.

"I never want this to end, you know," he says.

I gulp. "Nor do I. I want to stay here forever."

"You'd get hungry, though," he points out.

"I have you to satiate me."

He lets out a short laugh. "Not *that* kind of hunger. Besides, I need clothes—I can't exactly go running around in a jumpsuit."

I hadn't thought of that. I pull myself up, looking for my clothes. I find my jeans, rifle through them, and—yes, it's still there: my wallet.

"I'll buy you some clothes."

"Sure. You know my size, right?"

I remember that day—it seems so long ago—when I'd bought him a shirt, and taken him to a restaurant. How rebellious I felt, to be in love with a Fallen. If only I had known that he's so much more than that.

"I'll be back," I say.

"Wait," he cries out. "Do you know where you are?"

"No, but I'm sure I can find human civilisation."

"I have no idea where I flew, Conall." I shiver as I realise that he had *flown*, not walked. It seems so strange to say it like that, and know it's true.

He continues: "There could be mutants. I'll have to come with you."

"Naked?"

He pauses. Something strange is going on: it's like he's listening to something. He stands perfectly still—impossibly still, almost statue-like—and then, right before my eyes, he's clothed. He's picked light jeans and a white T-shirt.

"How did you…"

"It's not real," he tells me. "You can feel it."

I walk up to him, placing my hand on his abs. There's no hint of any fabric, even though I can see the whiteness of the T-shirt as if it were really there.

"Glamour?" I ask, incredulous.

"Something like that," he agrees.

I shake my head. "Come on then, my fair prince."

"I didn't know I was royalty, Conall."

"A prince of Faerie," I say.

"More like a prince of darkness," he mutters quietly.

✶✶✶

We walk for what seems like a long time; I estimate we've travelled a mile, but all we see is green fields. He sighs, annoyed.

"Let's fly," he says simply.

"Fly? With you?"

"I have no trouble carrying you," he tells me. In the blink of an eye, I find myself in his arms. I hadn't even seen him move; in fact I'm slightly dizzy.

"Look," he says. He grips my bum with one hand, lifting me up—I balance precariously on his arm. There's no hint of effort on his part.

"Damn it, Mark, I knew you were strong—"

"But not like this." He grins, like a pleased feline. He draws me into his chest, and wraps his arms around my back.

"What if I fall?" I ask, suddenly scared.

"Are you afraid of *flying*, Conall? You, who pilot giant electric dragonflies?"

"They're called ornithopters, actually."

"I'm not going to drop you." He gives my shoulders a squeeze.

"Okay," I agree meekly.

Without warning, he leaps into the sky.

I thought I'd be afraid, but I'm wrong. The feeling is exhilarating. The speed of it is one thing—he flies like an arrow, straight, unwavering. The wind whips past my face, so unlike the climate controlled interior of the flying craft. I'm laughing with joy. He laughs with me, the vibrations of his voice rumbling through me, setting my languid body on fire.

I could live like this.

Then, suddenly, it stops. I look around; we are next to a road. Dazed, I climb off him, finding my feet unsteady on the ground.

"A few minutes on my wings and you've already forgotten the ground," he comments.

"That was... wow. Flying ornithopters is a joke compared to that."

"I agree. Anyway, you said you wanted to buy me clothes?"

I blink. "I did. Can you hide your wings, though? I think it will draw even more questions than you being naked."

I watch, eyes wide, as his wings collapse into his back. It's not like a bird folding its wings; it's more like a curtain being drawn. One moment they're there, and the next, he looks just like an ordinary man. A very attractive one, perhaps, but ordinary nonetheless.

We walk, until we spot a shopping centre. Time to buy him some real clothes.

✷✷✷

I start by getting him some boxers, a few socks, and a T-shirt. He initially tries to go for a plain white one—the same as his glamour—but I refuse. Instead I pick him a dark red one, with a picture of a motorcycle riding into Hell.

"It's a bit literal, don't you think?" he complains.

"Shut up. I like it."

"I thought I'm supposed to be wearing it, though."

"Yes, but I'm *buying it*. Here—go into the changing rooms and try these jeans." The trousers in question are a deep blue, almost black, and cut in a slim fit. He obliges willingly. It's strange: I can still see the glamour-jeans, like an optical overlay, on top of his real jeans.

I shake my head. "Slim-fit always works well for me, but you're too muscular. Put them back."

I drag him to the jeans aisle again, and pick out a boot-cut. I choose some boots to go with it—short, thin leather ones. As I'm deciding what colour everything should be (should I go for red-accents or stick to plain black?) I notice a girl. She's pretty, and young, perhaps sixteen. She's looking at Mark, and me too, though not as much.

"That girl has a crush on you," I whisper.

He doesn't turn round, though he seems to know. "The one with brunette hair? I noticed."

Feeling suddenly brave, I kiss him. The girl's cheeks flame red.

"Come on," I say, "you're too good-looking to stay here."

"Damn right I am," he agrees with pleasure.

✷✷✷

"So where to next?" I ask.

He stops, thinking. "Well... I want to see my uncle. I think he knows a lot more about what's going on than I could have guessed."

"Really? Why would your uncle know about any of this?"

"Trust me, Conall."

I shrug. "My parents won't mind my absence, for the time being at least. Go. Or do you want me to come with you?"

But before he can answer, a voice interrupts us. A voice that is soft, feminine, and croons with a chilling power.

"Hello boys."

Chapter Two

Kaylin

My visions had not provided any more clues—I saw only wings, as far as the eye could see —but my men had easily been able to trace Mark and Conall through banal means. And so we find ourselves sorting through the wreckage of what had, not long ago, been a Party interrogation room.

"This is quite something," Diana comments.

I nod, silently. Around us, there is destruction. There are several dark corpses splayed across the floor; the ceiling is crowned by a large hole, where the early morning sun shines happily, seemingly untroubled by the carnage. There are blood stains everywhere. The Commissioner himself is the most mutilated of the corpses: the right side of his skull has caved in, leaving only one eye, staring emptily into space.

One part of me is chilled by the brutality, but another part of me can't help appreciating the power. The Party tried to cover it up, but we saw everything.

Two boys, one with wings. Mark, and Conall. We saw the power he could wield; we understood everything.

I had been right, of course. This is bigger than any of us. Mark is unstoppable. Whatever he is—and I have a strong suspicion it's not pretty—Sheilia wants him. I also have no illusions that Sheilia is acting alone. Everything about this seems too well executed, too well-planned, and driven by motives I cannot yet fathom.

"You saw, didn't you?" I ask her.

"I saw Mark kill that motherfucker, burn through a roof, and fly the hell out of there."

"You understand that he's powerful—and therefore valuable."

"I get that. I just don't understand... well, everything. What exactly does she want with him? How does she plan to get it? Is she acting alone?"

"All excellent questions," I agree. "So let's see if we can find more information."

We walk through the wreckage, my Glamour keeping us hidden from the indubitable prying eyes the Party had left behind. The banal evidence is scant: only inexplicable destruction. With a grim chuckle, I realise the Party will be completely unable to figure out what happened.

We, however, can see beyond the physical evidence. We both feel it: two powers, like ours, but somehow darker, more potent. And both going in one direction.

We lock eyes. The question is unmistakable: should we follow it? And the answer is equally obvious. *Of course.*

✲✲✲

We take one of our patrol cars, the distance being too significant to cover on foot. We explain the situation to our HQ via the intercom.

"Are you sure about this?" asks Grumman, my lieutenant. I valued him for his ability to assess risk and look at a situation with an eye for what could go wrong—an ability that, in this case, is inappropriate.

"Yes, Grumman. We were already too late to intervene when Mark was abducted; we can't repeat that mistake. We're in the dark, trying to make plans on inadequate information—trying to pre-empt a force we do not understand. We need to act unpredictably, and quickly."

"Don't you want backup?"

"Negative. If we can't handle this... then involving you would cost needless lives."

"Kaylin, listen to me. I've never seen you like this—I've never known you to take stu -pid risks. If we lose you, this is over. Our mission, our organisation, everything. Do you understand?"

I swallow. I believe what I said, but Grumman is right: this is a big risk.

"I understand, Grumman. And you're right. I just don't see the point."

"Take Shadow, at least."

"Okay."

Another one of our patrol cars pulls up, and we travel in a pair to our destination. Abruptly, I tell them to stop. We're close now—I can feel it.

"Diana, Shadow, are you ready?"

"I'm ready for the bitch," Shadow replies.

"I'll always be with you," Diana assures me.

Since my visions had not proven useful, I had studied the Black Book instead; there I had discovered a new spell. I close my eyes, take a deep breath, and prepare my magic.

Chapter Three

Mark

It all seemed so perfect. I escaped prison; I killed my worst enemy, saved Conall, and everything was going to turn out happily ever after.

As if it were going to be that simple.

"So at last we meet," she continues slyly. "The boy everyone is talking about. And I see you have a lover, too. Master will be so very pleased."

"I don't know who the feck you are, you manky bitch, but I want you out of my sight," I growl. "Also, if you touch him, I will rip you limb from limb."

"My, that was uncalled for. But, well, that is to expected; it was very inconsiderate of Moloch to leave you in the dark. You must be confused." She pouts in sympathy.

"You bet I am."

"So allow me to explain," she croons, almost like the mother I'd never known. "You, Mark, are a the son of a demon. This is quite unheard of, and Master is therefore interested in you greatly."

"Why should I care?"

"Well, he has a lot to offer you. He can tell you who your father is." I wince—she got me there. "He can offer you riches, power, and even a role in his kingdom. You can be with your boyfriend openly, not only tolerated, but admired. You will see how very retrograde these humans are."

"Mark, don't listen to her," Conall whispers. "She's a manipulator—can't you see?"

I blink, and somehow, the doubts surface.

"What will all this cost me?" I ask.

"Well, this isn't really for me to discuss. You will have to ask him yourself."

"Why doesn't he come meet me?"

She sighs, patiently, and gives me a look of heartbroken sadness. I almost believe it. "He cannot, alas. You will learn everything soon—but until then, you must follow me."

"To where? Who is your master?" I ask.

"Come on Mark, the answer is obvious. She wants to take you to Hell," Conall points out.

She turns her head towards him, examining him with new eyes. "You are clever; I can see what he wants in you," she comments.

"I'm clever enough to see you're a liar."

She shrugs. "I assure you everything I have said is true."

"It doesn't matter; you can lie by omission and subterfuge. We can't trust you."

"Perhaps too clever," she says. Suddenly, her wings unfurl. I stare at them, surprised. Sure: it should be obvious. She's a demon. And yet—somehow—I thought of her as sweet, reasonable, and friendly. Those wings make me realise what she's really capable of.

"I think a demonstration is in order," she continues. "You really don't know a thing."

"Oh, I can give you a demonstration," I growl. To Conall, I whisper, "stay behind me."

She laughs, but I cut her off with a charge. I close the distance almost instantly, and grab her by the throat. I pivot, driving her face into the asphalt. It cracks, loudly.

She just laughs.

"Oh, that was a good attempt." Then she's out of my grasp, and aiming a punch at me. I block—it's a surprisingly clumsy punch. I retaliate hard, each fist exploding into her body like an earthquake. But then there's nothing to punch: she's no longer in front of me. I spin, and find her next to Conall.

"You can't protect him—you don't even understand your own power."

"Get the fuck away from him," I warn her. Fear lends me speed; I fly into her, grab her by the arm, and pull. There is an audible crack as I break her arm.

"Ouch," she exclaims. Enraged, I ply my arms around her neck, trying to literally rip her head off. But nothing seems to hurt her. Instead, she relaxes; I feel her body soften against mine, almost like...

"Are you trying to fucking seduce me?"

"Perhaps. Do you want me to?" I feel a bizarre temptation to pin her to the ground and teach her some manners. I don't have the time to act on it; again she re-appears next to Conall, like she can fucking teleport. There's nothing I can do—she has his throat.

"I could kill him instantly. You can't protect him: stop this madness, and let me show you who you are."

Anger, fear, and confusion war within me. Can I trust her? What if she hurts him?

In the end, it makes no difference. She screeches, withdrawing her hand away from him: a black mark is on her wrist.

"Hey, wing girl! Why not take someone your own size?"

I swivel my head, and stare in amazement. A woman—her hair dark brown, her eyes glowing electric blue—is smiling at me. I spot Conall looking at her with amazement of his own, and something else: recognition.

"And who, pray tell, are you?" the demon asks.

"Someone who will send you back to where the Hell you belong."

The demon laughs, but soon her laugh turns into a chortle of agony. Fire, crimson red and potent in a way that makes my hair stand on end, explodes from the other woman. The demon claws at her face, her skin molten like a candle.

Before she can retaliate, another woman appears behind her. Black-clothed, black-

215

haired, and mesmerisingly deadly, she places a hand on the demon's throat. Another dark mark appears—larger this time, its form sprawling and spidery—and we all watch as the demon disintegrates. It's as if whatever was keeping her together simply forgot to exist, and in its place only cold silence remains.

"Well," the fire-woman says, "that was quite something."

Chapter Four

Conall

I drink the tea, enjoying the warm caffeine. Mark is to my right, looking shaken. In front, there are two women: Diana, my tutor, and someone else. I examine her perfectly straight black hair, and the pale blue iridescence of her eyes. There's something uncanny about her —not just in her appearance, which is strange enough, but also in the way she holds herself, the way she exudes power. In a strange and frightening way, she reminds me of the person we'd just met.

"Can someone tell me who you are? What's going on?" Mark asks them.

Diana only sighs; the other woman says nothing. They have brought us here, to a hidden base in the middle of the city. I stared at the invisibility field that surrounded this place, though considering the present turn of events, maybe I shouldn't have been surprised.

"We are... members of an organisation, dedicated to fighting the Party and all its evil. Conall, I believe you have already met Diana, your tutor and my dearest friend." I nod.

"So you know them, Conall?"

"He does not know me. My name is Kaylin; I am gifted."

"I got that from the stunt you pulled," Mark retorts.

She closes her eyes, smiling. "You didn't tell me he was like this," she says to Diana.

The other woman is also smiling. "No, I didn't."

"But to answer you, Mark, the 'stunt' I just pulled involved destroying a being so powerful, I had no idea if my magic would even have touched her. It is fortunate that it did, and we are here right now."

"This does not answer many of our questions, however," I point out. "The demon"—I choke out the word—"told us several important things before she perished. For which we do thank you, by the way."

"She told me she knew who my father is," Mark says, his voice husky with repressed emotions. I can imagine what he's feeling: fear, hope, confusion.

"Unanswered questions, indeed," Kaylin agrees, "and questions which, alas, I cannot help you with. What we can do is ascertain what information we have, and why it matters."

"I know it's hard, Mark," Diana starts, "but please bear with us. This is much bigger than any one of us."

"What do you mean?" he demands.

"What we mean," Kaylin responds, "is that Sheilia, the demon, was not acting alone. And she wanted something from you—wanted it badly."

"She said... she promised me that if I went to her master, he would give me a role in his kingdom."

"Are we talking about who I think we're talking about?" I ask. "As in, Satan, Lucifer, the Devil?"

"The very same," Kaylin replies. "And don't be so surprised, Conall. Your boyfriend *is* a demon."

"I'm still getting used to all this," I point out.

"So are we. Everything has changed because of it."

"What do you mean?"

"We used to believe... that the Party was everything. That's why we exist—to fight them."

Silence falls on our small group. Everything is too much: the demon, Mark's dad, the

218

things they speak of. All I wanted was to fall in love; to be with Mark. Why did he have to kill someone and go to prison? Why did he have to be a demon, of all things? Why do we have to be caught up in a *rebellion*, orchestrated by a clandestine organisation run by a witch?

I shake my head, feeling as exhausted as he is. "So let me get this straight: you are a witch."

"Something like that, yes."

"Your purpose was initially to usurp the Party, but now you are more worried about this demon."

"That is correct."

"And now... you want *us* to help you?"

"You are involved, whether you like it or not. Mark, you are a demon—or a half-demon—and as such you have considerable power. Someone is clearly interested in that power.

"I know you want to be teenagers; I know you want to be in love and pretend everything is fine. But Fate has not spared you that luxury, as she has not spared us. We all have a duty."

"Kaylin, I think that's enough," Diana interrupts. "They're just kids, you know. Come on, you two: walk with me. We can leave this for later."

She sits up, and leaves. We follow her.

✷✷✷

The city around us continues on with life: there are people walking to work, cleaning streets, shopping, and staring at their com phones. The sun shines, the first rays of autumn a deep gold, though the trees remain verdant. High above, Big Brother's tower looks down.

"Diana… why didn't you ever tell me about this?" I ask her.

"Come on, Conall, think about it. What reason would I have had to do that? Would it not have put you in unnecessary danger?"

"Why were you my tutor, then? Was it just money, or a way to pass spare time?" She can hear the skepticism in my voice.

"No; I won't lie. We thought you might be helpful to us. But I would never have endangered you."

"You didn't tell him about your power," Mark whispers.

"No, I did not. Like Kaylin, I am not an ordinary human being."

"What you did—" I say.

"I can control the elements, to answer your question. Fire is my main weapon, though not my only one."

"And it hurt her," Mark continues.

"Yes… that was unexpected. The plan was merely to distract her, and let Kaylin sneak up behind in order to place her rune."

"How did she do that?" I ask, still determined. "We never saw her."

"Some things are best kept secret."

"Some sort of invisibility, I would guess, Conall," Mark suggests.

"And what did Kaylin do to destroy the demon?" I continue asking.

"You will have to ask her; I don't quite understand it myself. We are all very new to this."

"And we all seem to be in some trouble," I add.

"That's your way of saying we're all fucked, Conall." Trust Mark to be blunt.

✦✦✦

Kaylin and Diana say goodbye—apparently, they have much to work on—but give us a parting gift.

"Wear this," Kaylin orders. She hands us a black medallion, bound on a chain. I take it, and Mark takes his own identical copy. The material is not metal; its a deep, smooth black, likely jet or some other volcanic stone. It feels strange in my hand, almost alive with some alien power.

"What does it do?" I ask.

"It is connected to me, and acts as a warning beacon. Additionally, it has wards that can protect you."

"From demons?"

She laughs bitterly. "No, that is beyond my power. But it will protect you from more banal forces. We failed you once; I hope we will not fail you again."

"Wait, you mean you knew I was going to go to prison?"

"We... well, not really. But we should have seen it."

"Thank you," I say to her. "This is still more than we could have hoped for. Without you, we're alone—right?"

"Don't talk about this to your parents, Conall," Diana warns me. "That would be a bad idea."

"I never intended to, don't worry."

"What about my uncle?" Mark asks.

"We... do not know," Kaylin says, massaging her temples. I never quite realised how fallible she is—I thought, from her inscrutable demeanour and obvious power, that she would be above doubt. Clearly she is not.

"I want to ask him," Mark continues, "about everything. He knows—I'm sure."

"I will need to See before I can give you advice," Kaylin says.

"I'll take that as a yes."

"Very well," Diana interrupts. "It was nice meeting you two, even in the circumstances. Try and stay out of trouble. We will be in touch with you again soon."

"Good bye, Diana," I say.

Then Mark grabs my hand, and we leave.

✷✷✷

"So this is it," he says.

"What do you mean?"

"This—everything. Me being a demon. Wanted by the fecking devil himself. I thought prison was bad enough, but—" He shakes his head. "This must be too much for you."

"Do you think I'm going to leave you, Mark?"

"I don't know, Conall; I wouldn't blame you if you did. You've got your life ahead of you. You've got it all: money, power..."

"Fuck that, Mark." He flinches at my language. "I want *you*. Prison didn't stop me."

"You said some horrible things to me."

"I did, and I'm deeply sorry about that."

"Did you see someone else?"

"What?" I stop, the world suddenly going off-kilter.

"I said, did you see someone else?"

"Why would you ask that?"

He shrugs, and that makes it worse. "You can tell me."

"I..."

"Who was it?"

"Someone from my school. His name is Jake. But Mark—it was a mistake. It didn't work out. He was a bastard."

"I understand, Conall," he says quietly.

It does not surprise me when he goes to his uncle, and I, to my parents.

Chapter Five

Mark

I feel like an idiot.

Why did I have to ask Conall if he had been with someone else? I had been in prison; I thought I would be there forever. He would have made sure of it. If Conall had been with someone else... surely I should have been happy? You're not supposed to share misery—that's stupid.

But for some reason, I did ask him, and I did care. Maybe I even know why. It's as if I don't really believe it still: that we can be happy. That we can be together. I want to push him away; I doubt myself.

I shake my head. Conall could wait—I have other doubts to put to rest now. I need to ask uncle... who I really am.

I walk confidently through the street, feeling a strange sort of invincibility. It's weird: for so long, I've been afraid. I've tried to keep my life a secret, to stay away from my uncle, all just to avoid the Party and their stupid minions. Now I can crush them with my bare hands. I might be doomed for Hell, but at least Hell will be more fun.

Uncle's house is neat and tidy as always; I knock on the door, feeling strangely nostalgic. It all comes down to this.

He opens the door. "Mark? Is that really you?"

"Yes it's me."

"But... how did you get out? Weren't you on trial"

"I was."

"And... oh no."

I walk in, a slow anger beginning to burn. He knew—of course he knew.

"You need to tell me the truth, uncle."

He sits down heavily. He's not yet fifty, but he seems much older now: his hair is frazzled, his expression drawn.

"Can I get you some tea?" he asks, remembering his manners.

"Please do," I say. Even a demon needs a good cup of tea, I guess.

"Where to start..." he mutters to himself as I sip the warm liquid.

In a flash, my wings open wide. They look so strange here in uncle's house: perfectly black, huge, and so completely alien from the technology and white-washed interior. I see him gulp visibly.

"Who am I, uncle? Why do I have fecking wings?"

"Language, boy."

"I'm not a boy anymore, and we both know how easily I can kill someone."

"You're right." He seems to pull himself together. "Let me speak plainly, then, nephew. You are half-demon."

"I got that much."

"Your mother died giving birth to you; that's because humans can't give birth to what you are. Your father didn't even believe it was possible. Fool that he was."

"You don't like my father, then?"

"My sister died because of him—I shouldn't like him. But to see how she looked at him... well, I understood. She knew the risk, in the end. He told her it might mean her death; but she gave birth to you anyway. What's done is done."

"Tell me more about him."

"He loved her, and he loved you. It shouldn't have been possible: your father was a demon, a being so black and perverted as to not even know the meaning of the word. But he did, somehow."

I mull in his words, trying to come to grips with my life. It seems impossible—a dark fairytale where I used to believe was only gritty reality. I imagined my dad was some sort of bank robber or drug dealer; the truth is much grander, and somehow worse. Bank robbers I can deal with. Demons? Not so much.

"Did he tell you more about what he was? What I am?" I continue.

"He told me things—though not everything. He came from Hell, another dimension."

"What brought him here?"

"He was on a mission for his master."

"The Devil?"

"Basically. He told me that... his master couldn't leave. They didn't come from Hell originally—they were bound there, somehow. Don't ask me how. But his master can't leave, and even the weaker demons barely can. He was the strongest of the ones on Earth."

"What was his mission?" I ask, feeling morbidly curious.

"To compel humans to do evil, and swear loyalty to his master—either as demons themselves or as subjects. Apparently, that weakens the barrier."

This is only getting worse. As much as I want to know more, it's not easy to ask the next question.

"And did he? Compel humans to evil, I mean?"

"He rebelled once he met your mother."

"He could do that?"

"It wasn't easy." Uncle laughs bitterly. "He had to constantly watch over her, and try to stay hidden from those below. He destroyed more than a few other demons."

"We can be destroyed?" I already know this—I saw it—but I need to know more.

"Yes, but as I say—don't ask me how."

I fold my wings. "Well, thank you uncle. I'm glad you've told me everything."

"Are you really, though? Wouldn't you have preferred to live life as a human being? Your father wanted that, you know; he hoped you would be normal, or at least, unaware of the darkness within. That's why he left. He couldn't keep you safe, otherwise."

It's been the question I've always asked myself. Why had he left? Had I not been worth it? The answer warms me, but somehow doesn't bring me closure.

"Uncle, he left me, and condemned me to life as a Fallen. What existence is that? What kind of boy never knows his father, always believing he's a scoundrel, imagining he's a hero?"

"It sucks, I know. And I'm sorry—for all of this. I did my best, but Fate cannot be denied."

"No... it can't. But I'm tired of living a lie, uncle; I want this, even if it's hard."

"Even if you have to do the devils's bidding?"

"I will fight."

"Just like your father, then." He shakes his head, though I feel a grudging admiration from him. "If you accept this, however, it isn't within my power to help you. You need to meet your father."

The floor drops from underneath me.

"What?"

It shouldn't surprise me. I always thought father was dead—but why should he be? He's a demon. An immortal.

"You didn't really think your father was dead, did you? He would be too young even if he wasn't immortal."

"No, it's just... I always thought he was gone from my life forever."

"He's not."

"How do I meet him?"

He looks down. "It's not hard."

"Tell me how."

Chapter Six

Kaylin

I call it the Black Book, but really I should call it the Book of Secrets. I have known of my powers for a long time: my visions have been with me since I became a teenager. But the finer points of spellcraft—and the tantalising origins of my power—I discovered from the Book.

Long and mysterious is its history: I found it only by good fortune, and the words told to me by an old Tibetan monk. Getting a hold of it had been no less difficult; the Chinese authorities kept a close eye over their territory, and stealing a priceless artefact from under their noses had proven some work.

One thing did make it easier for me, though. I am convinced it has a mind of its own. Firstly, the writing proved indecipherable—even the finest linguists and scholars had failed to make sense of it. Except I could read it as easily as if it were written today. And for two, it had given me the spell.

I scan through it now, hunting for information. The spell I had used was a long shot— but even long shots hit their mark from time to time. It is titled "Destroying Immortals". I knew demons are immortal; but I know little else.

And I have no doubt that, next time, things won't be so easy. She had been surprised. Shadow had sneaked me in behind her, allowing me to place my hand on her throat, and cast the spell with its full power—as a rune.

Spells are complex things, and even now, I do not fully grasp their workings. I know that runes direct them, solidify them, and imbue them with the power of my will. A rune seen by my mind's eye, and cast from distance, is not as strong as a rune written on its target. (Though it is still greater than a spell cast wildly, undirected; it is why I have memorised so many of the elaborate shapes.)

I sigh. The book is huge; it seems unlikely I will find it.

"Not much luck, huh?" Shadows asks behind me.

I don't bother turning round; I've discovered that sneaking up is his passion. It doesn't surprise me.

"Sadly, no. This book, as you can see, is huge. And really, I've never found a useful spell of my own accord—they always seem to come to me."

"As in, a vision or something?"

I smile at his child-like question. "No... it's more like the book *gives* them to me."

"That thing is conscious?"

"In a manner of speaking."

"Grand."

"Is that all you can say?"

"I don't know anything about magic books, Mistress. I just sneak around."

I quirk my mouth in a smile. "True."

"Still, minding as I don't know anything about it, can I be suggestin' something?"

"Go on."

"Why don't you try... this is hard for me to say. Why don't you let *it* tell *you* what it wants to say? You're looking for something, demanding things, like a general. Maybe you should be more like a bleedin' scholar."

There is a wisdom in that, I have to admit—perhaps more than I expected from Shadow. So, I close my eyes. I empty my mind; I try and be receptive. At first, nothing happens: there is no hint of magic, no promise of divine intervention. And yet, when I open my eyes, I find the book on a different page.

"Did you see it move the pages?" I ask him.

"Didn't see anythin', Mistress."

"But..." I focus, and realise that although the physical *page* hasn't changed—the book is still open about two thirds of the way through—the information on it *has*. No wonder no one had been able to decipher it!

I begin reading, and slowly start to wonder how exactly this is relevant. This story— the book has a lot of these—is about a woman who commits various acts of evil, usually because of greed or pride. It seems like nothing more than a parable, until the events take a more... supernatural turn.

And so the woman discovered the Dark One, and he smiled, and promised her great powers; so she succumbed, agreeing to the many things he asked of her. Eventually, after many small deeds, it came to drinking from the Dark Cup.

I blink. Everything about it seems so cryptic, and I wonder how it can possibly be related to what I'm looking for. At the same time, some other, unconscious part of me wants to read more. The story is important—I just can't tell why.

"Mistress?"

"Hmm?" I realise I have been distracted, and Shadow has been watching me all along.

"How exactly did you kill that thing? I understand you cast some sort of spell on her, but... it's all pretty bleedin' strange to me. I can't do spells; how am I supposed to beat one of them?"

"I don't think you can. You know Mark?"

"That kid with his own wings?"

"Yes. He killed several men, then burned through a concrete roof and flew out of it."

He whistles.

"So I can't just hit them on the head?"

"No. I don't believe any weapon can hurt them."

"That... sucks."

"It does, Shadow. As for the spell, it was designed to destroy beings that are immortal. To be honest, I didn't know if it would work."

"Really? But you seemed so bloody confident!"

"A ruse, you understand. Once you gain power over others, you realise that appearances count. If I seemed uncertain or frightened, it would weaken you."

"And if it had failed?"

"Then it would have been my problem—and I would have fixed it."

"Well, good luck then. It sounds like we're dependin' a lot on you."

I look down. "You are right about that, and don't think for one moment that I don't know it."

He disappears, returning to the work I'd set for him. With a sigh, I get back to reading. If this is to work—if we need to fight them—then I'm going to need to find out as much as I can. I just hope this demented, cryptic book will let me.

Chapter Seven

Conall

I sit, watching father, along with Sianna, my mother. Looking at them together, I can see why they married: my mother is one of the few women who would give my steely-eyed father a challenge. In fact, I suspect she proved *too* much of a challenge—it's why they divorced.

"So, darling, you're telling me that your handsome boyfriend was on trial for murder, but apparently had the charges dropped?"

I try not to gulp. That's the lie; I'm willing to bet the Party won't let word of the escape get out, not even to lower ranked members like my father. Of course, I still have to convince my parents I'm not lying.

"I'm as surprised as you are, mother."

"And where were you all of yesterday?" My father continues.

I'd arrived late last night, and he had not asked questions then. I can't exactly say I was being chased by a demon—so I improvise.

"Him being in prison... put a strain on our relationship. We had to go through a lot to repair the damage." It's not a lie, but it's not the whole truth either.

"I see." Father had make it clear he didn't approve of a long term male partner for me, let alone a Fallen one. But then again: I can be just as stubborn as he is. And I'm not going to just let Mark go; I've gone through too much, and love him too badly.

"Well, that is awfully convenient," she continues with a twinkle in her eye, "but fortu-nate." I have a feeling I haven't quite fooled her.

"The good news is that you can go back to school now." Trust father to worry about school. At least he seems to be buying my story—or at least not looking too carefully into what's actually going on.

"Oh my, still going on about school?" Sianna enquires.

"It's important," father says gruffly.

"Of course it is dear. And *darling*," she says, talking to me now, "remember that I will always help you up on the ladder. If you are so willing to debase yourself."

"Thank you, mother."

"Are you going to bring your boyfriend here? You know to keep it discreet, okay?" Father again.

"Father—"

"You can bring him over to my place," Sianna interrupts. "I'd like to meet him."

I close my eyes. We have enough to worry about without my mother getting in the way.

"Whatever you say, mother. Now, do you mind if I meet a friend instead?"

She waves a hand in dismissal, and I quickly run out of the room. Being alone with one of my parents is bad enough; the two of them are totally overwhelming.

Pocketing my com phone, I message Stella. *Hey, I'm back. Want to meet up?*

Conall? Yes, please!

For once in a long while, I feel myself smiling. I don't know what the future has in store for me—but sometimes you have to just enjoy the present.

*✶✶

I'm wearing my favourite designer jacket as I wait for her in the park. Though it's still sunny, and moderately warm, a cold wind is blowing. The summer is finally gone, and autumn has taken over. Even in the glow of the sunlight, I feel a little of the oncoming winter.

"Hey? Are you okay?" She looks at me with those blue eyes of hers, concern plastered on her face. I'd not talked to her about anything in the past few days—including our escape.

"I'm pretty good actually. They dropped the charges."

"What? Really? That's... that's great Conall!"

"Yes... we did argue though."

"Why?"

"I was with someone else for a bit."

"Who? No—"

"Yes, it was Jake."

"And...?"

I shrug. "Jake is a loser."

She smiles widely at that. "Told you so."

"Indeed you did, but he was so charming and attractive... well, I lost sight of who mattered."

"So you'll make it up with Mark then?"

"For sure. It's just..." I ponder how much I can tell her.

"You sound like there's something else standing between you."

"Well, he's a Fallen."

"You always knew it wasn't going to be easy, Conall."

"I don't just mean that—I mean, Mark has a bad past. Some of those demons are starting to catch up with him."

"How bad is it?" she asks.

"Bad enough." I want to tell her more—to spill all these secrets—but I know that would put her in danger. And I can't do that.

So I change the subject. "But don't worry about me, Stella; I will manage. How are you? Has school gotten any more fun since I've been away?"

"Not really, no. Constitutional law is boring as hell, and it's not the same without you around."

"Do you have a special someone of your own?" I ask, realising I've not seen her with anything more than a summer fling.

"Actually, since you ask, there is someone."

"Is he cute?"

"You bet."

"And charming?"

"That too."

"But...?"

"I've just not known him all that along, that's all."

"And, knowing you, I suspect that's important."

"Not all of all us are love at first sight, Conall."

"You know what?" I say, realising something. "You've never met him, have you? Mark, I mean."

"No... I haven't. But you've told me so much about him, I feel like I know him already."

"That's not good enough, Stella. I want you to meet him—all four us."

I fish out my com phone. I call him, hoping he'll answer.

"Conall?" His voice is nervous, but also strange—almost excited.

"It's me. Mark... I want you to meet someone. She's my friend."

"Oh? I've never met your friends before."

"Would... would that be okay?"

"Sure."

Feeling happy, I close the com phone, texting him the address. Stella phones her boy-friend too, and so we wait.

***

Seeing him makes me start. Even though it's only been a day, I can recognise the differences. The biggest difference is one only I know—there's an air of power about him now, something that wasn't there before. I feel it prickling the back of my neck, sharp and impossible to mistake: demonic magic.

The other difference is obvious to anyone with eyes. Mark has always been attractive; today he looks like a God. His eyes are impossibly blue, the power beneath them shifting with the shadows. His muscles are strongly defined underneath his thin T-shirt, though they seem altered to me—better proportioned somehow, like a perfectly strung machine. Even Stella can't take her eyes off him.

"Hi," she says meekly.

"Mark, meet Stella, my friend. Stella, meet Mark."

They shake hands, Mark with an amused smile, Stella with shyness.

Moments later, Stella's boyfriend arrives. I take in the red hair, the freckles, and the forest green eyes. He's cute—in a boyish, harmless sort of way.

"Mark, Conall, meet Eoin, my boyfriend."

"Am I really your boyfriend, Stella?" he asks with a hint of sarcasm.

"Of course you are, you. Now, say hello to my friends."

He shakes our hands, his eyes staying longer on Mark. It could be Mark's power, drawing him invisibly, like the web of a spider. Or it could be simple good looks. I think Eoin is straight, but then—Mark looks good enough for anyone.

"Pleased to meet you," Eoin says. "How come Stella knows you?"

"Well, I've been her friend for some time," I reply.

"Five years, Conall," she adds. "In the prep school, and lower down."

Mark says nothing.

"This is Mark, my boyfriend," I add for his sake. Mark just grins, and slings an arm around my shoulder. The sudden warmth—the unexpected feel of his body—makes something inside me twist.

"Pleased to meet you," Eoin says again. "And I apologise in advance for what Stella may have told you—she concocts all sorts of stories." That earns him a punch on the shoulder from Stella.

We walk, threading our way through the trees, admiring the manicured grass. Above, the lights of the Upper Quarter shine bright, illuminating the implausible geometric shapes of the buildings. I wonder how Mark got through—probably he flew. Did he Glamour himself into invisibility? Could he do that?

"Tell me more about you," Stella says out of the blue, to Mark.

Besides her, Eoin shrugs. "See? She's not interested in me."

Mark only chuckles. "Don't worry, she's all over you. Anyway, thanks for asking, Stella. I guess I should tell you that I'm Fallen."

"I already know, don't worry."

Eoin is less sure, and raises an eyebrow, though he doesn't ask questions. I don't peg him for an Upperclassman himself—maybe a Technical or an Owner, I haven't decided.

"Great," Mark affirms. I meet his eyes, silently saying: *Yes, of course I told her.*

"He wasn't lying about you being attractive, either," she adds.

Me and Mark roll our eyes, while Eoin groans.

"Touché, Stella," I tell her. She blows me a raspberry.

Despite this, I can feel Mark doesn't want to talk to them—although he badly wants to talk to me. I exchange pleasantries with Stella and Eoin, and promise them we'll meet and talk more another time. With curious looks, they leave me and Mark alone.

✶✶✶

"So," I say, once they're far in the distance.

"Conall, I'm sorry," he begins. Before I can respond, he kisses me. His mouth is hot and salty on my own—in one way, human, and the Mark I know—but it's also smooth, and makes me burn with intoxication. I thread my hands through his hair, careless of who might be watching. We're not allowed to be doing this, me and Mark. But what can they do?

"So I'm forgiven?" I ask, feeling happiness overtake the last of my fear.

"You are. God, Conall, I'm stupid. I was in *prison*; yet you came, brought a lawyer, tried to save me, and almost got killed in the process. It's me, really. I'm afraid."

"Afraid of... them?" I ask, referring to the demons.

"That, and myself." He sits me down on a bench.

"Conall, do you remember when we—"

"First met?"

"No—although, damn, I remember that too. Saved me from being scarab dinner."

"And you saved me too, remember."

"Yeah. But I was thinking of that time when we realised... that we were really in love with each other."

"Oh."

"I don't want to lose that feeling. I don't care if have to fight the stupid Party, or if I have to go into Hell and kill Old Beezlebub himself. But I'm not leaving you, Conall. You'll probably call this cliché—heck, most people would call it stupid—but I love you, no matter what happens."

In a way, it had all been a game until now. We were teenagers, madly in love, thinking we could defy the Party and the world. But now, I realise the scale of what he's saying: we're not playing a game, and there are worse things out there than even the Party. Much worse —life, death, and the afterlife kind of bad.

And yet, now as then, my response is the same. "I love you too, Mark. I'm not going away."

So we kiss, me on his lap. I thread my hands through his stomach, and down into his jeans.

He smiles against me. "I really must be a looker if you want to fuck me in the middle of the park, Conall."

I pull back. "Well..."

But I sense he has one more thing he wants to tell me. Despite his smile, and the bulge in his jeans, there's something more behind those blue eyes of his.

"Mark? Is there something else you want to tell me?"

"Yeah. My father is a demon, and he's alive, out there somewhere."

"Okay."

"Conall... I want to meet him."

"What? How?"

"My uncle told me. He said—"

But he doesn't get the chance to tell me, because at that moment, several things happen at the same time.

Chapter Eight

Mark

"PUT YOUR HANDS BEHIND YOUR BACK! STEP AWAY FROM THE OTHER MAN!"
I watch as they pour in around us: Secret Police, armed and armoured. Their helmets glint black in the light, their faces obscured. They're mostly pointing stun guns at me, though I spot some full size lasers and rifles in the mix. They don't know how dangerous I am—they think they can take me alive, cowed by a few stunners.

They have no fucking idea.

But it's not me I'm worried about: it's Conall, who looks at them with trepidation. It's my worst nightmare come true; but I'm not afraid. I can protect him. They're just humans, playing at a game they don't understand.

"I REPEAT, PUT YOUR—"

I spread open my wings, covering Conall. He holds me tight. I can see this gives the men pause: they look at my wings, obviously unprepared, clearly unknowing.

"I REPEAT—"

"I heard you the first time, and the second." My voice is whisper quiet, but I fill it with power—it carries across, reaching deep into their minds.

It doesn't surprise me when they fire. The electric bolts hit me, but I barely feel them; it's like being hit by an angry mosquito. There's not much it can really do. A cold anger builds: I want to hurt them, to kill them all, and prove that I am God, while they are simply mortals. I even feel a whisper of the old voices, promising me release in mass murder.

But I hold it back. I know what I am—and I know I can choose not to be a monster.

Instead, I only touch them with my power, throwing them back like dominoes.

"Mark, we need to get out of here. I know a place—"

I can't answer, because at that moment, we hear something else: a siren. The sound chills us to our bones. We've all heard it before—in classrooms, in history books. The last one rang more than seventy years ago. It means the same thing now as it did then: mutants. Lots of them.

The police agents fall back, and stare at the sky. It looks like they're not interested in us any longer.

"Mark? How can this be possible? We're in the Upper Quarter; this place—"

"Doesn't get mutants," I say without conviction. Conall looks at the sky with me; we all do now. The sky is a living mass, shifting and moving in impossible ways. It's only once I begin to make out the individual shapes—the dragon-like mutants with leathery wings, the enormous wasps and beetles—that I really start to understand the horror.

"Sergeant? What should we do?" I hear one of them cry out.

"Focus on defending against the monsters!" the order gets barked out. I feel a grim sort of satisfaction as they all point their weapons skyward. It's their turn to feel hunted, to be hounded by invisible, watching forces.

The first of the wave hits the force fields and the gun towers. Explosions rip out—blue fire, laser flashes, and electricity illuminate the night sky like macabre fireworks. It doesn't seem possible that the mutants can break through—they've never gotten through into here, like Conall says—but as we watch, they do just that. Some inner sense tells me this isn't an ordinary raid, and those aren't ordinary mutants.

The blue fire I see isn't just laser flashes, like I first thought; it's coming from the mutants themselves. The dragons are breathing fire, burning through force fields and gun towers alike. There's power in there; I can feel it. Power like my own.

242

"Mark!" It's Conall again, tugging against my shoulder. "We need to get out of here!"

"But where, Conall? This has to be the safest place; it's the best guarded. Besides, Kaylin's medallions will tell her we're in danger." I touch my own, feeling the smooth, cool surface of the obsidian.

"It isn't! They're attacking this place deliberately; we need to get out of their way. I think we should go to my mother's house."

"What?"

He doesn't have time to answer, because they're on us now. The men fire their weapons: laser flashes and bullets explode from their barrels. Scores of the creatures fall, but more take their place. I watch as a giant wasp drives its stinger through one of the men, into his shoulder. The guy collapses, but he's not dead: he's writhing in agony, the venom killing him slowly.

More gunfire and laser beams erupt, and both human and monster fall together. The noise is incredible: men scream in agony, while monsters emit either high pitched chitters or deep roars of anger. Conall is holding me tight, and shuddering in fear. The maelstrom is all around us; we're right in its eye.

"Mark! Please!"

The air around us is thick with the mutants, but I see no other choice. I hold him tight; I open my wings wide, and power high into the air. The sun has set now, and the world around us is covered in thick darkness, alive with the fluttering of mutant wings. The air is cool against our skin, as I fly hard and fast.

"Do you know where East is?" he asks.

"I do, yeah."

"Fly us there, and low. My mother lives in the ocean."

"What? As in, literally—"

"Literally floating on and underneath it, yes," he replies. "You'll see the lights; it's well guarded, and very exclusive."

I drop us lower, changing our direction until we're heading straight east. I gain more speed; the air is like a hammer now. I can see the waves crashing not far below, and there—in the distance—a gleam of light.

But I also feel them. They haven't gone away; they're flying with us, like some sort of fucking swarm. They don't attack us, for some reason, though maybe I shouldn't be surprised.

For a harrowing few minutes, we fly. As we get closer, laser fire cuts through the sky, burning mutants.

"We're going too fast!" he cries out.

"Hang on." I spread out my wings, cutting our speed. We land, a little roughly, but mostly intact.

"We made it—"

"Don't hold your breath, Conall. They're not far behind."

"What's going on? Are they following us?"

I turn, and look up. Somehow I have a feeling I know the answer.

"Yeah, they are."

"Well, do something! People are dying."

So I dig in, reaching deep into that dark power within me. Blue fire travels across my arms, and lightning arks from my wings. The swarm is above me, but it doesn't attack—it hangs back.

"They're not attacking," he whispers.

"What do you want me to do?" I ask.

"Can you destroy them?"

"All of them? I have no idea."

As I prepare to hit the bastards with everything I have, they start to retreat. No: it's not that simple. It's like something is *making* them retreat. Conall would compare it to an orchestrator. I would compare it to a general giving out new orders.

Suddenly, a figure flies through the air. The speed is incredible; I don't have time to do anything, as it lands right besides us, folding its wings with a grace I could never match.

We lock eyes. He's different from me—his hair is black, not blond like mine, and he has a different shape to his body—but the eyes are the same dark blue.

My father.

Chapter Nine

Conall

Mark and the demon stand straight, staring each other down. And yet it is not enmity I feel from them, or at least not exactly; there is much more to it than that, some hidden history I don't know.

"Dad?" Mark asks.

I look at the other demon more carefully, unable to really believe my ears. He's so different—dark where Mark is light, and lithe where Mark is built—but those eyes can't be mistaken.

"Hello, son." His voice is strange: he speaks with a thick, fluid accent, and one beyond my ability to recognise. There is power in his voice too, like the air beneath a storm.

"Dad... I need to know your name."

"They used to call me Moloch when I was born, and when I was in Hell. But I don't like that name—call me Michael."

"I'm Mark."

"Yes... I know. I named you."

"Why did you leave?"

Michael turns away. "That's too complicated to go into right now."

"It was because of them, wasn't it?"

"Yes."

"And why are you here now?" Mark continues. "Because of the mutants?"

"To an extent, but that was only a temporary exigency." Again he speaks the words with a strange accent, but I think I can recognise it better now: Latin. Turns out those lessons were good for something.

"Michael? Mark?" I interrupt. They turn and look at me, two impossibly blue eyes, here above the ocean.

"Can we please discuss this inside? I believe my mother will let us in—she has more than enough space."

"Your mother?" Michael asks me, blinking.

"Yes."

"Who are you?" he continues directly.

"He's my boyfriend, and you should know that," Mark adds with a hint of steel.

"Your boyfriend..." A look of concern flashes across his face, but is gone in an instant, to be replaced with smooth formality.

"My apologies," he continues. "I am forgetting my manners here on Earth. I am pleased to meet you; please lead on."

I walk on the raised platform, holding one hand on Mark's shoulder, and another on the bannister. Though it's probably not necessary: the ocean is calm, and the sky is clear. I orient myself, eventually spotting mother's home. It's hard to miss.

"What happened to the mutants?" Mark asks.

"I ordered them to scatter."

"You did?"

Michael sighs. "That's one of the many things I need to teach you."

"We can *control* mutants?"

"Yes, albeit not very well. Partly, it's because they lack the intelligence; they are distorted beings, and much weaker than we are. They can only follow simple instructions given by the closest one of us."

"So you couldn't make them just kill each other?"

"No, but even if I could, they would simply be replaced."

"Where do they come from?" I ask. The answer to this question belongs not to me, not to Mark, but to all of mankind.

"They are created by the power leeching through the barrier."

"The barrier between our world and Hell, you mean?" Mark asks.

"Yes. It has weakened, and the power leaks in, contaminating wild animals."

I shiver, and not just because it's cold here. We'd always been unable to discover how and why the mutants were formed; the answer is terrifying.

"They are not strong," Michael continues, "but they are many."

"You're telling us," I mutter.

But we've arrived at our destination: in front of us, there is a large geometric building, shaped like three sails (or a snail shell, as I like to think of it). Lights burn everywhere. I look at Mark and his father, taking note to make sure their wings aren't showing. Mother would have a fit.

I press the intercom button.

"Yes?" a portly male voice answers—my mother's butler.

"It's me, Conall. I have some guests."

"Come in! I will inform Mrs Sianna."

The gate opens, and we walk through a glass tunnel, down into the ocean. The water is dark, though lights illuminate the interior. Another door opens, and we find ourselves in a reception room. Everything is white, and brilliantly lit; the place is bare save for a coat rack, and a smiling butler. He takes my jacket—the inside is warm—though neither Mark nor his dad are wearing anything more than T-shirts. The cold clearly does not affect them.

"Conall, are you sure about this?" Mark asks. "Now doesn't seem the time—"

"Hello, darling! And who have you brought here?" my mother asks, interrupting whatever he was about to say.

"I am Michael."

"Sianna Dannan," mother proclaims imperiously. "Pleased to make your acquaintance."

"Mother, this is Mark, my boyfriend," I say.

"I am *most* intrigued to meet you, darling." Mother shakes his hand, and Mark gives her a bemused glance.

"Whatever brings you all here?" she continues. "Not that I'm complaining, mind you: Conall so rarely visits."

"Mother, there was an attack. Don't you know?"

"The mutants? I can't imagine they got past the defences."

"I'm afraid they did," Michael interrupts. "We helped your son escape to this island."

"Why, thank you. I ought to return the favour, though I am at odds to do so. Would you like tea?"

So she finds us a table, and her butler serves us tea. There's no denying her once she asks, and besides: the tea is nice. Blackcurrant and cinnamon, by the smell.

"So, Conall, Mark, and Michael, whom I presume is Mark's father."

"You are correct," Michael confirms, one eyebrow raised. He doesn't know how perceptive my mother is.

"Conall," she says with disapproval, "has told me very little of you, Mark, and I would like to know more. Is it true you are a Fallen?"

"Yeah," Mark agrees. I notice Michael looking away.

"That is dreadfully unfortunate, though," she continues with a melodramatic sigh, "love conquers all, no?"

"Indeed," Michael agrees.

"Mother, we've been through a lot—the mutants killed a lot of people," I say, annoyed. "We just wanted a safe place where no questions would be asked."

"Is that all, dear?"

I look at her more carefully, noticing the white dress she is wearing, along with the steel in her eyes. She knows something.

"You didn't mention that your boyfriend is still wanted for murder, and that the Party sent a force to apprehend him," she adds, still smiling. Inwardly, I curse. Of course she would have found out.

The temperature seems to drop. My mother stands unbowed, the power of her Class evident in her posture. Mark also thrums with a power—one that suffuses the room, making it vibrate slightly, like a hornet's nest. Only Michael seems unaffected by the stand off.

"It was self-defence," Mark says quietly.

"So Conall tells me, and really, I believe you. My contacts inform me that the Commissioner seemed... obsessed with you. It's a very unhealthy thing, obsession." She shrugs. "I don't know what they want from you, or why, but you have best tell me if you desire my help."

"I don't need—"

"Mother," I interrupt him, "the situation is quite complex, and as I say, we are both exhausted. Can we please discuss this tomorrow?"

She looks at me, taking in my dishevelled state.

"Tomorrow, indeed."

With that, she leaves us, an apologetic-looking butler in tow. Mark has his head in his hands, while Michael seems confused. Apparently he doesn't know.

I shake my head. We have a lot to learn.

★★★

"Who is after you?" Michael asks him.

"You should know."

"I... am sorry. But I don't."

"The Party. Them and their fucking minions—who else?"

The old demon raises an eyebrow at that. He doesn't seem aged—his skin is supple, and his hair is a dark, healthy black—but it's obvious to me that he's much older than that. I wonder exactly how old.

"And to think I wanted a normal, human life for you..."

"Yeah, well, being human is kinda overrated *and all dat.*" There is bitterness in Mark's voice.

"You're of the Fallen class?"

"Damn right."

"It wasn't like that when I... left."

"They call it 'family friendly' policy," I add sadly. "If a spouse abandons his children, the children automatically become Fallen. The idea is to keep a stable, secure home for children."

"Or just to keep us in line," Mark mutters angrily.

"So you're Fallen, and they are after you. Why?"

"Why does it matter?" Mark asks coldly. "We have bigger things on our plate now."

"True. I had hoped you would manage to avoid this fate, but alas, it is not so."

"Stop telling me that."

"You want to be this?"

"I want you stop pretending that my human life was going to be great."

Before their argument can progress any further, I interrupt.

"Mark," I say, laying a hand on his forearm, "I know this is hard for you, but we have to focus on what's important. Michael, you said that the mutants obeyed whichever demon was closest. Well, I don't believe the attack was a coincidence; in fact, it seemed clear they were following us. Who set them up?"

"That... is an excellent question." He looks at me carefully, and I think maybe even appreciatively.

"You still haven't answered the question," Mark points out.

"I am not sure," he responds, "but I suspect it was Lucifer himself."

"What? From Hell? How?" Mark continues.

"As I say, the barrier is weakening; Lucifer grows stronger, and I think, more daring, though Hell knows, he was always daring." There is emotion in his voice.

"Who is he? How do you know him?" Mark asks, desperate for information.

"Lucifer is... someone I hope you never have to meet. He is a being of terrible evil, though—I have to admit—he is also beautiful, and charming, and brilliant."

"When... did you meet?" Mark continues.

"A long, long time ago."

"We are getting distracted," I point out. "Assume Lucifer did send the mutants. Why? What purpose could he have had?"

"To toy with you, most likely. He likes that; it amuses him greatly. He may also want to see what you are capable of—if you can destroy them, or control them."

"How did you know where we were? And why did you only come now?" Mark asks. I realise that his questions are just too pressing, too pivotal to his identity, to wait any longer.

"Did your uncle tell you how to summon me?"

That's when Mark shows me a small wing, made of a bright white metal—platinum.

"Uncle told me that I all I had to do was hold this, think of you, and you would come. I didn't really believe it."

"But I did come," Michael points out. "That wing is enchanted. It's the only connection I kept to you."

"So you came, and saw the mutant swarm," I say.

"Yes."

"Did you also know about the other demon?" I continue.

His head snaps back with a sharp sound. "Another demon?"

"A female one," I add.

"What did she do to you? How did she find you?"

"We killed the bitch," Mark says. "I don't know how she found us. But she told us that her master wanted to talk to me—said I should meet him."

"She must have been a weak demon, or you wouldn't be here," he says, closing his eyes.

"Be that as it may," I say, "what's important is that Lucifer knows about Mark, and wants him for some reason."

"I think I know why," Michael continues, opening his eyes again.

"Why the fuck?" Mark asks.

"The barrier isn't gone, you understand; it is only weakened. Weaker demons can get through, but the stronger ones—including Lucifer himself—are still stuck."

"And?"

"You can get through the barrier, probably far more easily than even the weak demons. And more importantly, you can *stay* here."

"What do you mean?" Mark continues, frustrated. "There's so much I don't know!"

"I mean, Mark, that demons can only stay a short time on Earth. The weaker ones will manage longer—days, perhaps weeks. But they will have to return to Hell; they cannot deny the barrier."

"You're here," Mark points out.

"That's... a special case."

"My mother," he breathes. "It's because of my mother, isn't it?"

Michael looks away. "Yes."

Silence falls, and the house is still around us. I can tell Mark wants to ask more; I can also tell he's afraid to do it, afraid of what he might discover.

"Mark," I whisper, touching his cheek. He looks at me, eyes shrouded in darkness. "This is too much for you; I can see it. Sleep with me, and we'll find out more tomorrow."

From the corner of my eye, I spot Michael watching us wearily. "In that case, I will leave. I can't hang around in one place too long, regardless."

"Don't you need sleep?" I ask curiously.

"No," he replies with an ironic smile. "*Bonam noctem,* my son, and you, Conall. I will make my leave."

"I knew you spoke Latin!"

He only chuckles, and then he's gone.

✷✷✷

The butler comes soon afterwards, apologising that my mother was occupied with business (I knew mother didn't tell him anything about her "business") but promising to find us a bedroom. I noted that he did not say "two bedrooms"—he was either observant, or well instructed by my mother. I couldn't decide which one.

So we find ourselves together in bed, me in his arms.

"So you're okay with all this—my father, my past, who I am; everything."

"You know my answer to that, Mark."

"Don't you ever wonder," he muses, "if we're naive? If we believe we can fight, and change the world?"

"Your father fought."

"Yeah..."

"You resent him for leaving, don't you?"

"I do," he admits. "I can understand why he thought he was doing the best thing for me, but... I still hate him for it."

"At least you have me," I point out, sitting up and kissing him.

"True," he agrees. "I don't know where I'd be without you, Conall."

"Now who's being cliché?"

He laughs. "Come on, you." He threads his body around me, encasing me in his warmth.

"It's been a long day," I say.

"You bet."

He closes his eyes, and I close mine. In the quiet darkness, I remember something. "Mark?"

"Yeah?"

"You could have killed those men who tried to arrest you, couldn't you?"

"I could have."

"But you didn't."

"No."

"Mark?"

"Yeah?"

"I want to feel your wings around me."

And so the warmth of his body is met with the silky softness of his wings, and I sleep.

Chapter Ten

Kaylin

We walk on the platform, hidden by Shadow's Ability. Below, the ocean rises tempestu-ously; above, the first pale rays of dawn touch the horizon. We can see our destination a few 'houses' away.

I came as soon as I could. The medallions told me that they were in trouble—and it did not take long before news of the mutant attack also reached me. People had been killed, many of them in the Upper Quarter. That in itself is highly unusual; the attack had clearly been targeted, and mutants never target their attacks. Stranger still is the fact that the swarm dissipated not long afterwards, despite having breached the defences.

Still, none of it matters as much as they do. I can feel it; I don't know why, exactly, but there are few certainties in my line of work. Only possibilities, probable and improbable.

I wonder what they are doing here. Clearly, they must have survived the mutant attack; but why did they flee here, barely a few miles away, instead of further afield? I did not have time to investigate; I simply took Shadow and Diana. Though now, looking at the bizarre spectacle of architecture in front of us, I'm starting to suspect I acted in haste.

"What now, Mistress?" Shadow asks.

"The medallions are inside, and I can feel Mark and Conall too."

"So you want us to break in?"

"It shouldn't be too difficult; you're the expert."

"That I am," he agrees with the pleasure.

"Are you sure about this, Kaylin?" Diana asks. "It's not like you, to just barge in."

"As I say, Diana, we must act quickly and unpredictably. Besides, since when are you so cautious?"

She shrugs. "If you say so."

Shadow makes good on his word: in a matter of moments, we're in, following on the footsteps of a sleepy-looking butler. I suspect the owner has them on shifts, to ensure twenty-four-hour service. The vagaries of the upper Classes know no bounds.

The corridor around us is nearly dark, the light above not quite penetrating the water. I follow the signal—it's like a pull, a faint, invisible string of magic. Just before we reach it, I feel something else: a much darker presence.

"On your guard!" I whisper, though Shadow's Ability conceals sound as easily as light. We find a hidden recess in the building, and we watch.

My eyes widen as I take in the figure: powerful, masculine, those dark wings exuding silent menace. I steel myself, preparing the spell I'd recently discovered. The Book had been cryptic, and it had taken much reading, but I know two important things now. How demons are created, and how very necessary it is to destroy them.

Like a well-oiled machine, Diana and Shadow move around me, ready to act. Shadow will keep us invisible until I cast the spell; then he'll move back, letting us work our magic.

I draw the rune in the air; it hangs there, glowing an ethereal blue. The demon freezes as the spell takes hold. I freeze as well. All magic has a cost—and the stronger magics have the highest cost of all.

Diana glows bright with fire. We'd seen how her Ability could harm them; and so we gambled, counting on her ability to destroy them while I kept them stunned.

Then it goes horribly wrong.

"Diana? What are you doing? No!" Mark's voice is deafeningly loud in the silence, though it is his power that stops her. She flies across the room, and hangs there, in mid-air.

I try and think. The spell won't hold forever; I can't do anything while I'm casting it. Shadow can't reach Diana. If she tries to attack anyway, Mark will probably kill her. And Shadow himself doesn't have the power to hurt either one of them.

In the end, the decision is made for me.

I blink, eyes burning in the light. A woman stands at the door: tall, richly dressed even in her nightgown, her eyes like winter itself.

"What, in the name of all that is good, is going on here?"

Chapter Eleven

Mark

Everything seems frozen in time: dad stays perfectly still, Diana I keep in the air, and Conall's mother has her hands on her hips.

"I said, what is going on? And what are you on doing on *my ceiling*?" she asks to Diana. She only puts out a strangled gasp, my power still locked around her throat.

Somehow, Sianna breaks the spell. I let Diana down to the floor; Kaylin seems to sway, and dad unfreezes. The world is back to normal—or what the Hell passes for normal in my life.

"You *all* have a lot of explaining to do," Sianna continues.

I turn my eyes to dad, who looks grateful, and Kaylin, who seems confused. Kaylin definitely has a lot of explaining to do.

⁕⁕⁕

We sit around a central dining table—me, Conall, who I've just woken up, along with dad, Diana and Kaylin. Light is starting to penetrate into the water, and I watch fish swim from the ceiling-height windows. Sianna is crazy; but somehow, I think I like her crazy. I wonder why Conall treats her like a mutant snake.

"So, allow me to confirm this," she starts. "You are Kaylin—a witch—and the leader of an insurrection."

"That is correct."

"Somehow, you contrived to enter my home uninvited in order to make sure Mark, and by extension my son, was in good working order—all because of the magic medallions you gave them."

Kaylin nods.

"Yet instead you found dear Michael"—she smiles magnanimously at him—"whom you attacked and attempted to murder."

"Yes," Kaylin replies, without any obvious guilt in her voice. I wonder what the Hell made her think my dad was a target.

"And whom you tell me is a demon." Sianna doesn't put that as a question; instead, she takes him in thoughtfully, like he's the answer to all her questions. And I guess he is—for both of us.

"I am indeed, Sianna," Michael responds.

"I presume, therefore, that Mark has some of it as well?"

"I do," I say, not letting him answer for me.

"So my son is in love with a demon." Other people would have been disbelieving, or gone into hysterics. Heck, *I'm* a demon, and I still don't really believe it all. But not her: it's like a lightbulb has gone off in her head.

"Excellent!" she announces suddenly. "It all makes sense now, my darlings."

"What do you mean, mother?" Conall asks with exasperation.

"Why Mark was put in prison, dear."

"I was there because I... was forced to kill someone." I gulp, beginning to notice all the things that didn't really make sense.

"It was self-defence, silly," she says, "and there was no evidence to the contrary. Besides, why would the Party Commissioner *himself* care about this 'murder' case?"

It's what I've been wondering all along. I remember his words, feeling cold all over. And I remember everything else too—the power I had felt in him, confusing him, controlling him.

"We figured that much out. What we don't understand is: how? It was as if everything she asked, they did." It's Kaylin who speaks.

We all look at my dad; he just sighs.

"I should have seen it. What you are describing, witch, is called Persuasion. It only works on those of weaker will, or those blinded by ambition. We can... manipulate humans —use their emotions to our advantage."

"So this Sheilia, whom I assume is also a demon, put them up to it. But why? I fail to see the purpose." It's Sianna again.

"Because Lucifer ordered her to," my dad says. "Mark... when did you transform?"

"What?"

"You weren't a demon when you were born. You turned at some point—something I knew could happen. Was it when you killed the boy who attacked you?"

I blink, remembering the dream, and the voices, and the pain. "Yes... that was it."

He curses something in a language I don't understand, and smashes the table. Sianna raises an eyebrow at the destruction.

"It was all part of the plan—the attack, putting you in prison."

"What do you mean, dad?"

"I mean, the transition doesn't just *happen*. You have to kill someone, harm others, commit evil."

"But... it was self-defence." I'm saying that a lot lately.

"Clearly, it makes no difference."

Sianna suddenly rises. "Well, clearly you have a lot more to be discussing, though it does not really concern me. I will leave now. And Michael?"

"Yes?"

"You owe me a new table."

As she begins walking, Kaylin stops her. "I did not release these secrets lightly, woman. And nor do I trust you: you have plans of your own, ideas I cannot see. What do you intend to do with this knowledge? It is a dangerous thing, not fit for personal advance-ment and political gain."

Sianna's eyes are stone cold. "My concern is for my son, witch. It always has been."

"You cannot keep him safe on your own; powers such as ours are beyond you."

"What are you saying?"

"I'm saying you need to divulge whatever information you have, and let *us* protect him."

"Even if this information includes the Party?"

"Damn right."

Surprisingly, she shrugs. "Very well."

Even Kaylin looks puzzled. "Aren't you going to protest?"

Sianna just laughs. "Oh, I always knew the Party was going to collapse eventually. They're too weak; their corruption has made them stupid. And these demons are a far greater force. I will form alliances, as I always do."

With that, she's gone. So we turn, facing each other. I need answers.

✶✶✶

"Why did you attack my dad?" I ask Kaylin.

"We thought..."

"You thought I was in Lucifer's pocket," my dad interrupts her. "And nor do I blame you, witch. Nearly all of us are."

"I'm still not entirely convinced," Kaylin says. "Mark may have turned, but he did not do so willingly—he was forced by circumstance and contrivance. You, on the other hand, *did* choose to become what you are."

"Dad?" I look at him carefully, studying the drawn angles in his face, the way he avoids looking me in the eye. I realise that I've still only just met him; I don't really know that much about him.

"Do not speak of this, witch. And I'm sorry, Mark, but I'm... not willing to tell you yet."

"You better fucking tell me!"

But he's shaking his head. "I'm sorry." To Kaylin, he adds: "Nice try, witch. You almost got me. But perhaps you ought to tell my son a few secrets of your own—including what your friends are. Because, while I've met witches before, I've never met anyone like *her*."

Then he's gone. I blink, looking everywhere; yet the room has only me, Conall, Kaylin, and Diana. Or does it?

*✶✶

Shadows twist in a corner, and then a guy is next to us.

"Whew! That's a hell of a woman, Mistress."

"Yes indeed, Shadow."

"And some dad you have there," he says, talking to me now.

"Who the fuck are you?" I ask.

"Mark, this is Shadow, one of my men."

"Pleased to meet ya, Mark," he says, "your fuckin' notwithstandin'." He winks at me.

"Sorry about him," Conall says. "I am Conall."

"I know you too, mister."

"And they call you Shadow?" I ask him.

"Yup."

"Shadow," Kaylin orders, "sneak out of here. You have some spying to do."

"On who, Mistress?"

"Sianna, for now, and Mark's father, once we find him."

He nods, and disappears into the shadows again. I can't believe it—I can't see him at all.

"I'm willing to bet you still have questions, Mark," Diana speaks.

"You bet."

"We need to tell him, Kaylin."

The other woman sighs. "Very well. You've always wanted to know more about our powers, and your father alluded as much. The truth is, we don't know everything. I've always had my visions; I discovered more of my powers in the Black Book, which has revealed many secrets to me. I am some sort of witch, though I suspect your father knows more than I do. As for Diana and Shadow—they are something else."

"Really?"

"Yes, I am sure of it. The Black Book has nothing on them; their power also seems to work very differently from mine."

"So you don't know what you are, Diana?" I continue.

She shakes her head.

"Okay... thanks for that. I appreciate it. But what did you mean—when you said my father chose to become a demon?"

Kaylin closes her eyes.

"You have to tell him," Diana whispers.

"Mark, your father had to commit an act of evil."

"What... what kind of evil?"

"You'll have to ask him. The Book calls it 'grievous'; it mentions murder, rape, and things besides."

"So what's why you didn't trust him," I realise.

"Yes. Now, if you'll excuse me, I have more to discover. I will be back."

"One more thing!" Conall calls out. "The medallions—they were far too inaccurate. We need to be able to speak to you."

She shakes her head. "That kind of spellwork is as yet beyond my ability; perhaps one of my technology experts will have a solution. I must go—there is much to do. I doubt the Party has given up on you yet, and they are getting in the way."

"Getting in the way, Kaylin?" Diana asks. "They used to be everything."

"I think we all realise that's in the past," she says with a trace of irony. Then they leave, and we're alone.

✶✶✶

"So this is what it all boils down to," he says, as we walk on the promenade.

The sun is rising; it casts a pink light on us, and the wind lifts Conall's brown hair into tufts. He's a wearing a jacket—it's made from tan leather, and is matched with dark blue jeans—and he looks good. He's never been what you'd call a model: he's too slight, his face more 'cute' than masculine. Still, I've always been crazy about him. Maybe it's the personality that does it; he's so confident.

"What do you mean?"

"A dysfunctional family"

I laugh, just barely. "Yeah, you could call it that. I don't think you can complain—your mother is a cool lady."

"Really, Mark? A 'cool lady'?"

"She gets what she wants."

"Through whatever amoral means come handy, right?"

"Sometimes we have to be mean, Conall."

He goes more quiet then. The wind picks up—it's always blowing here in the ocean—and I wrap an arm around him, to keep him warm. I'm only wearing a T-shirt, but then, I'm not exactly human.

"She cares for you, you have to admit that," I continue.

"I think your father cares about you too, you know."

"It doesn't really seem like it."

"Neither does it for me, but as I say: we have dysfunctional families."

"And a mad witch on top of it," I say.

"So did she really try to kill your dad?"

"Yeah, and I think she would have succeeded—it only failed because of me."

"Because you kept Diana in a Force choke?"

I can't help but smile. "Something like that, yeah."

"So many things could have gone wrong today..."

"Yeah, but they didn't."

He presses himself into me, stroking my jaw with his fingers. He kisses me underneath the chin; I close my eyes, savouring the moment.

"Let's hope things don't go wrong, okay?"

"Okay."

The wind rises again; the ocean waves grow fierce, almost as if they understand us.

Chapter Twelve

Kaylin

I may be a witch, but it seems I may as well call myself the Queen of Spies. I lounge on a leather recliner; the room around me is luxurious, being my home away from home here in the Dublin base. Shadow stands to attention, barely visible in a corner.

"So Sianna is entertaining senior Party figures, in an effort to glean information," I say, going over the meat of his information.

"That's right, Mistress. She's giving them a big fancy ball with all the bleedin' stops."

"In her home in the ocean?"

"No, she has some other location."

"That woman may be the craziest I've ever met, but she does have some sense. Always better to keep trouble away from home."

"You bet."

"If she discovers anything, and you find out what, report it to me immediately."

"Of course."

The past days had been hectic, our near-disastrous encounter with Mark's dad forcing me to learn more—as much as I possibly could. The Book gave up its secrets only slowly, though what I did learn has much potential. Shadow has been busy spying; I have offered him additional help in the form of technology, and the aid of my team, though he hardly seems to need it. He has discovered nearly everything about Sianna, even her darkest, dirtiest secrets.

Only the demon has proven immune to his espionage—and that solely because

Shadow hasn't been able to find him. I suspect Michael is not the kind of being to tarry too long in one place, nor take conventional means of transportation.

"Shadow, you may leave now. I will attempt to glean information about Michael through my visions."

"Good luck, Mistress."

"You too, Shadow."

He disappears once more, and I close my eyes, relaxing myself. It's never easy: the trance state requires calmness, an open mind, and a sort of perfect, unbroken concentration. Still, it feels even harder now—there's so much at stake, and so much hangs on my ability to See. It takes a good minute before the room around me blurs, and is swallowed by darkness.

I seek him through the ether, searching for answers. The world around me flashes: I see mutants hunted down throughout Ireland and the world; I see Party figures plotting, and soldiers being armed; but none of it is what I'm after. His thread seems elusive, a needle in a very large haystack. Maybe I don't have a strong enough connection: he eludes me, remaining just at the edge of my visions.

I pull back into consciousness, sighing in frustration. Perhaps I am too distracted; perhaps some more reading is in order. So I withdraw the Book, and seek answers in its pages once more. An electronic clock sits in one corner of the room, silently making its steady progress. The sun gradually lowers itself across the sky; yet I discover nothing more. The spells here are of love-potions, and the stories no more than various anecdotes about their dangers.

I close the book, focusing myself once more. This time, I slide into the trance state easily. Yet it is not Michael I see; it is someone much darker, someone so powerful I cannot perceive him directly, but only as an outline. Lights shift around me—a far cry from my usual clarity. Even the sounds are distorted, while scent—usually present, if vaguely—is altogether absent.

I do not have time to wonder why this is so; the conversation is too important to miss.

"So they have destroyed her, and evaded my mutants."

"Indeed, Master."

He does not seem angry; in fact, he seems strangely pleased.

"He is proving quite a challenge—I daresay I am relishing it."

"If you say so, Master, though I think we are wasting too much time, and too many resources, on this."

"Now, now, *Amata*—" He says her name endearingly, though I sense some hidden undercurrent in his tone, "—don't be spoilsport. He will prove a valuable asset. For now, we must send him one last test."

I see no more, for the vision collapses into shards of light. I breathe quickly, my heart rate rapid. All magic has a cost; but I suspect there is more to my reaction than the normal effects of the spell.

"Mistress?"

I jump when he says my name. "Shadow?"

"I came here because I just spotted Michael—he was flying down to Sianna's."

"That is good news. Bring Diana; we are going to meet him."

"Why now?"

"You will soon find out."

Chapter Thirteen

Conall

They arrive at the same time: Michael, on his wings; Kaylin and Diana by Q-car, which I strongly suspect is illegal (and I strongly suspect Kaylin doesn't care). They watch each other wearily, their near-fatal encounter no doubt still fresh in their minds. Still, Kaylin obviously has something important to tell us: she makes her way to me and Mark, her stride quick and determined.

"I had a vision. We will be under attack."

"From whom?" I ask.

"From demons," she says.

"You saw Lucifer?" Michael asks, sounding surprised.

"Mostly I just heard him; what difference does it make?"

"I've never met a witch who could see into Hell."

"Well, pity that. The point is this: we need to be ready."

"And how do you plan on doing that?"

"You tell me."

Michael sighs. "Normally, I would leave—go somewhere far."

"How far exactly?" Mark asks.

"Japan, North America, Australia," he suggests.

"I'm not going anywhere," I say.

"Neither am I," Mark agrees.

"Michael," Kaylin says, sounding surprisingly civil, "we cannot leave. Breaking

271

ourselves up would weaken us, and I have too many responsibilities here. Besides, from what I gleaned, Lucifer is no fool—he will have anticipated this, knowing you."

Mark's dad looks away. "You are right, much as I am loathe to admit it."

"We need to be able to fight them," Kaylin continues. "I have... discovered another spell. If you agree, I would like to test it."

"On me, witch?"

"It's a defensive spell, demon."

They square off, Michael exuding dark power, and Kaylin possessed of a power of her own—something strange, subtle, but also very tangible.

"Dad, we don't have time for this macho bullshit. I want to fight too; teach me. Teach us both."

Michael closes his eyes. "You are right, although I wished it didn't have to come to this. Very well, Kaylin: show me what you can do."

We both watch as Diana moves away from her, and Kaylin begins writing a complex pattern in the air. It hangs there, glowing a peculiar, iridescent blue.

"Attack me," Kaylin orders.

Michael only raises an eyebrow, but does as she orders: he lifts his hand, where a bright ball of blue flame has coalesced. It flies out of his hand, and slams against the rune. Only to break apart, doing nothing.

"Again."

This time, Michael hits harder—a bolt of black power slams into the defensive rune. It shatters. Still, I see the rune is less bright; it seems to flicker in the air now, no longer solid. Michael throws a second bolt, and again it shatters, but again the rune grows dimmer. The third bolt finally breaks it.

"Not bad, witch."

"Isn't there more you can do? I was led to believe you demons were capable of various things."

Michael smiles, just a little, and I shiver. He's very civilised, and in a way, almost timid —but behind that there lies a powerful supernatural being, and a great deal of past evil. Kaylin is unfazed; she creates another rune, and waits. We watch as Michael changes: his eyes become black, like ink, or the darkest recesses of Hell. Yet nothing more seems to happen.

The blackness recedes from his eyes. "As I suspected. You are very fortunate to possess this spell."

"Oh? And what did you expect to happen?"

"Do you want to see for yourself?"

Kaylin shrugs, and dismisses the rune—it flicks out of existence, like smoke. This time, when Michael's eyes go black, she collapses. A second later, Michael's eyes return to normal, though Kaylin is still down. It takes a long while until she gets back up, gasping.

"Damn you, that hurt."

He shrugs. "Consider it payback for the spell you put on me."

"What do you call it?"

"The Dark Stare."

"An appropriate name. Is there... anything else? We need to know."

Michael disappears. He did that before, when he refused to answer Mark's questions, and I suspect Kaylin remembered. He re-appears next to Kaylin—he has his hand round her throat.

"We can teleport. And break your neck."

"Believe me, I know." A second later, Kaylin touches him, and we watch as he collapses, stunned.

"I have a few tricks of my own."

"Yes," Michael says, coughing, "but can you use them before one of them kills you? We're fast; you won't have enough time."

Kaylin shrugs. "I know—it's why I chose to ambush you. But you have not yet seen what *Diana* can do."

"Indeed," Michael agrees, and we watch as Diana smiles, exuding confidence. The wind seems to pick up; the waves grow more aggressive. It's strange: I always knew there was *something* about her, something that didn't make sense. Now I know why. Even her eyes aren't the same—they're a pale, platinum blue, so very different from her usual brown.

We watch as Michael's own power rises to match hers: his is a malevolent blue fire, slithering over his wings, and covering his upper arms.

Diana lifts her hand, and the air explodes in violet fire. It meets the blue fire head on; the spectacle is awe-inspiring, the power beyond anything I can fathom. The world seems to shake from the onslaught. Yet neither of them are harmed—in fact, Michael doesn't seem impressed.

"That may be flashy, but it won't help you," he tells her. Then, before I can comprehend what he's doing, he's high into the air. Several blue fireballs rain down like asteroids. Diana fires back, but can't hit him—he's too fast, a black mark across the sky.

Diana purses his lips. She grows still. A split second later, I feel it: a wave of power, building everywhere. In an instant, the sky darkens, and lightning bursts across the clouds. Not natural lightning—something much worse.

Michael lands back on the ground. "I don't know what you are, but you'll be the death of me."

"You were beginning to annoy me with the flying," Diana explains.

She doesn't have time to say anymore, because a black bolt shoots out from Michael's hand. It narrowly misses—instead it strikes the concrete, and blows clean through.

"Your abilities, whatever they are, do impress me," Michael continues, "but you are too confident, and demons are nothing if not deceitful. We are masters of it."

He turns to us and Mark. "I have shown you enough; I do not know your powers, so it is down to you to make the best of what you have learned. Now, son, I need to teach you what are you capable of."

I feel Mark's emotions: he's full of anger, but also excitement. I can tell he's been wait-ing for this. Inside, I worry. This is a dangerous game he's teaching us to play at.

∗∗∗

I stand back, watching the two along with Kaylin and Diana. They stand a little apart. Mark is brimming with repressed emotion; Michael is concentrating intensely. Sparks fly from Mark's hands.

"So, *dad*, you're finally here to tell me how to fight."

"Yes." Michael's voice is very quiet.

"Well, you're a little late to the party." A split second later, Mark attacks. He flies into Michael. He moves too fast for me to see—there's only a flurry of punches, kicks, and then Michael is flying through the air. He collides with the concrete platform; the noise is deaf-ening, like a divine hammer punishing the Earth.

Michael gets back up, and dusts himself off. "Aggressive, I see. Fast, strong. No doubt it served you well against humans."

"It wasn't easy," Mark says, breathing hard. "A lot of people wanted to hurt me."

"But what you know won't help you now," Michael continues, as if he hadn't heard. "You cannot harm a demon with physical means. You can shoot us, stab us, dice us, burn us, throw us into buildings—and still we will carry on." He shrugs. A moment later, something dark jumps out of him, flies through the air, and explodes next to Mark. He falls to the ground—I feel his confusion.

"It is your power—your ability to wield demonic magic—that can harm other demons," Michael continues, walking over to him.

"Fuck you."

"I appreciate the sentiment," Michael responds dryly. "Come on. We have a lot of catching up to do."

Mark rises, and the two share a look. Even far away as I am, there is no mistaking its intent.

Chapter Fourteen

Mark

I feel alive. I haven't felt like this in a long time—not since Conall and I first got together, really. But then I went to prison, shit happened, and I lost a little bit of that magic. Except now I can feel it, burning through my veins, my wings fluttering with excitement.

It feels good to have power.

"So how am I supposed to fight you?" I ask dad.

"The single most effective attack you can employ is known as a shadow bolt."

"Really?"

"You will see why. Put your hands together, and concentrate. Draw some of your power—focus it as far as you can." I do as he tells me. I feel my power coiled inside me; it practically purrs when I draw it out. The bolt in my hand quivers, like it's alive, and desires only one thing: to destroy.

"Throw it," he orders.

It explodes from my hand, heading straight for him. But then it hits a concrete barrier, destroying it.

"Turn around."

I turn around, finding him behind me.

"The teleport, huh?"

"Fading, officially, but the modern English term will suffice. It is a powerful tool in our arsenal, if mastered."

"How do I do it?"

"You should understand that it requires knowledge of a place; you must be able to visualise it, in great detail, from the sound of the waves to the feel of the wind. Also, you cannot Fade to or from Hell."

"The barrier, right?"

"Yes indeed. Now, focus on the area where I was a moment ago. Try to imagine yourself there."

"Is that all there is to it?"

"Yes, but it's not as easy as it sounds."

So I concentrate, imagining myself right in that little spot. The world around me seems to waver; it's like I'm not quite here anymore. I concentrate more intensely: I imagine the way the light shines on it, visualising the dust particles, the sea spray, its relation to me.

The world seems to go sideways, and suddenly, I'm here. I blink, feeling a little dizzy.

"We all feel that the first time, but you will get used to it."

"Great. So I can teleport, and throw magic bolts. Can I also do that stare?"

"The Dark Stare? It is fairly trivial—I imagine you may have already done it without realising—but it does not work against other demons."

"I still have those Party bastards. How does it work?"

"You have to want someone to hurt—badly."

"I can do that."

"I know, but be careful."

Before I know it, he's Faded in front of me. For the first time, he touches me, on the shoulder.

"Mark," he whispers, "they don't understand, except for the witch, who won't tell you this the way you need to hear it. We are beings of darkness; and our free will—our ability to do good instead of evil—is something that carries on from human life. We can choose, but the choice is often not easy, and against our nature."

"Why are you telling me this?"

"Because you must understand it—you must, or you will hurt people, even innocent people, and barely realise it. You may come to enjoy it; once, I did."

"Will you tell me—about what you did, to become a demon?"

This time, he looks me in the eye. I wonder how we can be so different, and yet so alike.

"I will, soon, but not now. It's... not easy for me."

He backs away. "In any case, I have only taught you the basics. I do not have time to teach you the finer points of the dark craft; only the most crucial elements. There is one more thing, which I have mentioned, but not really addressed."

"And that is?" I ask. My voice is more subdued, as is the power inside me. I realise he was right.

"How to destroy us. Even with magic, it is not that easy—it requires strong magic, and the stronger the demon, the greater the magic. That witch and her companion are very powerful for what they are; even so, I doubt they could destroy the strongest demons.

"As for us, you have to understand that we are average. We are stronger than virtually any of the demons he can send on Earth, but in Hell... we are not the strongest."

"So how do I kill the strong ones?" I ask, feeling frustrated.

"Weaker demons, as you have seen, can be destroyed with even a stray fireball. A medium demon, like you or I, can be destroyed by a concentrated bolt of demonic magic. Remember that: you are not unstoppable.

"As for Greater Demons, including Lucifer himself, only great acts of magic have ever been able to compromise them."

"What exactly is that?"

"It's not the kind of magic you can just conjure up, like you do fireballs or bolts. It requires three things: planning, activation, and sacrifice."

"Sacrifice?"

"Yes. The sacrifice can vary, from a drop of blood to a life given. Don't ask me more; I don't know."

I think over the new information, feeling troubled. Nothing is ever simple, I realise.

"Mark?" It's Conall: he seems worried.

"Hey," I say. Smiling, I focus, and manage to Fade next to him. He jumps a little.

"So you learned that new trick?"

"Yup. Isn't it cool?"

"That's one way of putting it."

I thread my arms around him, kissing him on the cheek. Everything is complicated, except Conall. Because for all that life has thrown at me, and at him, one thing remains simple: I love him.

"This isn't a game, you know," he says. "It's life or death."

"I know that, Conall," I say, in a lower tone now. "But you have to make the most of life—you have to have fun, even when it's bad."

"You sound like a poet."

"I just know life."

"Anyway," he says, and now I sense what's making him uncomfortable. "Kaylin is having a vision."

We turn our eyes to her. She's sitting crosslegged, her eyes staring into... nothing. Then the moment is over, and she's back to normal. She blinks, looking weary.

"What?" I ask.

"Sianna is coming, and she has news."

"What news?" I continue.

"Ask her yourself," she says, and then we see the Q-car. It lands next to her house, and Sianna walks out, looking very determined. I have a bad feeling about it.

✷✷✷

"What's going on, mother?"

She sighs deeply. "I tried to convince them, to use my contacts and find a sympathetic ear. But they've outsmarted us dear."

"Who?" Conall continues.

"The demons of course. They have someone planted high—at the top. Big Brother himself has ordered your boyfriend captured, alive... or dead."

"What do we do?"

"We should leave," Kaylin states. "I have a Q-car ready to fly us out."

"What? But... there must be another way. Even if we could escape—and I don't think we can—where would we go?"

"Conall has a point," I say. "America, Russia and what else remains of the world are wastelands teeming with mutants. The Chinese are hostile. Anywhere else in Europe, and we'll be extradited back to Ireland."

"What about Spain?" Kaylin asks.

"Fool witch," Sianna tells her. "The Communists are not trusted by anyone; they are only part of the Superstate because it is in their geopolitical interests. They will not compromise that for the sake of one boy."

"Why not go to Russia?" Michael asks. "Mark, it may be a wasteland, but you are immortal; you cannot freeze or starve. The mutants are not a threat to one of us."

"Oh yeah? But what about Conall? He still needs to eat, and stay warm, and be kept safe from the mutants."

"He is in more danger here. They will use him to get to you—be sure of that."

I don't have time to argue more, because Kaylin suddenly closes her eyes. Another vision.

"What is it?" I ask.

"They're coming."

***

I close my wings around Conall, protecting him. My father opens his wings wide, and shoots into the air. Diana is on fire, and not figuratively, as Conall would say; while Kaylin draws her runes of protection around us. They glow a faint blue, but soon disappear.

"They are not gone," she tells us, "as you will find out if you try to leave their confines."

"What?" I ask.

"All magic has a cost, Mark. Or, at least, the magic I do. No one may pass the barrier I have created, not even I, unless I dispel it. No magic can cross it."

"Not even your own, right?"

"Precisely. So let me put it this way: there is no point in you staying here. You are much more valuable to Conall by letting him remain safe here, and by helping us fight them."

"But can I really trust your spell to keep him safe? I saw how my father destroyed your wall."

"Your father is rather more powerful than they are, and he did not destroy it easily."

"Mark," Conall whispers. "It's alright. Go: give them hell."

The power inside me rises at that, and I know it's the right decision. I kiss him, quickly but firmly.

"Call me if you need me," I tell him.

Kaylin makes a temporary gap in the wall, and I'm out, soaring high into the air. The night sky seems alive: stars shine brightly, and the cool air feels good against my skin. I can see them coming: three Q-craft, a fighter and two assault carriers. I fly next to dad.

"Mark!" he shouts. "Let me handle the fighter—you take care of the other two."

We fly together, and then pull apart, him heading right for the fighter; I take the left, putting me on course with the other two. I build speed, going faster than I've ever gone before. But the Q-craft are faster still, faster than sound. The first one fires a plasma ball at me. They look slow, only they aren't. Rather than try and dodge it, I do something else: I launch a fireball of my own. The two meet, and disintegrate in a shower of sparks.

Not that I should have bothered. I'm hit by a laser flash—the world around me explodes in light. Except I feel nothing.

I laugh. I know it should be wrong, but I can't help it: for so long I've been terrorised by them, only to discover how weak they really are. I twist, intercepting one of their craft. It tries to evade me, but assault carriers, I know, are good at one thing: carrying lots of soldiers and equipment. They're not dog fighters.

For a good second, I'm level with it, and I take the opportunity to fire a bolt. It smashes through the force shield, and turns the aircraft into dust.

I see a flash, and realise that dad has destroyed the fighter. That leaves the second assault carrier, heading fast for Conall, Kaylin and Diana. I accelerate, but it's getting harder: the air is fighting me now, and I realise I can't break the sound barrier.

Dad flies next to me. "I'll deal with it: you should try and Fade back to the platform. They need your help."

"What? I thought—"

"The air attack is just a diversion; they also have a submarine. Diana has her work cut out. Go."

I focus, imagining the spot where I'd last Faded. Practice makes perfect, I guess: there's that weird sideways sensation again, and I'm there. I still have my momentum though; I land hard against the concrete. The concrete cracks thanks to the impact, but I remain unharmed.

Turns out dad was right. Diana is on fire, but she's also surrounded, each Party soldier pointing a weapon at her.

"Now, miss, if you'll come with us..."

"I will burn you to a cinder before you threaten me."

"Oh? What if we threaten your friend?" Several more men traipse from below, and point their weapons at Kaylin and Conall. I know I have to trust her spells.

"Hey, bastards, forget about me?"

"Oh, you're a wanted man, Mark," the same guys speaks again, and I realise he's the captain. There's very little to indicate he's human: he's covered head to toe in black armour, his visor obscuring his face. His voice is projected by microphone, to make it louder. Cocky bastard.

Before he realises what's going on, I slam his head against the concrete. Both the con-crete and his head crack. (His helmet didn't do him much good.) This does the job: they all start firing at me. Bullets and laser flashes hit me, but do nothing, as I've come to expect.

With their attention off Diana, she happily burns them alive; their armour is no match for her fire. But then she cries out. Distantly, I realise she must be injured. The thought doesn't bother me as much as it should: it is revenge that occupies my mind. The men that threatened Conall will face a worse fate than a quick death by fire.

Realising they can't hurt me, they shoot at Conall instead. My rage burns brighter still. Luckily, Kaylin's spell holds: the bullets simply disintegrate against her shield. I smile darkly; they're going to pay. Two I simply burn. Another two I grab hold of, and decapitate them. I rip off the last guy's visor, and pin him to the ground.

"So Big Brother himself sent you, eh?"

"That's right, sir."

"And what did he tell you?"

"That you are to be brought alive or dead." He adds, with a gulp, "Sir."

"Do you know what I am, soldier?"

"N-no."

"I'm something bad."

I feel my power coil itself, like a snake ready to pounce.

"Mark, don't," Kaylin orders. "It's part of their plan."

"Did you see that, witch?"

"No, but I can guess."

"She's right," Michael says, dropping next to me. "If you kill him..."

"Why not? He would have killed me if he could, or Conall if he couldn't."

"They shot me," Diana calls out. "But that's not enough to kill a man in cold blood."

They don't convince me; I tighten my hold on the guy's throat, feeling his blood pumping through his veins, realising the fragility of his bones. The power inside me sings. If I crush his throat, he will suffocate to death more slowly than if I simply ripped his head off.

"Mark, don't do it." It's Conall. "It doesn't matter if you're right about him; this is about *you*. He doesn't present a threat, and you don't need to kill him. This is about *desire*, not need. And I know you wouldn't kill someone just because you *wanted* to."

I hesitate.

"Mark, I can wipe his memories," Kaylin tells me. "Just let him go."

With disgust, I let go of him, and take to the air. I need to clear my head.

Chapter Fifteen

Mark

I fly hard and fast, heading west. My mind is in turmoil. Those men had deserved to die—Party lackeys *always* deserve death, and more. Even so, I could see Conall's reaction; he had been horrified, in shock, while I revelled in the killing.

Kaylin, that witch, had kept her calm perfectly, like the professional she is. Even Diana had managed to contain herself and not kill the last guy, even though she had been shot.

Harder I fly, reaching my maximum speed. The air buffets me—it's like moving through concrete. But I ignore it, and focus on the thrill of the speed. The ocean lies far below me; I am alone with the moon and the sky.

I fly for a long time, gradually abandoning myself to the sensation. Slowly, my mind begins to clear. I breathe a little more easily; the power that had begged to be released subsides into blank calmness.

✳✳✳

Time passes, and the horizon begins to lighten. It's dawn, I realise. I've been flying full speed all night. I know that a human should be exhausted by now—but then again, humans don't have wings and can't fly at five hundred miles per hour. It shouldn't surprise me that I don't need to sleep.

I also realise that there's something else visible on the horizon: land. I realise that my course must have taken me to... Greenland? No, it must be America.

I dive, at breakneck speed, then fan out my wings. I still hit the ground hard—far harder than I would have risked with Conall—but, of course, I'm indestructible.

I pause, listening. I hear nothing. No birds, or buzzing insects; even the wind is quiet. I scan the terrain around me—it's wet marshland, dotted with rivers and lakes. If uncle's geography lessons were any good, I'm probably in Maine.

The morning is still cold, though it doesn't bother me, even in my T-shirt. I walk around, but see nothing of interest. No humans, no animals.

Again I take to the air, but I fly low this time, and slowly. At points I even hover— something I didn't know I could do. The landscape stretches out far beyond me.

Not much is known about the Americas these days. The nuclear apocalypse had killed most people, we think—there's definitely no trace of civilisation left. No cities, no new nations, no outside communication.

The chaos, I know, had also spread to Canada, although they remained neutral in the conflict with Russia. The Canadian government still exists, but their economy has been decimated, and many people either live in the wilderness or have emigrated to Europe. Mexico has suffered a similar fate.

There's nothing here, I realise. Not the in the US, which is a wasteland, judging by what I can see. Maybe in Canada or Mexico, but would Conall really want to live there? He lives a life of luxury, and has lived it all his live. I don't need luxury; I only want to wake up with him in my arms every day. Enough for me, but not fair on him.

Damnit! I know so little. Maybe South America would be better? But the Party has kept contact with the outside world limited. Much of the Internet is firewalled and mon- itored (I'd even tried it once, out of curiosity). South America could be paradise for all I know, or just another mutant-torn emptiness.

The Chinese are too dangerous, and they administer all of habitable Asia—including Japan and India, excluding the wilderness of Russia, another apocalyptic hell. Most of

Africa and the Middle East is colonised by the European League of Nations (France enjoys it most). Australia fell to the Chinese as well. Which leaves Antarctica and some remote islands.

No, I have to fight for Conall. I close my eyes, imagining the ocean, and Conall's bright eyes; I Fade instantly.

Chapter Sixteen

Conall

I stand still, numb with shock. Mark is nowhere to be seen. Kaylin has broken the spell around us; instead she is in front of the last soldier alive, writing spells on him while Michael keeps him pinned. (Though the soldier does not struggle, doubtless realising the futility.) Soon Kaylin is done, and Michael drags him off somewhere else.

Mother finds me, and tells me to come inside. I obey without thinking. The butler serves me tea; I drink it without tasting it.

"Darling, don't be in such a state."

"They killed so many..."

"Don't be naïve—those were professional soldiers, and their job was to kidnap you, likely so that Party torturers could have their way with you. They deserved their deaths."

The logical part of me realises the truth in her words; yet another part of me—the one that saw the broken necks, the decimated skulls, the charred bodies—denies it. Most of all it denies that it was not a monster, but Mark, the man I love, who killed them.

Mother tuts, but does nothing more. It is not in her nature to be nurturing, or to show physical affection: that time is long past, if it ever existed. Instead she leaves me to myself. I realise that I need someone else to talk to—someone who understands.

I find Michael outside, standing perfectly still. The wind lashes him with sea spray, and the waves below are alive with violent energy; but still he stands, an immovable, implacable force. I always thought that power *acted*: it let you bend others to your will, to move mountains or cure the sick. But now I realise that power also means *free will*.

There is no point in exerting control over others if you are yourself controlled. He could have been just another one of Lucifer's lackeys, his power a convenient illusion.

"So that's what it's about?" I ask.

"Power, you mean?

"Of course."

He smiles darkly. "It would have been so easy. He promised me everything: riches, women, and of course, magic. That's the most seductive drug there is, you know. Humans may be greedy, but greed is nothing compared to being a god."

"Only you would have been a demigod, subject to his will as surely as humans would have been subject to yours."

"Precisely. Only I didn't see that, at the time. He played us all."

"Lucifer."

"The light-bearer; the beautiful, the all-knowing, the glorious and the tragic."

"Is that how you think of us, then?" I ask. I'd suspected he didn't approve of our relationship; I needed to confirm it.

"You don't honestly believe you're going to live happily ever after, do you? My son is not an angel, Conall. He cannot protect; only destroy. If I were you. I'd get out of here. Ask that witch to help you."

"I haven't fought for him just so I could give him up."

"He may be the death of you, in the end. Either that, or Lucifer will want to keep you alive: he will then eventually succeed in turning you."

"Into a demon?"

"Yes."

I gulp. "It's like vampirism, isn't it?"

He chuckles darkly. "A good analogy."

I shake my head. "You're wrong. Didn't *you* fall in love? Didn't *you* father Mark, and keep him safe all these years?"

"And looks where it's come to. My wife died, and my son is now like me."

I've had enough. I leave, finding my way to bed. I dream bad things, that night; I hunt humans, drink their blood, and revel in it.

✶✶✶

The morning sees me awake, though tired. Light comes in through the window, filtered by the ocean water; it seems strangely beautiful, and I regret being unable to appreciate it. I eat breakfast quickly, thanking the butler for his prompt service. Then I am outside, savouring the cool morning air, the tang of salt.

It doesn't surprise me when, out of the blue, Mark lands next to me.

"Should I ask where you were?"

"Flying," he answers simply.

"All night?"

"I went to America."

"No! Really? What did you see?"

"Miles and miles of ocean, and then... a wild place."

"Some people still live there, apparently."

"It looked so empty... And I thought: I can't take you there, Conall. You deserve better than that."

"I talked to your father," I admit.

He perks up. "Did he tell you anything?"

I sigh. "He doesn't think this will work."

"What? Us you mean?"

"Yes."

"And do you believe him?"

"No. I didn't fight for you just to give you up."

"It would be easier," he points out.

"Lots of things are easy; that doesn't mean we should do them."

"I always knew you were a philosopher, Conall."

"Yes, well," I say, and he notices my discomfort.

"What is it?"

"I didn't always know you were an axe murderer, either."

"So that's it." He looks away.

"You wanted to kill him, didn't you?" I ask. "Not because you should, but because you could."

"My dad was right about this much. It's part of me, Conall: the desire to kill. It's in my nature, like a cat catching mice."

"But do cats ever become friends with mice?"

"That's the million euro question, isn't it?"

I embrace him, suddenly, unable to contain it any longer. His hair is soft against my hands; his body is still and statuesque.

"Make me a millionaire, Mark."

"Oh, I think you already are, Conall."

Then he kisses me, deeply, and I forget about the world. There is only him: impossibly perfect, unholy, and yet still the man I know and love.

"Mark?"

"Yes?" he whispers.

"Take me flying."

✶

We fly, the wind whipping past my face. Below, we see the coast: it is rocky, the land jutting defiantly out against the sea. The sun shines autumn golds across the sky. The moment is so perfect, I wonder how it can be real.

"So this is what it means," I say.

"What?"

"To be divine."

He laughs. "Don't get ahead of yourself, Conall. We're all here on this Earth."

"Put me on the beach," I ask him. "So I can be on *terra.*"

"Your Latin again, am I right?"

"You should ask your father for help; he is a native speaker."

"Oh? Wow."

Moments later, we are on the sand, and I'm splashing him with water.

"Have some fun," I say.

He smiles. "Let me show you fun."

I watch as he takes to the air again, gains altitude, and then dives. He hits the water with a deafening boom. Seconds pass; the world holds its breath. Then he surfaces next to me, wet as a seal.

"I take it you enjoy the suicidal forms of fun," I remark.

"There are some things you can't experience when you're only human."

I laugh, though his words strike a chord. Would I be content with remaining human? Or would I always desire to be more? Because, in the end, a cat must catch mice.

Chapter Seventeen

Kaylin

They say that mad ideas are born of desperation, of other options attempted and extinguished. It would not be fair to say that I was desperate, or that I had tried everything; but even so, I believe this is the right course of action. We must kill Big Brother.

You must understand that attempting to kill the Grand Leader of the Party, and Ireland's head of state, is no easy task. Indeed, many would think me insane; I had not contemplated it until now, and for good reason. He is very, very well guarded. He claims to live in the Tower—the tallest building right in the centre of the Upper Quarter—but he is rarely there: ascertaining his location will require some spells.

But there is no other alternative. While he lives, he is a menace, not only to me and the people of this country, but also to Conall. We cannot protect him forever. Escape is possible—but foolish. The Spanish government is unlikely to take to them kindly (and for reasons I understand all too well).

We also have the best weapon we could ask for: not one, but two unstoppable demons.

I walk into our main antechamber. My men—the men I found, trained, and armed—stand tall, speaking quietly among themselves; they go silent when they see me. It's time to make my announcement.

★★★

"I have decided to kill Big Brother." They do not react to this; I continue speaking.

"This is no easy task, and it will require preparation. We will need to determine his locations; I expect Shadow, along with the hackers, to perform this task. I want to know what we'll face."

"Death, that's what," mutters Grumman, my lieutenant.

"Not long ago, I would have agreed with you, Grumman. However, we are not doing this alone; indeed, our main role will be to obtain information. The attack will be carried out by Mark and Michael."

"The demons?" he asks.

"The very same."

"Just the two of them?" he continues.

"You haven't seen them," Diana tells him.

"Of course, we need to convince them to help us," I point out.

"I don't think that will be difficult, Kaylin. Mark hates their guts; Michael also has every reason to want him and his Party gone."

There is more muttering, but I feel I have their acquiescence. My men have always been loyal. After all: power is the greatest motivator there is. The Party understands that all too well. Soon, they will learn another important lesson—that a snake cannot live without its head.

I order them to find information, and they get to work, moving like a well-oiled machine. I feel a surge of pride. I leave them to their work: I need to consult my own sixth sense.

✳✳✳

In that quiet corner, I go, the world around me suddenly becoming calm. Even in the midst of my plans, I am capable of finding that peculiar, tranquil place inside me—that thing which sees no barriers, and feels no fear. I close my eyes; the visions come.

A distant part of me remarks that I have never gazed upon the face of my enemy, despite all these years fighting him. He is, really, very pathetic: he is small, old, and sickly. Yet he inspires fear, and radiates a cold, calculating brutality. His generals and assorted lackeys are around him, taking orders.

The vision shifts, and I see my attack. The details are blurry, except one thing: the rune of a spell, burning clearly. Around it, shadows shift; above, the sky is pitch black, and darker than any ordinary night.

Soon the vision is over, and the world around me returns to its normal shape. Visions are always strange, peculiar things, but this one is clear: I need to find that spell.

The Book waits for me, as it always does, though this time it seems especially keen. Again I wonder if the thing is in some way sentient. Who created it? What was it doing in a remote mountain in Tibet? Despite all the answers it's given me, it remains shrouded in mystery.

"Now, you strange magical book, show me that spell," I mutter quietly. I find myself half-surprised to see that *indeed* the book opens, all by itself, to reveal a hitherto unseen spell.

I begin reading. It takes me a while to comprehend what exactly it does; it seems to be a "spell to conceal and enshadow" which is rather vague. What's clear is that it's not an ordinary spell, like Glamour: its effect is much wider than that, affecting everything within a large area.

"Having much luck?" I look up to see Diana. She seems a little troubled, and sports a bandage on her left arm.

"I've discovered a rather intriguing spell, though I'm uncertain as to what exactly it does."

"What's the use of a spell you don't understand? Besides, from what you tell me, you need to have a good idea of a spell in order to cast it."

"A good idea, yes, but not necessarily a perfect one. Magic has a mind of its own, sometimes."

She shrugs. "Try it; there's no other way."

So I stand, raise my hand, and focus myself on the task at hand. My finger tingles as the power of the spell acts, forming a glowing blue rune. It hangs for a moment, and then disappears. Nothing seems to happen.

"Well, that was pointless," she says.

Moments later, one of my men comes running in, looking frightened.

"Mistress?"

"Yes John?"

"All our electronics are down. We think—"

"It's my spell." Then I raise my hand, and cast the spell again, though this time I make sure to draw it incorrectly. It glows blue, then shatters. Realising what's going on, the tech-nician takes out his com phone—it's working.

"Well, Mistress, I raise my hat."

"That's a hell of a spell," Diana remarks. "How far does it go?"

"We'll find out soon," I say.

✶

The spell knocked out the entire city's electronics, and most of Ireland's too. It acci-dentally harmed our own efforts to locate Big Brother, though further efforts—and a few hints from my visions—eventually took care of that. Now it's time to convince the most important people in our plan: Mark and Michael.

The latter is now in our Dublin base, standing in front of me, eyebrows raised.

"This is quite impressive, witch. A base in the beast's belly, and concealed so well by Glamour, even I did not 'spot' it, as you say in English."

"I'm glad you like it," I say, "though that's not why I asked for you."

"I thought as much. So, why *did* you bring me here?"

"We have been able to ascertain the location of Big Brother; we want you, and Mark, to kill him."

He laughs. "That's it?"

"This is no easy task! We would never have dreamed of attempting it."

"That is because you are mortal. We are not."

"So that's why you should help us."

"I don't think you understand: I am perfectly happy to kill this Big Brother. He and his Party sent my son into the underclass. But he is a distraction; we have worse things to worry about."

In truth, I had not really thought of that. The Party is everything I strived against—to destroy them seems like the ultimate victory. And it's a victory I can't let slip past my fingers.

"You may be immortal, and we are strong, but Conall is neither of those things. You've seen how your son looks at him. Do you think he would ever forgive you if the Party killed Conall?"

The demon sighs, looking very human at that moment—very much like a father. "I tried to separate them, but... it can't be done. I of all people should know. So yes: I will help you kill this maniac."

"Excellent," I say. A small cheer breaks out from my men, nearby.

"This just leaves Mark," Diana points out.

"I can kill Big Brother on my own," Michael points out.

"Maybe," Diana continues, "but I don't think Mark will want to miss out on the fun."

I sense that she would have liked to join in as well, but that her injury has made her more cautious. I place my hand on her good arm, directing her out of the main chamber.

"Are you OK?"

"My hand is fine, the wound will heal." She speaks with an air of nonchalance, and I give her a look.

"Okay, it could have been a lot worse," she admits grudgingly.

"You're not immortal, Diana. Not like them. You can't just ride into battle; your fire can destroy anything or anyone, but a stray bullet will still kill you."

She sighs. "You've always protected me, Kaylin, especially during my worst moments. But this is war now: you've just ordered the Party leader and head of state dead. This isn't clandestine operations, lurking in the shadows stuff anymore.

"And in war, we will always be in danger."

I am left stunned. Not because Diana spoke her mind—she always does—but because of how wise she sounds. She sees things I cannot, even with the gift of Sight.

Chapter Eighteen

Mark

"Mark? We have something to tell you." It's Kaylin who speaks.

Me and Conall are on a sofa, making the best of the underwater views. It doesn't surprise me to see Kaylin, Diana, and my dad in here; they've become regular visitors, like we are. The butlers don't even bother to ask Sianna if they can come in.

"Yes?" I ask. Something tells me this is important.

"Me and my team have been able to discover where Big Brother lives."

"In the Tower?"

"No, he's rarely there. He is in a secret location in Ireland right now."

"So?"

"We want to kill him."

Time seems to stop, and then restart at double tempo.

"Say that again?"

"You and Michael are immortal; I have also discovered a new spell. We did not have the ability to attack him before."

"And now you do."

I can't believe I didn't realise it before. Big Brother always seemed so far away—an invisible menace, ruining my life without even knowing it. But now he knows me, and I know him. It's time to settle the score.

"I'm in," I say.

"I thought as much," Kaylin mutters.

"Mark? Are you sure?" Conall asks.

"Come on! I know that, for you, Big Brother doesn't mean what it does to me. You didn't grow up with life in the underclass. You didn't face separation from your family. You don't *hate* him, Conall."

"That's what I'm afraid of."

"Why? They can't kill me."

"No—not that. I mean... you hating him."

"Some people deserve to be hated."

Suddenly, Sianna interrupts the conversation.

"Oh hello darlings! What are you all doing here?"

"Sianna," Kaylin begins, "it's best you don't know—"

"Too late. I overheard you. For a witch spy-queen, dear, you are very sloppy."

Kaylin sighs. "In that case—"

"I am onboard. I cannot protect my son from the Party any longer. My contacts cannot contradict the man himself; it only stands to reason, therefore, that we should get rid of him."

Sianna's attitude to these things always amazes me: she's so matter of fact about it all. I can see why Conall doesn't like her. I love her.

"Then it is decided," Kaylin says. "Mark, Michael, I will contact you when the time comes. And it will be soon, rest assured. Now, make the best of things." With that, she turns heel.

Conall touches my arm. "She's right, you know. I think you should tell your uncle."

Uncle. I'd almost forgot about him.

✳✳✳

I fly over the city, trusting my Glamour to keep me safe from prying eyes. (I'd gotten very good at it.) I pass the Refuse; the place where I spent my teenage years, an outcast from my own family, and even from myself. I thought I was a failure—even my own father had abandoned be. How little I knew!

I make a flyover of the large, ugly building where I'd lived with the drug-dealers, and killed Finn. The place where it all began. I wonder if they're still there—the drug dealers, I mean. I even consider going in there and killing them. They'd been all too keen to believe Finn, beat me up, and throw me to the scarabs. But then: what's the point?

Besides, I'd ended up meeting Conall. Surely that was worth it?

I keep flying, finding my way to the Middle Quarter, and my uncle's house. I land in front of the garden—the roses are still beautiful—and knock on the door. He opens it immediately.

"Mark," he says simply.

"Hello uncle."

"I heard from your father."

"Really?" I ask.

"He came to visit me, after he'd found you. I understand you've had quite the adventure."

"Yeah."

"Well come in—let me make you some tea."

So I find myself facing him, both of us sitting on the white sofa. The sun shines a golden light outside; I see the first leaves of autumn in the garden. I wonder how something so beautiful can exist in a world so terrible. Conall would have an answer. Me? I just make the best of life: it's what I've always done.

"There's a reason I'm here," I begin.

"I gather as much. Conall must keep you busy, as must your father."

"I'm going to kill him—Big Brother, I mean."

"You can do that?"

"I'm immortal, and Kaylin knows where he is. Did my father mention her?"

"He did say something about some witch. I didn't even know they existed; I'm a doctor, not some mystical scribe."

"Believe me, I was as surprised as you are. But you haven't said anything about..."

"Killing Big Brother? Go for it. God knows, the bastard deserves it."

For a time, there is silence. Then, I get up.

"Wish me luck," I say.

"Oh, I will. But I don't think you need it." He seems strangely nostalgic then—as if remembering my father.

Still, I don't have time for nostalgia. I head outside, opening my wings; the sky greets me with a kiss of air.

✶✶✶

I find Conall back at the mansion. I remember, as if by magic, the first day we met: how I'd taken my clothes off in front of him, not knowing, but suspecting, his reaction. The place had seemed huge to me; the wealth, insane. Now I find it a bit silly. I evade the cameras, the guards, and the androids, my Glamour hiding me from all. I sneak in through the back door, and find myself in Conall's bedroom.

"Had trouble sneaking in?" he asks. He's sitting on the bed; the light throws him into silhouette.

"No. I'm pretty good at this Glamour thing."

"To have that kind of power…" He shakes his head. "They're nothing compared to you."

"The Party, you mean?"

"Yeah."

"They'll deserve what's comin' for dem, den?"

He smiles at my Fallen accent. "You should tell my father," he says suddenly.

"What? And say I'm going to kill his boss?"

"Tell him everything."

"Why?"

"It may seem strange to you, but my father is not that powerful. There are much bigger fish in this sea—not least Lucifer and his demons. Much as I dislike my father, I don't desire him dead. He needs to know if he is to survive."

"Fine. How will he react?"

"We'll have to find out."

So he leads me across the hall, down a storey, and to his father's study. He knocks on the door. We wait in silence, but not for long; in a few moments, the door opens.

The man behind it seems pretty ordinary to me. His hair is greying at the edges; there are no smile lines on his face. He raises an eyebrow when he sees me—a gesture I recognise as being very Conall, despite the obvious difference between the two.

"I take it you're the boy who put my son through so much trouble?" Again the resemblance is uncanny.

"I am."

"I don't know what to make of you: a Fallen boy, right?"

"In more ways than you can imagine."

"Well, come in. I want to meet you, at least."

We walk into his office. The place is dark; there's wood panelling everywhere, and even some velvet. The place is actually pretty small, though the tall ceiling makes it seem larger.

"Father, Mark has something to tell you. Something very important."

"What, you killed someone to get out of prison?"

"I did, actually. He was the Party Commissioner for Crime and Justice."

He freezes. "You can't be serious?"

"Oh, I am." I unfurl my wings: he stares at them, unable to believe it.

"You see, I'm a demon."

"This has to be a joke," he declares, "albeit in poor taste. Son, I'm disappointed in you. Now, I'm calling—"

I lift him in the air, though without moving. He hangs there; and for once, he looks afraid.

"You won't," I say, "and believe me, I can do far worse than this. Now, here's the deal: I am a demon, and I am going to kill Big Brother."

He's in shock, though still listening. "You must also know that I am not the only one. There are others—in the pay of Lucifer, not free, like me. You have worse to worry about than the Party."

I let him go. He holds a hand on the table, unsteady on his feet.

"Son?" he asks.

"Yes, father?"

"Remind me not to ask about your boyfriend, ever again."

"Yes, father."

✷✷✷

"Was I too harsh?" I ask him, once we're back.

"No, actually. Father admires power—always has. He will thus admire you, and take your advice very seriously indeed."

"Glad to hear it."

"But there's something else," he says, and I hear a catch in his voice.

"Yeah?"

"All this talk of death saddens me. I want life."

"Does that mean what I think it means, Conall?"

He smiles, and I see the seduction written plainly on it. "Oh yes."

I will remember that night for what it was: passionate, almost desperate, his body craving mine like a drug. I will remember the way he looked at me, like it was the last time he'd see me. And I didn't know it then—but he was right.

Chapter Nineteen

Kaylin

It is time; it is the day. My men have acquired Big Brother's location; they have determined the scope of his defences; and they are ready. Michael is at my side: he looks agitated, pensive even. I blame it on the excitement. As for Mark, he is together with Conall, both of them standing together on the sea platform where we've decided to meet.

"Time to kick ass," Mark says.

This elicits a raised eyebrow from me, but a chuckle from his father.

"If you say so, son. What about Conall?"

"What about me?" the boy in question asks.

"Will you watch? Will we have to protect you somehow?" Michael continues.

"I... I'm fine without watching, thank you." He sounds slightly perturbed.

"But if we're gone, someone might want to target you—either the Party or Lucifer's agents."

"I believe I can help," I interject.

Conall smiles. "Your shield spell again, Kaylin?"

"Indeed. Come with me."

I take him to Sianna's living room—she briefly takes note of us—and explain things to him. "I will spell this room, as it is much easier to cover a cubic volume. Ask your mother to stay with you while we conduct our operation."

"I doubt she'll agree to that, and I doubt anyone wants her dead anyway."

I sigh. He's probably right. "In that case, whatever you do: don't leave this place."

"Got it."

✶✶✶

And so me, Diana, members of my team, and the two demons board our Q-car. We fly high but slow, keeping all of our stealth technologies activated. Michael seems a little bemused by it all: the holographic projections, the blinking lights, the screens, the vertiginous height. Mark seems awestruck in comparison.

"Wow," he exclaims.

"Believe me, I had the same reaction," Diana replies.

"How long have you guys had this thing?"

"Less than a year—it was one of Kaylin's accomplishments." I smile wistfully at the memory.

"It's amazing," he continues. "And we're so high! Even I've never flown this high."

Still, his wonder does not last long. Soon my driver is bringing the Q-car into a descent; the ground gradually materialises before us. We park the Q-car in a secluded wood, and get out. The air smells fresh; the world is ripe for the taking.

I know that Big Brother is not far from here, though we've avoided getting *too* close, in fear of setting off alarms. Our Q-car has impressive stealth capabilities—including invisibility—but the Party has access to an excellent array of sensors. Nor have I ever been able to Glamour Q-cars; the magic seems to resist attaching to it.

"So it all comes down to this," Mark says.

His comment brings forth memories.

✶✶✶

Why does an Owner-class woman become a revolutionary? In the beginning, I had no reason to hate the Party: their regime benefited me personally, as my family's wealth could testify. Waxing lyrical about equality is all well and good, but in the end, that only happens to other people.

Two things changed me, and turned me into what I am now. The first were my visions. They began when I was sixteen: at first they were vague, mysterious, and seemed like madness to me. I tried to ignore them; I tried to pretend they didn't exist—that I was just like everyone else. But I see now that I wasn't like everyone else, and that Fate had other plans for me.

The visions allowed me to see what grotesque things the Party did, not only to Fallen, drug addicts and prostitutes, but also to political dissidents and whistleblowers.

The second reason is Diana: as a Technical, she is very different from me. Work is a reality for her. Meeting her brought a new perspective on my life: it taught me that, for many people on this island, life isn't rosy or easy. And even she lived in a different world from what the Workers and the Fallen were put through.

∗∗∗

I return to the present. The past is the past; it makes us who we are, but it does not determine the future. That rests on the present.

"You both understand the basics of the plan?" I ask them.

"You get intel, disable their communications, and we go in and kill the bleedin' fuckers." Trust Mark to be blunt about these things.

"I believe I do understand it," Michael says, more cautiously, "though forgive me—since I am no expert—how do you plan on destroying their communications? I've been on

Earth long enough to realise that government equipment is better protected than that."

I only smile. "See, and learn."

I raise my hand, and concentrate, letting my magic take hold. My finger glows blue—something I've learned is visible only to those with magic of their own. I form the sprawling, unfamiliar lines of the rune. It hangs in mid-air, and then... changes. The proportions seem subtly altered, the geometry a new one.

The hairs on my skin stand up. I feel the spell's influence growing, emanating a strange power. Before our eyes, the sky changes: it darkens, the sun blotted out as if by ink. The world around us gains a pallid shade, as if illuminated by a permeant greyness.

"I don't think that was meant to happen," Diana says.

"Something has gone wrong," I agree. I raise my hand again, attempting to dispel it.

But nothing happens; the spell refuses to obey my command. I feel a queasiness settle in my stomach.

"What is this?" Michael asks. We both watch as he attempts to form a fireball—and fails. His blue demon fire only fizzles uselessly.

"Kaylin, I can't use my magic either," Diana says. "That spell does a lot more than we bargained for."

"I agree, but... I don't know what to do." I've never felt so helpless in a long time. My own magic, and I seem unable to control it.

"Let's get back to base, and you can consult the book." Trust Diana to keep her wits.

We go back to the Q-car, but our driver gives us a panicked look.

"It's gone. All of it," he says.

"The electronics you mean?"

"Power, control, navigation, weapons, stealth..."

I realise now the full gravity of our predicament. In casting the Spell of Silencing, I had hoped to disable the Party's weapons, allowing our magic to gain full advantage; but instead I have weakened both of us, and lost control of the situation.

"We need to call this off," I say.

"No," Mark says. We all turn to look at him.

He unfurls his wings, and takes to the air. He circles above us, like a supernatural bird of prey. Then he dives; we drop to the ground as he collides with the earth, the resulting explosion shattering our ear drums.

Through the dust, he rises, smiling. "I don't need my magic to kill them. I'm still stronger than they are."

I wanted to tell him to no; to say that it was too dangerous, too out of my control. But did I not say we needed to be unpredictable? That our enemies were one step ahead of us? In the end, though, it wasn't about that—Mark wanted them dead, and nothing was going to stand in his way.

Chapter Twenty

Mark

We like to pretend that we do good; that we're not selfish, not interested in power—that we act with the motivation of a hero and the methods of a saint. I never believed it. Conall always talked about philosophy, and poetry: the ethics of war or the virtue of Greek heroes in the *Iliad*. But I know we're just human (and I include the demons). In the end, I only care about one thing: revenge.

Me and my dad walk to the secret location; Kaylin and Diana have stayed behind, useless without their magic. I don't care: this is about me and the Big Man. Our destination is actually pretty innocuous—a small concrete bunker, like the ones that used to exist in the early days of the mutants. If not for Kaylin, we would have no idea there's a whole underground network below it.

They told us we should expect resistance the moment we got in sight. But nothing happens; the place is deathly quiet, and the sky above is deathly black. It's as if we've stepped into an alternate dimension. I imagine Hell is like this—though I don't have time to ask dad. I don't think he'd like the question anyway.

"The witch is right, you know," he says. "Something made her magic act in that way."

"I understood it's a new spell and she hasn't got the hang of it yet."

"Maybe," he agrees, though he's not convinced.

"Anyway," I point out, "it's not like we're at a disadvantage. Those Party bastards can't do a thing without their tech."

"But we *are* at a disadvantage," he says, "because the situation is out of our control."

He doesn't have time to say anything more, because at that point, a voice challenges us.

"Halt! Who are you? Who gave you authorisation to be here?" The voice is male, though I can't tell where it's coming from.

I pretend to go along. "We've been ordered here. We can show you our papers."

"Come here," he orders. A man steps out from the bunker; I notice several more behind him, armed with rifles. I can't see any drones, which are much stronger guards than human soldiers. And obviously don't work because of Kaylin's spell.

We walk up to him; he raises his hand, expecting official documents. Instead he gets a punch to the head. He crumples to the floor without a sound.

The other guys cock their rifles, but they're simply too slow: my father breaks their necks instantly.

"Well, that wasn't much of a fight," I say.

"They are weakened without their drones, yes, but this is just the beginning." He points to a door inside the bunker. He drives a fist through it; the metal screeches, but the door holds. It takes several blows until it fails.

"Likely one of their alloys," I point out.

"Tough," he agrees.

We walk inside. The place is mostly bare concrete: there are some weapons in various places on the walls, and a couple of inactive drones. They stand still—silent sentinels, Conall would say. I just think they're creepy.

It takes a few attempts to locate the trap door, and to punch through it. A wide, dark space opens below us. Cold air seeps through; I shiver, even though the cold doesn't make me uncomfortable in a physical sense.

"Welcome to Hell," I whisper.

He smiles darkly. "You're closer to the truth than you imagine."

Then he goes down the rabbit hole, and I follow.

⋆⋆⋆

The world underneath is very different from the one above. It's dark except for a series of lights inset into the concrete; they give off a pale white light. I imagine they're running on backup power. (Though what the hell do I know? I'm not a witch.) Eventually the tunnel, which is almost sheer and vertical, mellows out into a gradient.

My father puts a hand on me, and hides me against the wall. A handful of soldiers pass next to us, somehow failing to notice us. They look like they're in a hurry.

"Without our Glamour," he says, "we cannot simply walk through here and locate Big Brother. We need information."

"You're right," I agree. I never imagined that Big Brother would be running away from me when I meet him, but now I realise that's the likeliest outcome. He wouldn't be alive this long if he didn't know not to stare death in the face.

"Normally I would be able to obtain the information with my magic," he says, "but the traditional method will have to do."

"Torture, you mean?"

"Yes."

I gulp. Here I am, ready to kill, but not to inflict pain.

"Let me handle it. I need you to distract them."

He explains his plan; I nod, and get ready. Soon I'm tearing through the place, making a huge racket. A group of soldiers then arrives, but I don't fight them: instead I simply push through them, like a freight train. In the ensuing chaos, Michael grabs one of them.

I follow him, both of us moving like wraiths. We find a side-room—another weapons cache—and I stand guard next to the door. Michael has his hands wrapped around the soldier's throat.

He explains the situation to the man in very simple, and very chilling terms. "Good day, human. We are looking for your Big Brother." He spreads his wings wide, and engulfs him, like a mother bird taking care of its chick.

"If you don't tell me where he is, well... things won't be pretty."

Neither of us expects the answer.

"I'll tell ya where he is. I don't like him, not one bit."

My dad raises an eyebrow, and the soldier continues. "He's not in the main secure room, but in the smaller one just below it. You can't get to it from the main—you have to take the 22nd corridor." He continues sprouting details, and we nod, taking it in.

"Why are you telling us this?" I ask him. "You're a feckin' soldier—you're supposed to be loyal."

"Yeah, well, he's not been treatin' us so well. Besides, this guy looks pretty fierce," he says, referring to my dad.

"Don't you understand..." My father seems confused, and I don't blame him. If I were confronted with the supernatural, I would be in denial as well.

"Let him go," I say. Michael releases the soldier; he tips his hat, and disappears into the tunnels.

"Humans are peculiar," he says.

"You've not been here long enough," I mumble.

Shaking his head, dad leaves, and I follow him, returning to the mission at hand.

✱✱✱

The tunnels are silent. There are no alarms, no troop movements, nothing. I realise that without their technology—without radios, microphones, cameras—they really are in the Dark Ages. It's only once we follow the soldiers' instructions, and find ourselves in front of the second secure room, that we meet real resistance.

You can always tell professional soldiers from amateurs. After all: why would anyone else be here? We don't wear uniform, don't carry weapons, and don't follow protocol. We can only be one thing—a threat. They start shooting the moment we get near them.

Not that it does them much good. The bullets feel more like stings than lethal projectiles; it makes killing them only too easy. Their training, armour, and armament just doesn't prepare them for a fight against supernatural beings like us. After a few seconds, there is nothing left except blood and silence.

"Do you think he's heard us by now?" I wonder.

"The shooting might have alerted him that something's up, but I doubt he comprehends the scale of what he's up against."

"Do you think we should show him?" I ask dad, pointing to the big metal door where the second secure room must be.

"Be my guest, as they say."

This one is even tougher than the door above ground. My first punch only dents it; my second dents it a bit more, and it's only when I shoulder charge it that the alloy gives way. (I imagine it could have survived a nuclear blast. Too bad it didn't survive me.)

The room beyond is straight out of my nightmares. Holographic projectors and computer monitors are everywhere, though they are dark, disabled by the power of the spell. Drones—some in designs I've never seen before—are scattered across the place, like pale blue statues. The air is cold; the light is dim, barely allowing even my senses to penetrate deeper into the gloom.

But my eyes are better than a human's, and I do see the figure perched at the very end of the antechamber.

I expected Big Brother to be, well, big. I always saw him as a hulking, shadowy figure —like a vampire or a member of the Russian mafia. Instead, the man that stands before me is short, fragile, and *old*. His hair is pale enough to resemble snow; his skin is folded with numerous wrinkles.

It's only the eyes that scare me. They're bright blue, full of wicked cunning and inhuman brutality.

"So it's you," he says, not sounding surprised.

"Yeah, it's me. I'm the Dark Angel, come to take your feckin' arse where it belongs."

He only laughs. The sound makes me cold: it's like icicles scraping broken glass.

"Oh, my. They told me you were a Fallen. A wounded puppy, ready to bite the hand that feeds it."

"You little cunt," I say. "The only thing you and your regime ever gave me was pain, brutality, and contempt."

My dad interrupts us. "Who told you about him?"

"Oh, I can't possibly reveal that," Big Brother responds with a chuckle.

"What if I make you?" I ask. Before he can blink, I'm across the room, my hand gripping his throat.

To my surprise, he ignores the pain, and stabs me with me a syringe. I raise an eyebrow at the liquid that pools across my feet, burning through my T-shirt and shoes.

"Acid? Really?"

"It's the best I can do," he offers. "They didn't warn me that you were going to disable all of our technology. Though, then again, I ordered the army to take you out—and the only thing they succeeded in doing was losing two Q-cars."

"I'm going to make you suffer, you know," I tell him.

"Go on. I don't care."

"Why? Are you insane?"

"Many have thought so, but they were wrong: I am entirely sane. Evil, perhaps," he adds with another one of those laughs, "but evil is very sane, I assure you."

"They promised you, didn't they?" Michael asks at that moment.

"Promised me what?" Big Brother asks.

"That you'd die and go to Hell. There, you'd be treated like a king."

Big Brother giggles, but he sounds worried this time.

"How did you know that?"

"Because I was one of them."

"Ah." Somehow, that makes him nervous. "They told me there was only one of you, and that he was barely half-demon. They told me I could kill you."

"They lied," my father tells him. I can see something that looks a lot like pity in those eyes of his.

"Come on, son. We need to leave. Lucifer expected something like this, and, well, I don't know what he's planning."

"What? Do you think I can just leave him alive?" I shout, anger boiling through me.

My dad only shrugs. With a cry of rage, I hurl Big Brother across the room. His body collides with a concrete wall; we hear his neck snap. His broken corpse falls, limp, to the floor. I'd done it—I'd killed a dictator, saved Ireland from tyranny, and got my revenge.

But it doesn't make me relieved; it doesn't bring me happiness. Some things are more important than revenge. And I feel that, somehow, I've made a mistake.

Chapter Twenty One

Conall

I realised something was wrong immediately. I felt it like a shockwave: a debilitating wave of energy. I saw the shield spell around me flicker and go out. But did I do anything? Did I run, hide, warn them that something was wrong?

That's what annoys me most, you see. I know something is wrong—and yet there's nothing I can do. My com phone, along with all other electronics, is down. I try Kaylin's enchanted medallion, shaking it in frustration; but it's as useless as her shield spell. And where would I run? It would only make it more difficult for Mark and Kaylin to find me, and I doubt I could fool anyone if they came looking.

So I pace around my room, frustration coiled through me. Everything is beyond my control, my fate in the hands of impossibly powerful external forces.

In the end, I try reading something. It's been a long time since I opened a physical book: I'd forgotten the experience—the fragrant smell of printed paper, the rustling of pages, the solidity of a a physical object. I barely even follow the story (a romance of some sort?) but I am, at least, doing something.

The minutes pass, and eventually an hour ticks by. My worry mounts; I feel it in the pit of my stomach, gnawing at my bones and whispering dark things into my subconscious.

I almost miss that tell-tale feeling, ascribing it to my own paranoia. But I simply could not mistake it—I had, after all, become familiar with it. The sense of darkness in the air; the faint smell of hellfire and tobacco. The charged energy that surrounds them.

Demons.

★★★

I know I can't fight them. I'd seen firsthand what they could do against armed and trained soldiers supported by the best of modern technology; it hadn't been pretty. Running is out of the question—they'll see me, and swoop down on me like vultures. So, I hide. Luckily, my mother's house is enormous, and crammed full of nooks and crannies. I find an enormous storage room, and climb to the top shelf, where I sit still and try not to breathe. A grill lets me see out into the main living area.

Like shadows, they slither in, silent and strong. I count four of them—way too many. I wonder if they can hear my heart beating.

"He's not here," says a male voice.

"He must be," replies a female voice. "Keep looking."

I wonder how I ever got used to beings like them. Darkness oozes from them in invisible tentacles, cloying the air. Had I ever considered it attractive? The power of their evil; the temptation of their sculptured forms and seductive smiles?

But then, neither Mark nor his father are anything like them. Mark loves me. These beings aren't capable of love: they're capable of seduction, yes, and sex no doubt, but love?

I hear the creak of a door opening, and spot the dark form of a demon below me. I close my eyes; I try to conceal myself, imagining an invisible cloak around me. Kaylin had her Glamour, as did Mark, and Shadow could fool anyone. But I'm not blessed with magic. What can I do?

To my surprise, the demon leaves. "He's not here—we need to look elsewhere."

"It'll take too long, you fool," the female voice responds. "We've already looked through the other mansion. For some reason, we can't Fade, and flying is too slow."

So whatever spell had taken out the shield had clearly also affected them. Does that mean that Mark can't Fade either?

"Flying is not that slow," the other demon says. "The Barrier won't drive us back yet."

"Really? Because it makes me feel sick."

"I've been to Earth before—trust me. And who appointed you boss, Adrianne?"

"I'm the strongest one here."

"You're also the least experienced. Now come on, let's go."

They begin to leave, and I let myself breathe a little. Hopefully, if they look elsewhere...

At that moment, my foot hits something, and I fall. I grab the next shelf, arresting the drop, but the damage is already done.

"Did you hear that?"

I curse myself. Then, I start to pray. If there was such a thing as divine power out there, I needed its help now.

✶✶✶

Mark

We leave the bunker, and find ourselves in the outside world again. I would say that I'm glad to be away from the place—it gave me the creeps. But on the other hand, the outside world seems to be no better: the sky is black as pitch, the spell still strong. And I feel something worse than the cold disgust of being in that dungeon.

I started this day with fire and vengeance. Now I'm afraid. I don't want to admit it, because to admit fear is to give it power over you. (I'd learned that a long time ago.) Still, it's true. I can feel it—something is happening around me. Here's another lesson I learned as a Fallen: just because something is invisible, it doesn't mean it can't hurt you. In fact, the invisible threats are the worst.

We find Kaylin and Diana where we left them. I can see the questions on their faces.

"He's dead," I state simply.

A ragged cheer passes between them, though they can tell there's more to it than that.

"But," I continue, "Lucifer's agents manipulated him to believe he could kill me. They must have anticipated we'd do this."

"Lucifer is cunning like that," Michael says. "Which is why I'm worried."

Kaylin is thinking, her eyes closed in what I assume is a vision. She shakes her head.

"Events have become out of my control," she says. "And I cannot See, thanks to this damn spell. I'm sorry, Mark, but I can't help you until I find out how to reverse it. Michael, can you fly me back?"

"Yes, but only one of you. Normally, I would be able to lift you both into the air."

"How so?" Kaylin asks curiously.

"Demons don't actually fly with their wings, contrary to what you assume. Our wings are the embodiment of our power, yes, but we fly by manipulating air and gravity. Without your spell, I could have made you fly without lifting a finger. With it, however, my magic is capable of acting only on me."

"So the spell does not actually nullify magic, only limits its ability to influence the external world," Kaylin muses.

"Something like that, yes. Your kind of magic is mostly beyond me, I admit."

"So let me get this straight," I say with frustration. "You need both of us to fly you two back."

"No." Kaylin shakes her head. "Diana, you will have to stay here until I unravel the spell; then you can take the Q-car. Mark, you should go back to Conall."

"Is he in trouble?" I ask.

"I... don't know, unfortunately. But something tells me he is."

With that, Michael wraps his arms around Kaylin—she winces a little—and swoops into the air. Me and Diana share a look. There's sympathy in her eyes, and maybe pity too.

I unfurl my wings, and take to the air. I have no time for pity. If Conall needs me, I'll be there.

✦✦

I hurl myself through the air, determined to reach him quickly. The sky is a pool of infinite black; and I'm like a comet, casting light wherever go. Granted, comets are supposed to be one of God's omens—and I'm anything but angelic. Still, I feel like an angel, ready to bring salvation to the weak, and death for the wicked.

The feeling doesn't last. Soon, I'm descending, and my heart sinks with me. There are four demons—and two are holding Conall.

✦✦

Kaylin

I want to burn it. I want to rip its pages from its spine; to mutilate it and declare it worthless.

I don't, of course. I need the Book. And besides, it's me I should be blaming: it was my responsibility to understand the magic and what it did. Now, I can only hope that the Book will take pity on me, and get me out of my hole.

Even before I reach it, it flips open, the words re-arranging themselves on the page.

(I've never actually *seen* it do this, and somehow I feel it represents the gravity of the situation.) I begin reading immediately. The spell, thankfully, seems simple: it reverses other spells. The Book explains that not all spells can be so reversed, specifically, "Those Spells cast by Great Magic, are to be undone only with Great Magic."

Reading further, I realise that the spell I so ignorantly cast is in fact not Great Magic: "Great Magic is defined by Sacrifice, Foresight, and Fulfilment."

"Any luck?" Michael asks.

"Yes," I say. I don't bother explaining more; instead, I lift myself up, close my eyes, and try to cast the spell. Nothing happens.

"Kaylin?" he asks, with concern.

The Book flips pages audibly, and I sigh, getting back to reading. I should learn my lesson: real magic is complicated and hard. I must read both carefully and comprehensively; that is what the Book is trying to teach me.

The next page isn't about a spell per se, but rather magical theory. It all seems arcane, until I get to this: "A Spell, excepting special kinds of Great Magic, does not exist independently of the caster; indeed, to act, a Spell must be part of the caster's conscious awareness."

"Michael?" I ask.

"Yes?"

"You mentioned that you thought my spell acts to block magic from acting externally, but not internally?"

"That's the only way it makes sense."

Realisation dawns on me.

"Of course!"

Again I close my eyes, but this time, I don't try to form the spell in the air; rather, I try to form it *in my mind*. I picture the swirling shapes and lines, and burn the outline into that strange, subconscious part of me.

The spell acts, moving through me like a purifying elixir. Clarity is injected into the world. Even the sun comes out, flooding the room with light. It feels good to have my magic back.

At that moment, all our electronics come back online. What we hear makes us go cold.

"Let him go!"

✦✦✦

Telepathy comes in useful at the most unexpected of times, and Michael easily under-stood my unspoken order: *Go get Diana*. He Fades immediately, and I focus on their con-versation.

"Now, Mark, we can't let him go that easily. We want something in return."

I fumble for the electronic switches, and a holographic projection comes into view. It's as I expected: the computer system is connected to Conall's com phone, and the boy has managed to turn it on. Smart kid.

"If you don't let him go, I'll send all of you back where you came from."

"We know you're powerful, and we all know you're not *that* powerful."

I realise that Mark isn't thinking straight. He's angry; his boyfriend is in danger. He should be stalling for time, not provoking them, or being a braggart.

"Good day, gentlemen," I say.

For a brief moment, I relish in their confusion.

"Who is this? Where are you? Is this magic?" one of them asks.

I suspect they don't know what a com phone is or how technology works, so I go along with it.

"I am a witch, and this is one of my rather trivial pieces of magic." All true. "I have an interest in the boy you are holding, and I think we should settle our differences."

"We don't negotiate with your kind."

"Oh, but you may have to. I have the capability to destroy you."

"Prove it."

That would not be easy, but at that moment, Michael and Diana arrive.

"You fools!" we hear one of them say. "It's his phone."

The line cuts off, and I quickly brief the two on my plan.

"So you expect us to fight them?" Diana asks, with fire in her eye.

"It will come to that, but I hope to give you an advantage."

"We're risking a lot on you, Kaylin," Michael says.

"You're just going to have to trust me."

They Fade away, and I focus on my task. The Book actually floats towards me, opening itself to a page full of text. I don't have time to ponder this new miracle; I only read. They think I know everything—Diana, Mark, even Michael. But the truth is, I know very little.

I have no plan waiting in store. I'm just going to have to hope the Book knows more than I do.

Chapter Twenty Two

Conall

I thought the worst part about being caught and held hostage would be the fear. But no: it's being so utterly helpless that really grates. I'm worse than useless; I'm a liability, putting Mark and Kaylin in danger.

Two demons are holding me. One is male, and built like a tank. The other is female—a dainty little thing, with light black hair, and vaguely Middle-Eastern in appearance. (Apparently her name is Aisha.) She looks weak, but her hands have the strength of iron.

And boy, I hoped I'd be glad to see Mark when he came flying down: an Avenging Angel, come to rescue me from the forces of darkness. Yet instead I'd felt terrible dread, and agony. Whatever their plan is, he's fallen right into it.

Then I realised that my com phone should be working, and I surreptitiously turned it on. Kaylin's voice surprised me, and brought me hope: if anyone could get me out of this, it would be her.

"Where is it?" they ask me.

They soon find the phone, and crush it in their hands. It doesn't matter: Michael and Diana are now here.

"Maybe *I* can't kill all of you," Mark points out, "but the *three* of us can."

The demons share a look, and the male demon takes his grip off me, joining his companions. The female demon, however, seems to grip me harder. Bitch.

"Don't be a fool," the demon I recognise to be the leader speaks up. "We have your lover. And we can kill him easily."

"What do you want?" Diana asks.

They look at her curiously, realising she is human, and yet that she's powerful in ways no human can be.

Then they turn their attention back to Mark.

"We want *you*, Mark. Join us."

"It'll be a cold day in Hell."

"Stranger things have happened."

"Let me tell you *this*, you fuck-face. The Earth belongs to people, not demons. My friends can destroy you."

"You seem to be forgetting the small matter of your boyfriend."

The demon twists my arm then, and agony splinters down into the bone. I bite back my voice, but they all hear me whimper.

Mark's reaction is instantaneous. My eyes can't even follow the punch, but it hits the other demon like a wrecking ball. His eyes stare into me, his head twisted backwards by the force of the blow.

Then he smiles; I shudder. There's an audible snap as his neck twists back into shape.

"That was unwise of you, but can be forgiven. Nothing has changed."

I want to say something, but fear holds me back. They won't kill me—I'm sure of that. If only Mark will call their bluff...

At that moment, I feel it: a dark, impossibly powerful presence, gaining shape in front of us. Shadows thicken, imbued with a power not of this world; they coalesce around a shape, turning nightmare into reality.

"Oh hello!" His voice is melodic, and smooth like burnt caramel. A peculiar accent graces his words—almost like Italian, but not quite.

"Who are you?" Mark asks, though we all know.

"I am Lucifer. Pleased to make your acquaintance. I've been waiting a long time to meet you, you know."

✱✱✱

Meeting the Devil calls to mind certain images. A dark pit, somewhere deep in Hell; fire, preferably with brimstone, should be present, along with some horns and tails. A pitchfork might be cliché.

But Lucifer is nothing like that. The being that stands before us is indescribably *elegant*. It's not just his clothes—tailor-made by the look of it—or his hair, which is perfectly coiffed. It's in the bearing, the way he holds himself: with a poise that no human can match, a grace that defies mortality.

And, much as I am loathe to admit it, he is also undeniably gorgeous. His eyes seem black, but on closer inspection, I see the details: the depth, the twinkle of rainbow colours, the agelessness. His body radiates evil—I feel it like a profound sickness in the universe. And yet it doesn't stop me from noticing the perfect lines of his muscles, the athletic composition of his legs, or the hard curve of his jaw.

Lucifer is terrible not because he is ugly, but because he is beautiful.

"It's you is it?" Michael asks.

"Hello to you too darling. Don't worry—I haven't forgotten about you. Your time will come. For now, it is your son I am interested in knowing."

"Oh, I doubt that very much, *vanidicus*."

"Calling me a liar? Well, you'd be correct, but I hardly think it's fair. *Tu quoque*—or, as they say in English, the pot should not call the kettle black."

"Mark, ignore him," Michael orders. "He is no more than a Projection, sent here to deceive us."

"Is that so?" Lucifer asks with a sardonic smile.

"What's a Projection?" Mark asks.

Though the question is not aimed at him, it is Lucifer who replies. "A Projection is a Sending to Earth by a demon in Hell. Your father believes I am one such, since I used to suffer the ignominy."

"So does it mean you're not really here?"

"In a manner of speaking, yes. Projections are merely illusions."

"What do you want, Lucifer? Leave my son out of this."

"You know I can't do that," the demon responds. "Mark, you are a very special being. You belong to this Earth, and yet you also belong to me—it is my power that courses through your veins."

"I don't care," Mark says. "You're not even real."

"Oh, but I am. Your father is quite mistaken."

"Prove it."

A sly smile, and Lucifer conjures a fireball. It glows a sparkling, iridescent blue, seemingly animated by a power of its own.

"Theatrics," Michael says.

I feel a cold stab of fear as I watch it. Something tells me that's no conjurer's trick.

Suddenly, it collides with a concrete barrier. The explosion would have sent me flying, if not for the demon holding me steady.

"Still theatre?" Lucifer asks.

The expression on Michael's face worries me. Before, he had been dismissive, even confident; but now that emotion melts slowly, morphing into icy fear. His entire body seems to collapse inward: the powerful, God-like being I had known becomes a coward in front of our eyes.

"Dad?"

But Michael is shaking his head. I don't hear the words, but I see them said: "I'm sorry, Mark."

Mark tries, but it's too late. His father Fades away.

Inadvertently, my eyes turn back to Lucifer. He has one eyebrow raised, as if in amusement, or maybe pity. I wonder what being he is, to turn such a strong man into flee-ing and abandoning his son. Is he so powerful as to make all opposition futile? Is he so evil that death is a better option than surrender?

I have a feeling I'm about to find out.

***

Kaylin

My men have apparently already installed cameras and microphones in Sianna's home—without any orders from me, since I'd forgotten. I want to curse my oversight, but also praise them for their intelligence. I settle on neither, instead watching the holographic monitors carefully.

The sight isn't pretty. Lucifer has appeared, his words grandiloquent, his power equally grand and far more terrifying. The cameras don't really capture him: they see the beauty, the grace, the masculinity, but not what lies beneath. It is my sixth sense which can feel it—a blight on the world, seeping into every living thing like black poison.

The Book lies open in front of me. I'd found no magic spell that could paralyse four demons at once, or take down whatever Lucifer is. Instead, the book has provided me with a different spell: remote teleportation. Provided that I have good knowledge of the target and the destination, I can whisk them away to safety.

It has a cost, as all spells do: I won't be able to use the spell again for a day and a night. It's now or never. The plan is straightforward—I get Conall out of their hands, and let Diana, Mark and Michael do their best. It's a terrible plan, with many avenues for going wrong, but it's the best I have.

As I prepare to telepathy my plans to Diana, it all goes wrong.

I never expected Michael to be a coward, nor to abandon his son. But he does exactly that; I am left jaw-struck. Lucifer now has his sights set on Diana: he's holding another fire-ball in his hand, playing with it the way a man might play with a tennis ball.

"Will you also run away, little girl?" he asks her, in the same tone of voice a father might use.

Diana looks worried—almost scared, and I've never seen her truly scared. Conall looks terrified. And Mark? Mark looks furious.

I close my eyes, and think. The choice is hard, and I regret it bitterly; but I see no alternative. Diana and Mark cannot defeat the four demons and the thing that is Lucifer, even if Conall were taken out of the equation. I must save her: the woman who became my friend, who fought with me through hardship and terror.

I tell myself that they will let Conall go, and we will rescue Mark when we are better prepared. But the words lack conviction; they cannot rationalise my choice.

✶✶✶

Mark

How could he? But then, why wouldn't he? He abandoned me when I was a baby, condemning me to life as one of the Fallen; he never told me who he really is, why he fell in love, or why he fought Lucifer. He's a coward by nature, an opportunist by nurture. I'm almost surprised to find out that I'm angry. I should've expected it—but it still enrages me. I wanted better; I wanted him to be my father, and not a self-serving demon.

When Diana disappears, taken away by one of Kaylin's spells, it's simply too late to feel more anger. The rage has overtaken me, defined me, shaped my purpose: to destroy.

"Oh, Mark," Lucifer says, with strange pity. "It does not surprise me; I have known your father far longer than you."

I only turn my eyes to the sky, and roar. And I really do mean *roar*: it's not a human sound, not the cry of a young boy who has just lost his dad. I was that young boy, once, but that was a long time ago. This is a howl of pure rage, and it holds a power that no kid could dream of. Birds scatter; the ocean heaves; the concrete beneath my feet shudders.

I've always felt it—the darkness. I started to be aware of it once I became a demon, but now I realise that it was always there; it only hid itself, suppressed by my human instincts, kept away by uncle's love for me. Now it's here, and guess what? I want it. I welcome it with open arms, and it rewards me with power.

"Get away from him," I order, and my voice sounds alien to my own ears. It's far deeper, reverberating with darkness, echoing my true nature.

Lucifer vanishes; I ignore him. The demons looks at themselves.

"There are four of us, and only one of you."

Before I know it, I've Faded next to Conall and the small female demon. I grab her arm; with glee, my power comes to the fore, ready to obey. I order it to destroy her, and she is destroyed.

The other three attack at once, at first trying to physically overwhelm me. I move through them like a scythe; they scatter like wheat stalks, each too slow, too weak, to fight me individually. Seeing my opportunity, I grab for Conall, and prepare to Fade.

His power collides into me like a freight train.

I fly into wall; it crumbles underneath me. I try to rise to my feet—to shrug it off. But my body lacks its normal strength. The world seems to swim before my eyes, like I'm not quite in it.

"Oh, you're strong. So very strong." He smiles brilliantly, and I see the demented gleam in his eyes. Lucifer wants me, and he wants me bad.

"Fuck you." I'm not going to be his puppet, ready to serve evil as he wishes it.

"And brave, too! Far braver than your father. Oh, if only you'll join me."

"You're a monster."

"So are you, *meu amator*. It is a very human thing, to fear monsters; but being a monster is really quite fun. You will rule instead of being ruled. You can have all that you desire —even this boy Conall. I only ask that you join me: accept me as your master, and embrace your real self. "

I shake my head, and summon my power—all of it. It builds inside me like charged lightning. The weakness disappears from my body; pure strength replaces it. Blue fire burns through my body, illuminating my outstretched wings.

The sky above is dark, now, and the stars shine brightly. I used to think I was just a human, subject to their whims: a mortal among the gods. But now I feel like my power rivals even theirs.

"Take this," I whisper.

A column of blue fire erupts from my hands, and slams into Lucifer. He just laughs.

"You try, oh you try! But you cannot defeat me, Mark; I am greater than you, greater than all."

His own power rises like a hungry beast, stretching out, dark and malevolent. I close my wings around me, focusing my power into a point.

It's like being hit by a battering ram, but I don't fall. I don't even squirm. I'd faced viol-ence before—I've been bloodied and beaten. Magical or not, this isn't any different.

"Stop it," he orders. "I will destroy you eventually, and that would be a terrible pity."

"It's a price I'm willing to pay," I say through gritted teeth.

"But it's not a price *I'm* willing to pay!"

I freeze. Here I am, ready to be the martyr. I'd never considered Conall, never realised he would value my life more than I would.

"Don't do it, Mark. Accept his offer. Just—please don't leave me."

I close my eyes, knowing I'm defeated. I push the words out.

"I will—"

"You will come with me, Mark, to Hell. To my kingdom, and your rightful place."

"I will come with you."

One of the demons—the one I recognise as their leader—walks up to the pier, and draws a symbol on the concrete. It's not like Kaylin's spells, which, chaotic as they are, still have obvious order. This is a simple, ugly mark.

The demon closes his eyes, raises his arms, and falls to the ground. In front of him, space seems to rupture, and bend, turning into a whirling, circular shape: a portal.

Lucifer walks to it, and turns to me, a question on his face.

I look him in the eye. The being within seems impossibly aloof, a true god. But some-how, he understands me perfectly; his features even soften in sympathy.

"Go on. Let him be," he says to the demons.

I walk to Conall. I follow the slight curve of his jaw, the angles of his cheekbones, the shade of his brown hair; I trace his lips with my finger, and look him in the eye. He's afraid, but brave. The emotion in his eyes is plain to read: love.

"So this is it," I say.

"Don't forget about me down there."

"Oh, I wouldn't worry about that, Conall."

"Tell me. Tell me that—"

"I love you, Conall."

I kiss him, then; his lips part softly, his mouth scorching hot. Soon the heat melts into languor, and then—ever so quickly—into sweet remembrance. I walk to the portal, feeling his eyes on me. One last time, I turn around. He can't hear the words, but his eyes widen, recognising the meaning on my lips all the same. *I will return.*

Then I cross the border, from Earth into Hell; from the old life, as a human, into a new one, as a demon. Is this the Fall? Or does love conquer all?

To be continued...

Acknowledgements

Authors usually like to thank all the people who helped them turn a book into reality. I would like to thank Molly Fennig and Teresa (alias "Fallen Angel") for reading the manuscript and providing in-depth feedback. I also appreciated the comments by Rena Violet, in case you are reading this! Hampton Lamoureux also deserves thanks for working so hard to meet all of my requirements for the cover. Annie Nybo's editorial feedback was most welcome; Peter Wells knows what he did to help.

Special thanks goes to Jeanne Smith, for whom I am truly grateful. To Tim Putney: thank you for choosing the Arch Demon special. Can you guess which character he could represent in the second book? Share your thoughts on Twitter or Facebook.

I must also thank Charisse James and Glenn Guzier for backing me on Kickstarter. You two are awesome!

This book did not come to be in your hand easily; its tale is a long and fraught one. Initially, it did not start out by the name *Fallen Love*. In fact, it began life as a totally different book: that story was named the *Ark*, and I can only describe it as a work of self-indulgent poetry. An expensive mistake, if you will—it took nearly 60,000 words, and the editorial feedback of a talented editor named Matrice, to figure that out.

Fortunately, inspiration came to me in the form of a dream. Well, not really: this is an apocryphal myth I encourage for marketing purposes, and the aforementioned self-indulgence. It would be more correct to state that it came in a conscious state just prior to dreaming.

I began the *Ark* at age 17 (from early 2015), and I started writing *Fallen Love* in October of 2016, just two months after starting university. I completed it after my 19th birthday, in nine months. This was a tumultuous period in my life, you understand: I moved to Amsterdam, visiting my family in Scotland and Romania during my holidays. I accepted to join a rather prestigious—and academically demanding—university college.

This was, still, the least of it, because my efforts to secure a trade publisher for *Fallen Love* proved fruitless; for two years I tried, to no avail. My first novel, the *Necromancer*, had met the same fate, but I ascribed that to being 14 when I wrote it. What was big publishing's excuse this time? Should I have written adult colouring books instead?

Still, I did not give up writing my first novel when I was 14, and I wasn't going to give up now. By crook or by hook, I was going to get this book published, and now you hold the proof in your hands.

What more can I say? If you liked this book, feel free to write a review on Goodreads or Amazon. And if you *loved* the book, why not share it with friends, acquaintances and family? You can also share it on Goodreads groups, blog about it, or share it on Facebook and Twitter. I really do appreciate any effort you can make! Remember: it is readers that make or break a book, not marketing budgets!

About the Author

Alex Stargazer is an author of dark, fantastical tales that snare you in with epic world-building—and keep you reading with funny anecdotes and beautiful love stories. He currently hails from rainy Scotland, but he can be found all over Europe. Since publishing his first novel—the Necromancer—at 14, Alex has released two short stories and an upcoming new novel, named Fallen Love.

When not establishing the finer points of magecraft or the peculiarities of dragons, Alex is working hard on getting a Master's degree in boring topics like economics. In his spare time, Alex enjoys exploring the wilderness of Scotland—though Austria, Italy and the Nordic countries fascinate him most. If he really needs to blow off some steam, Alex will shoot zombies in his favourite shooter, Left 4 Dead 2.

Alex can be found on Twitter @AlexStargazerWE or on Facebook at Alex Stargazer Writes Books. Check out his website at www.alexstargazer.com. If you want to shelve his books and leave him reviews, head over to his Goodreads profile or his Amazon page.

Other Books by Alex Stargazer

The Necromancer:

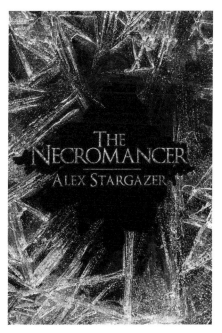

The wind of the North whispers a name, and all who hear it are frozen in fear. It is the name of the Necromancer. And it means death...

In the South, Linaera dreams of becoming a healer. A novice at the Academy of Magic, she skips most of her battle magic classes (because who needs battle magic any-way?) When her mentor, Terrin, decides to send her on a quest to the icy North, Linaera will have to learn far more than a simple fire spell to survive the ravenous undead.

Even so, Linaera will have to face greater dangers if she is to prevail. There is a dark secret hiding in the depths of the North; a secret that will make her stronger—or destroy her.

Magic and adventure beckon in the world of Arachadia. There's dark humour for the cynics, and a sweet love story for the romantics. If you like stories about mages, bad-tempered ghosts, dragons, elves and thief guilds—you've come to the right place.

Buy now on Amazon.com or Amazon.co.uk

The Sandman: Check it out on my website, alexstargazer.com.

The Vampire Eirik:

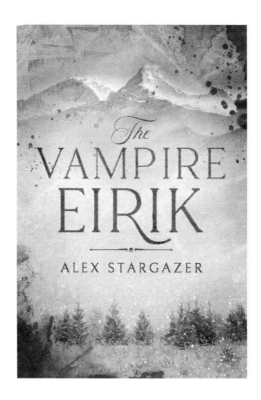

For Peter, a young, carefree engineering student, Norway means a chance for a better financial future — and the opportunity to see a beautiful landscape of fjords, primeval forests, and windswept peaks. A friendly vampire on the other hand — that's just an unexpected perk.

Yet the landscape conceals a darkness, a hidden ferocity: nature is older than man, and it does not always welcome him. To survive, Peter will have to rely on Eirik. But Eirik is still a vampire, and nature always wins in the end...

A tale of friendship, intimacy and magic, the Vampire Eirik is a short story that's perfect for bedtime reading.

What readers have said...

★★★★★ "I enjoyed the sexual tension between the characters, it was exquisite."—Margaux, Goodreads Reviewer.

★★★★★ "I was riveted to the drama; it is my hope that their story has just begun."—Teresa, Goodreads Reviewer.

If you sign up to my mailing list (http://eepurl.com/gE5Rg9) you can get it for free! You will also receive behind-the-scenes announcements, special review or beta-reading opportunities, and promotions.

Printed in Great Britain
by Amazon

42312350R00197